MURDER AT THE WEDDING

A MISS MERRILL AND AUNT VIOLET MYSTERY

ANITA DAVISON

Boldwood

First published in Great Britain in 2025 by Boldwood Books Ltd.

Copyright © Anita Davison, 2025

Cover Design by Head Design Ltd.

Cover Images: Shutterstock

A CIP catalogue record for this book is available from the British Library.

Paperback ISBN 978-1-83678-354-1

Large Print ISBN 978-1-83678-355-8

Hardback ISBN 978-1-83678-353-4

Trade Paperback ISBN 978-1-80656-037-0

Ebook ISBN 978-1-83678-356-5

Kindle ISBN 978-1-83678-357-2

Audio CD ISBN 978-1-83678-348-0

MP3 CD ISBN 978-1-83678-349-7

Digital audio download ISBN 978-1-83678-351-0

This book is printed on certified sustainable paper. Boldwood Books is dedicated to putting sustainability at the heart of our business. For more information please visit https://www.boldwoodbooks.com/about-us/sustainability/

Boldwood Books Ltd, 23 Bowerdean Street, London, SW6 3TN

www.boldwoodbooks.com

Hector and Madeleine Merrill request the pleasure of your company at the wedding of their daughter, Hannah Mary Cordelia

to

Mr Darius Alexander Bartholomew Clifford at St Nicholas Church, Chiswick, on Saturday May 4, 1918, at 2.00 p.m.

1

Although jittery with nerves, Hannah attempted to remain perfectly still while her sister, Iris, secured her headdress with several dangerous-looking pins. Her sister turned away briefly and, taking advantage of her distraction, Hannah tweaked a thorn that scratched her temple.

'Don't touch!' Iris slapped her hand away. 'You'll ruin it.'

'Sorry.' Hannah grimaced and dropped her hand into her lap, gripping it tightly in the other.

'These pale pink rosebuds complement your dark hair beautifully,' Iris said, evidently delighted with her handiwork.

From the corner of her eye, Hannah spotted her mother approach, holding a length of Honiton lace. 'Mama, we've talked about this!' she said through gritted teeth. 'I'm not wearing Grandmama's veil.' She pulled back her chin as a distinctive smell of mothballs reached her.

'Don't look so disapproving, darling,' Madeleine said dismissively. 'You'll change your mind when you see what it looks like on.'

Iris suppressed a cough, covering her nose with one hand, the other still clamped on the headdress to keep it in place.

'It is rather – yellow.' Norah Atherton, Iris's sister-in-law wrinkled her nose and fingered the lace with mild disgust. 'It won't go with the gown at all.' Hannah had included Norah in the wedding party as a courtesy; a decision she now regretted.

'It's a family heirloom,' Madeleine's upper lip curled as she snatched the veil from Norah's hand. 'And it must be over fifty years old.'

'It certainly looks it!' Aunt Violet muttered from a chair in the corner.

'Not today,' Hannah said in an undertone, summoning patience. 'Mama, I'm sure you and Grandmama both looked wonderful in it when you got married, but it's not what *I* want for my special day.'

'I've waited so long for this day,' Madeleine whined, the veil hanging limp between her hands like a dejected ghost. 'I want it to be special.'

'It *will* be special. To Darius and me.' Hannah removed the hand mirror from her lap and dropped it onto the dressing table hard enough to break, but it stayed intact. 'And I'm twenty-five, hardly a spinster of the parish.'

Madeleine continued to stoutly resist Hannah's desire for a small, intimate wedding, on the basis an extravagant display was inappropriate for wartime, with more than one argument on the subject conducted publicly in a department store.

For years, Hannah was constantly reminded that Iris had fulfilled their mother's ambition by marrying the son of a wealthy landowner at eighteen, with a wedding that would have made Gloria Vanderbilt's mother proud. To make matters worse, Iris was now the mother of four beautiful, healthy children.

'I hope that spinster remark wasn't aimed at me?' Aunt Violet lounged in a slipper chair in the corner; her stockinged feet crossed over a footstool and her luxurious chocolate-coloured hair wound into curling rags.

'I'm sorry, Aunt Violet. I didn't mean to imply anything.' Hannah groaned inwardly, aware her nerves had made her voice sharp.

'I was only joking.' Her aunt laughingly waved her off. 'It's not as if I haven't chosen not to marry, although my forties sneaked up on me rather sooner than I imagined. Anyway, weren't veils devices to prevent the groom balking at first sight of his bride at the altar?'

'Mr Clifford won't change his mind, surely?' Penny Wells, Hannah's sixteen-year-old bookshop assistant, said from where she was folding Hannah's trousseau into neat piles on a chest of drawers. 'I know it's been a long engagement, but as my father always says, when one overthinks a decision, doubts can creep in.'

Penny wore a pale-blue frothy dress and matching hat, her toffee-brown curls bouncing on her shoulders. Vanity had made her leave her spectacles at home for the occasion, and with her expressive brown eyes and dimpled cheeks, she resembled a figure from Kingsley's *Water Babies*. After months of silent devotion to Archie, their bookshop manager, they were now officially walking out.

'Penny!' Iris snapped, her vivid blue eyes wide in horror. 'Don't even suggest such a thing.'

'She's right, though.' Hannah sighed, accustomed to the girl's habit of saying exactly what was on her mind without thinking. At her age, she probably did the same herself. 'I've often wondered if this day would come. And don't worry, Penny, I'm not offended.'

Although she was. A little.

Her fiancé's work at the War Office meant Darius was frequently called away at short notice, which had disrupted their wedding preparations three times thus far.

'There! It's finished.' Iris inserted the last pin and stepped back to admire her work. 'What do you think?'

Hannah swung her head from side to side, examining the result in her dressing table mirror. 'Iris, it's perfect! Exactly what I wanted.'

A wide satin band encircled her forehead, dipping slightly towards the back of her head, and the right side was adorned with a swathe of tightly furled white, pink and yellow roses. 'Don't you think so, Mama?' she asked, shooting her mother a look that dared her to find fault.

'Hmm. It's pretty enough, I suppose,' Madeleine replied grudgingly. 'I still think rosebuds are a strange choice. Wedding roses should be gloriously full-blown and of the deepest scarlet. You don't even have any bridesmaids.'

'Mads, do stop complaining.' Aunt Violet made a face at her sister. 'It's far too late to change things, and should anyone want *my* opinion, I think she looks lovely.'

Hannah threw her a grateful smile and Madeleine retreated to the far side of the room, tutting to herself.

'Oh, Iris,' Hannah whispered low enough so her mother would not hear. 'Why does Mama make everything so stressful?' She raised her hand to eye level. 'Look, I'm shaking!'

'She was the same on my wedding day.' Iris stroked the round bulge beneath her dress with one hand, her resigned gaze going to Madeleine. 'And when this little one makes an appearance, no doubt she'll be offering endless unwanted advice, despite it being my fifth.' Iris unhooked a gown wrapped in a muslin sheath from the front of the wardrobe and carried it back to Hannah's chair.

'Now, let's get you into this dress. I know it's early, but then we'll have time for any last-minute alterations.'

'You're a darling for keeping me grounded,' Hannah whispered, stepping gingerly into the gown that Iris held open at her feet. 'I'm so glad you're here.'

'That's what older sisters are for.' Iris deftly fastened the row of fabric-covered buttons that ran from the neckline to waist, then swung the cheval mirror closer so Hannah could view the full ensemble.

'Oh!' Hannah gasped, hardly recognising herself in the glass. 'It's nicer than I could ever have imagined.'

Fashioned in ivory satin with a scooped neckline and full skirt that skimmed her slender figure, the gown was lightly cinched at the waist. A floral organza lace overlay embroidered with forget-me-nots and leaves flowed in gentle folds to the floor. Elbow-length bell sleeves in the same organza completed the look.

'It's exquisite.' Norah sighed. 'You look quite lovely. Almost ethereal.'

'You'll do very nicely.' Aunt Violet nodded sagely; the equivalent of a compliment from her.

'You don't think it's too simple without a train, do you?' Hannah pirouetted in front of the cheval mirror.

Madeleine choked on a sob. '*You're* beautiful.' She clasped her hands beneath her chin, her eyes suspiciously wet. 'And I was mistaken about the veil. The gown looks much better without it.'

'You'll float down that aisle like a duchess.' Iris bent to tweak the skirt into place, then winced, a hand below her bump.

Hannah's eyes widened. 'Are you all right? Is it the baby?'

Iris straightened and shook her head, though her smile was strained. 'A brief pang, that's all. I get them every time I'm expecting, so nothing to worry about.' Her gaze went to their mother in a 'don't mention it' look, but Madeleine was busy correcting Penny's packing technique.

Hannah chewed her bottom lip gently, uncertain whether to pursue it, but Iris seemed to recover quickly. And she had been pregnant four times before.

'I will be all right, won't I?' Hannah asked, her heart thrumming faster in her chest. 'I keep dreaming that I'll trip and fall flat on my face in the middle of the aisle with everyone watching, and —' She broke off as a clatter of gravel at the window sent her jumping back in alarm.

Tutting in annoyance, Madeleine strode to the window and pulled up the sash as far as it would go and leaned out. 'Whatever do you think you're doing, young man— My goodness? Darius, is that you?'

Aunt Violet left her chair and joined her, followed by Iris and then Norah and Penny, their combined feminine rears crowding the opening as they stared down into the front garden below.

'What's he *doing* here?' Hannah rose and skirted the dressing table, mindful of her skirt snagging on the furniture. 'He's supposed to be getting ready at Cavan's house.'

Hannah had retained her friendship with Dr Cavan Soames in the two years since the murder of his wife. Lily-Anne Soames had been Hannah's best friend, and her loss still hit Hannah hard at unguarded moments. Cavan had kindly offered his impressive house opposite the church for the reception; Hannah's charming home by the river being unsuitable for a large gathering.

'He mustn't see you!' Madeleine intercepted her, arms spread wide to block her view of the window. 'It's extremely bad luck.'

'When did I ever believe in luck, Mama? Good or bad.' Hannah attempted to ease past her without success. 'Let me pass. Something must have happened.'

'You stay right there. We'll handle whatever it is.' Madeleine held up a finger in warning before adding her rounded backside to those lined up at the window.

'Why didn't you knock?' Aunt Violet demanded, her upper body so far out of the window she was in danger of toppling onto the lawn below.

'I did,' Darius's deep, disembodied voice replied. 'No one answered the front door.'

'This is most irregular, Darius, dear,' Madeleine said haughtily. 'We're trying to get ready, and there's still a lot to do.'

'My apologies, future mother-in-law.' Darius's melodious voice created a flutter in Hannah's lower belly. Did a last-minute summons from the Admiralty bring him, or was he having second thoughts, as Penny had suggested? If so, she couldn't blame him. Hannah had experienced moments of doubt herself accompanied by sheer panic as the day grew closer.

'I see he omitted to add a visit to a barber in his preparations,' Aunt Violet muttered, a smile in her voice.

Impatience spiked Hannah's already tight nerves and she pushed between them and leaned over the sill, her gaze finding Darius on the path below – all six feet three inches of him in an old jacket and collarless shirt, his longer than fashionable hair uncombed. Catching sight of her, he grinned, creating more butterflies in Hannah's stomach. 'Well, don't you look splendid with those flowers in your hair!'

'Thank you, darling, but why are you here?' Her voice rose in panic. 'Please don't say you've been called back to the Admiralty?'

'Thankfully, no.' Darius rubbed the back of his neck with one hand. 'However, there might be a slight hiccough regarding the ceremony.'

'It's not Xander, is it?' Iris clutched her neckline, her motherly instincts rising. She had left her husband, Mycroft, at the Coach and Horses in Kew with their eldest son, Alexander, who was normally the least likely of her offspring to cause havoc.

'Unless the boy is swinging on a rope from the altar cross, Iris, what possible trouble could an eight-year-old cause?' Madeleine said with ill-concealed scorn.

'Xander's perfectly fine, Iris, as far as I know,' Darius replied. 'But, um...' He scanned the road both ways before continuing. 'There's a slight problem with Reverend Aldrich.'

'How slight?' Hannah conjured an image of the handsome, young vicar, who, despite being new to the parish, fitted in well with the community. 'Where is he?'

'That's just it – we don't know.' Darius flung both hands in the air in resignation. 'No one has seen him since ten this morning. I don't suppose anyone here has seen him?'

'Maybe he had an early morning assignation?' Aunt Violet suggested. 'A man that handsome and on the right side of thirty is bound to set a few hearts fluttering among the congregation.'

'Violet, have some respect!' Madeleine snapped, aghast. 'He's a man of the cloth.'

'But still a man, isn't he?' Aunt Violet lifted both shoulders in an exasperated shrug.

'I wish it were so easily explained.' Darius bit back a laugh.

'He certainly isn't here,' Madeleine said, shoving Hannah to one side. 'Well, don't just stand there, Darius – find him. He cannot have gone far.'

'He's not a stray dog, Mama,' Hannah muttered irritably, then louder, 'perhaps he was called away to an emergency?'

'I agree. That's possible. And you're right.' Darius shoved a hand into his hair, distracted. 'He probably ran out of communion wine or something equally trivial. I expect he's already back at the vicarage.' He scuffed the toe of his shoe against the dirt path. 'Apologies all, I'm probably panicking over nothing.' He turned to walk away, thought better of it and returned to the gate. 'By the way, I meant it, Hannah. I've never seen you look so beautiful.'

'I appreciate that, Darius, even though only half of me is visible from down there.' Hannah relaxed, strangely emotional and suddenly shy. Perhaps they should have gone to Caxton Hall to do the deed with Aunt Violet and her partner, Aidan, otherwise known as Detective Chief Inspector Farrell, as witnesses after all? An option that had been seriously discussed at one point.

'Now go away! We'll see you in the church later,' Madeleine called, then slammed the window down with a bang, narrowly missing Hannah's fingers.

'That will cause a right hoo-ha at the church if the vicar is missing.' Penny slumped onto the chair Hannah had just vacated and poked her fingers into a powder puff on the dresser.

'That's enough, Penny!' Aunt Violet glared at her but, undeterred, Penny merely shrugged.

'Not missing.' Hannah's voice shook slightly. 'I prefer to think of it as a temporary delay.' She paced the floor while picking at a hangnail. 'I'm sure there's a reasonable explanation,' she added with more confidence than she felt. 'Reverend Aldrich will turn up at the last moment and all this drama will have been for nothing.'

'Then where is he?' Madeleine snapped. 'I asked after him earlier when I went to check the flower arrangements. He wasn't there.'

Hannah mentally altered the word 'check' to 'supervise' and suspected the vicar had made himself scarce when he saw her coming.

'There's still plenty of time.' Madeleine guided Hannah back to the dressing table, dislodging Iris without ceremony and giving

Penny a hard look. 'Sit down and finish your toilette, darling. Everything will be fine, I'm sure.'

'What if they don't find him?' Hannah's scalp itched, but she resisted the urge to scratch her head for fear of ruining her sister's careful work. 'The ceremony will have to be postponed! Again.'

'Can't the churchwarden step in and officiate?' Iris suggested.

'Don't be silly, dear,' Madeleine tutted. 'It has to be an ordained priest, not a lay person.'

'It would be a shame to waste all that food everyone collected for the party.' Aunt Violet sounded mildly put out – not that she had been responsible for preparing any of it.

'I could always call my papa?' Penny said into the brief but tense silence that followed.

'That's most kind of you, dear.' Madeleine's patronising laugh made Hannah flinch. 'But unless he's an ordained Anglican priest, I doubt he'll be of any use whatsoever.'

'Well, actually, he is.' Penny eased backwards onto the bed, her hands braced on either side of her knees, her feet several inches off the floor and her legs swinging like a schoolgirl. 'St Hilda's is in the same parish, and Papa has stepped in for the previous minister before. Would you like me to call him?'

'Oh, Penny, would you?' Hannah pressed her crossed hands to her throat. 'I hope we won't need him but having him on hand would be comforting.'

'Excellent!' Penny launched herself onto the floor, landing with a surprisingly solid thump for someone of her size. 'I won't be long.' She turned back at the door. 'At least I hope not. Only sometimes he forgets we have a telephone at all and asks what that strange noise is.' She hunched her shoulders before disappearing around the door jamb, her rapid footsteps retreating down the stairs.

'I had completely forgotten her father was a clergyman.'

Hannah twisted in her chair to face Madeleine. 'And I hope you're ashamed of yourself, Mama. You were rather condescending to Penny just now.'

'Oh, pish! How was I to know?' Madeleine slumped back against the buttoned upholstery of her armchair. 'Is it too early for a sherry?'

'I sincerely hope not.' Aunt Violet held up a half-filled glass. 'This is my second. Although, to be fair, it's not sherry... it's gin.'

2

'Are you certain your father said he could get here on time, Penny?' Hannah's hands inside her gloves felt clammy as she gripped her bouquet and prepared for the short walk from the lych-gate to the church door.

'I'm sure he will, Miss Merrill,' Penny insisted, but there was trepidation in her voice. 'Even wearing his cassock, he can work up a fair lick on his bicycle.'

'I hope so.' Hannah toyed with the image of a middle-aged man in a long gown pedalling like fury, but with her nauseous stomach she could not conjure a smile.

The small entourage exited the house, her mother in a pale lilac suit with a gigantic hat that bounced as she walked. Aunt Violet followed in a subtle, sage-green tunic dress; a new fashion that had yet to take hold but guaranteed to draw both admiring and outraged looks since she had dispensed with a corset.

Madeleine tutted disapprovingly. 'Violet, you cannot leave the house half-dressed!'

'Tunic dresses are all the rage now,' Norah interjected. 'Corsets are going out of fashion.'

'It's not as if she needs one anyway,' Iris added to the anti-Madeleine brigade. 'She's so tall and shapely. I'm quite envious, especially when I look so matronly.' She looked down at the bump beneath her dress.

'I think you look lovely, all of you.' Hannah turned at the front gate and surveyed the outfits, each one in a different pastel shade which reflected those of Hannah's bouquet.

'Here he is.' Madeleine breathed a sigh of relief as a sleek forest-green Daimler stopped beside them. A wide white ribbon ran from the roof to the end of the bonnet, where it was tied into an enormous bow. Through the window she spotted her father, Hector, in full top hat and tails on the back seat.

'Mama, was this your idea?' Hannah gasped. 'I don't need to be driven; the church is barely a five-minute walk away. As soon as I get in, I'll have to get out again.'

'Of course you do,' her mother said, sounding suitably outraged. 'You cannot possibly walk to your own wedding.'

'At least that's something we can agree on,' Aunt Violet muttered, looking up from where she was attaching her corsage to her dress.

'I've instructed the driver to make a slow tour of the area to settle your nerves and give us all time to get there before you. By then Penny's father should have arrived.'

Madeleine fussily tweaked the folds of Hannah's skirt.

'I'm hoping we wouldn't need him.' Hannah tugged the fabric out of her mother's fingers and climbed in beside her father. 'Although I assume that means there's still no sign of Reverend Aldrich?' She addressed the question to her small entourage, but it was her father who answered.

'I'm afraid not, darling.' Hector shook his head and slid further along the leather seat, giving her space to spread her skirt to avoid creases. 'But don't you worry. Everything will be fine.' He clasped her free hand and squeezed, not letting go until the vehicle pulled up on the road outside the church.

The Daimler rolled to a halt beside the lych-gate, and Aidan – otherwise known as Detective Chief Inspector Farrell – wearing full morning garb, leapt forward and flung open the door.

'No need to panic, Hannah. Reverend Wells arrived a few minutes ago. He's happily ensconced in the chancel ordering choirboys about, so we're all set.'

'That's a relief.' Hannah exhaled a calming breath, finally able to summon a smile. 'You've been wonderful, and I know it's been a fraught morning for everyone, but—'

'No time, Hannah. I'd better get back.' Aidan saluted her smartly. 'Having the best man pelting through the church has already unnerved the guests. I'll see you inside.' Before she could utter another word, he was halfway back down the path.

A group of locals had gathered on the road, and a wave of sighs and a few gasps erupted as she alighted from the motor car and walked up the path on her father's arm, pausing inside the porch which smelled of dust and the scent of roses.

'Well, this is it, my darling,' Hector whispered as the opening chords of the bridal march drifted along the aisle. 'You know it's not too late to—'

'Papa, as if I would. And anyway, Mother would kill me.'

'And me for letting you.' He leant closer, his soft moustache tickling her cheek. 'And if I don't get the chance to tell you later... you are the most beautiful bride I have seen in my entire life.'

'That's very sweet, Papa. But I'm quite certain you said the same to Iris when you escorted her down the aisle.'

'I don't recall.' He feigned a frown. 'And why would I, when you have always been my favourite?' His eyes, like her own, sparkled and her throat closed with emotion. Suddenly unable to speak, she gripped his arm tighter.

Forcing her feet to obey, she walked slowly towards the altar where Darius waited with an amiable-looking man shorter than both Aidan and Darius by several inches, his round face beaming a smile of welcome whose vestments swamped his compact frame.

Darius's gaze remained fixed on her throughout the seemingly endless walk across the tiled floor towards him, his expression of a mixture of pride and admiration that made her heartbeat quicken.

Reverend Wells conducted the ceremony with a large dose of humour and a penchant for inappropriate side comments which created bubbles of laughter among the guests that made everyone relax.

The ceremony passed in a blur while Hannah's focus stayed solely on Darius's face. His low, melodious voice soothed her as he spoke his vows, her hand in his. The small congregation behind her faded away, and she became conscious of only the subtle perfume of the arches of blue, yellow and pink flowers – that must have decimated every florist in Surrey – combined with the musty smell of old stone and dust, as spring sunlight slanted through long stained-glass windows creating jewel-coloured patterns on the stone tiles.

After Hannah and Darius were declared husband and wife, Reverend Wells embraced his adopted role with enthusiasm and corralled the guests into the porch to pose for photographs, giving orders like a ringmaster.

The process ended with a collective sigh of relief, and the photographer rapidly repacked his equipment while muttering about another event he was due at.

The guests drifted onto the path and over towards the lych-gate where they congregated in small groups to chatter, which prompted Reverend Wells to call them all back again with a frantic waving of arms.

'The wedding breakfast will commence in a while, but would everyone remain here, while the bride and groom adjourn to the south side of the churchyard for a private moment.'

Accompanied by smothered laughter, smirks and some raised eyebrows, Darius took Hannah's hand and drew her back into the church, along the aisle and into the vestry. They took the side door into the churchyard to where the Benthall Mausoleum occupied a small clearing with no nearby graves, the area surrounded by thick hedges where the nostalgic smell of newly cut grass permeated the air.

A slab of polished Portland stone that reached Hannah's chin bore a pensive angel reclined on the top, her gaze fixed on the far distance, set within wrought-iron railings. A gate at one end led down three steps to a thick wooden door with brass studs.

'You don't think this is macabre, do you?' Hannah tightened her grip on Darius's hand as they approached the tomb. 'Lily-Anne would have loved being here today, and I wanted to remember her in some way.'

'Not at all. As I said when you first mentioned it, it's a beautiful tribute to her.'

'I'm mildly annoyed at Reverend Aldrich for letting us down so badly.' Hannah fingered the satin ribbon that held her bouquet together. 'If he didn't want to officiate, he had only to inform us.'

'Perhaps he had an emergency and had to leave? We'll probably find a note under a pew later, apologising.'

'Then he should have delegated the task to another minister.' Hannah realised she was being uncharitable and softened her tone. 'Although actually, Reverend Wells was a perfect substitute. It was so nice of him to step in.'

'It was, but all I really care about is that after all the false starts, delays – not to mention the murders – we're finally married.'

'You always were a sentimental old thing, deep down.' Hannah slid her hand into his and drew him closer to the railed enclosure of the tomb where her best friend lay.

'I'll always remember you, Lily-Anne.' Hannah blinked away welling tears as she stooped and placed her bouquet of pink and yellow rosebuds, forget-me-nots and dianthus at the base of the gate. 'I cannot believe it's over two years since she... died.' The words 'was murdered' stuck in her throat. 'I still expect her to walk up my garden path in one of her frilly white dresses, floppy hat and one of those ridiculous parasols she loved.'

'Her flamboyance added to her charm,' Darius said with a smile in his voice. 'But Lily-Anne wouldn't want you to be upset, not today.' He ran a finger down her cheek, then leaned down to brush her lips. A soft, gentle touch which lingered for a few seconds then became more urgent as the moment stretched until at last, she pulled back, her cheeks hot.

'We'd better get back,' she said, slightly breathless. 'Our guests are waiting.'

'I suppose we should. My father brought a fine blended malt whisky from his cellar, and I've spotted several of the men eyeing it.'

Hannah cast a final look back at the tomb as she stepped onto the path and halted. 'Darius, wait. The door to the tomb is open.'

'I doubt it.' He shrugged lightly. 'It's set several feet down, so it's probably just a shadow you can see.' He reached to grasp her hand again, but she pulled it away.

'No. I'm sure it's open.' Hannah returned to the surrounding railings and pushed the gate with her hand. It creaked open a few inches. 'This gate is always locked.'

'Maintenance, perhaps?' Darius offered, though it was half-hearted. 'Come on, we have a reception to attend. Cavan's staff has been working all morning, setting out a spread.'

'There's no reason for the tomb to be open.' Hannah shifted her vantage point so she could see inside. 'They locked it after Lily-Anne's interment and hasn't been opened since.'

At the bottom of the steps lay the distinctive outline of a sole of a shoe. A man's shoe. Her stomach knotted. 'There's someone down there, and he's not moving.'

Darius was halfway to the vestry door, but her tone halted him. Turning, he returned to her side. 'Are you sure?' He peered over her shoulder. 'You're right. He's lying on the floor. And by the look of it, he's wearing a cassock.'

'Could it be Reverend Aldrich?' Hannah gasped, instantly regretting her earlier comment.

'I don't know. Let me take a proper look.'

She started to follow, but he held up a hand. 'No, you stay here. I'll go.' He swung the gate inwards and descended the steps.

Hannah halted and chewed her bottom lip, hoping she was mistaken, but knew she was not.

Darius returned almost instantly, his expression grim. 'It *is* him. And he's dead. I'd better fetch Aidan.'

Hannah's knees gave way, and she lowered herself onto the top step leading into the vestry. A gentle wind rustled the hedges and the tops of the trees beyond, and a flap of wings and a distant birdsong contrived to make it a perfect spring day... apart from the dead body inside the tomb.

Conscious she was being unreasonable, even callous, her mind raged, *It's not fair, it's our wedding day.*

* * *

Hannah had no real sense of how much time passed before Aidan appeared at the vestry door, followed by Darius, Aunt Violet and Cavan, all with concerned, puzzled faces.

A commotion erupted behind them as some of the guests tried to follow, while Reverend Wells flapped his arms like an agitated penguin in an attempt to hold them back.

'Ladies and gentlemen.' Darius raised both arms and took charge. 'Would everyone adjourn to Dr Cavan Soames's house across the road while we await the police.'

'What's happened?' Madeleine demanded as she pushed through the small crowd, but Darius merely smiled enigmatically and ushered her through the side gate.

Aidan aimed a curt but understanding nod at Hannah as he strode past her and descended the steps into the mausoleum. Cavan looked about to follow, but hesitated, laying a comforting hand on Hannah's shoulder. 'Do you feel faint? Can I get you anything?'

'I'm shaken, but otherwise fine.' Hannah smiled weakly up at him. 'I only saw his feet before Darius insisted I should come away.'

'Is it true?' Aunt Violet reached her and looked from Hannah to Cavan and back again. 'Reverend Aldrich is dead?'

'I'm afraid so,' Hannah replied, just as Aidan reappeared, climbing the steps more slowly than he had descended them.

'How did it happen?' Aunt Violet asked. 'Did he fall?'

'At first glance it appears so, but we cannot be certain.' Aidan's gaze slid over Hannah and settled on Cavan. 'Dr Soames, could I ask you to confirm the death? And might I use your telephone to inform the police?'

'Of-of course. It's on the wall outside my study.' He remained where he was, frozen for long seconds. Then he swallowed, adjusted his tie and took a deep breath before taking Darius's place at the entrance to the tomb.

Hannah climbed to her feet and smoothed down her skirt with hands that shook while focusing on Cavan's rigid back. Would he seek out his wife's coffin where it had lain on a stone shelf between those of her deceased relatives for the last two years? Or would he consciously avoid it to focus on the dead man on the ground? Then another thought intruded: Why had Reverend Aldrich entered the tomb at all?

'Come with me, Hannah.' Aunt Violet wrapped a firm arm around Hannah's shoulders and forced her upright. 'Let's leave the authorities to do their worst.'

The mausoleum receded behind them, and they had reached the door to Cavan's house on the corner before Hannah said, 'Did you say worst?'

'I did,' Aunt Violet said, lowering her voice. 'The police will need to question everyone, and I suspect things are about to get awkward. Since there's nothing you can do here, we might as well get ourselves a drink.'

'That's the best suggestion I've heard all morning,' a commanding female voice said from behind them. Hannah turned to see Cavan's sister, dressed in a flowing pale-green silk dress decorated with red roses, her flaming red hair topped with a scarlet felt hat set at an angle towards her left eye making a vivid splash of colour among the dark suits and pastel dresses around her.

'Eliza. How lovely you were able to come.' Hannah pressed her hands warmly. 'I'm only sorry things aren't turning out quite as anyone expected.' Of a similar age to Hannah, Eliza had run away from home a decade earlier to become an actress and had since worked in several West End theatres, making a name for herself.

'It's not your fault, sweetheart, and tragedy aside, this is all quite the drama, isn't it? I'll certainly dine out on this one for a while. And Hannah, dear, you look exquisite. Doesn't she, Vi?'

'She does indeed,' Aunt Violet slipped one arm through Hannah's and linked the other through Eliza's. 'Now let's go and get some of that champagne I've been eyeing since I arrived.'

3

Following an unusually dry April, the early May weather had stayed miraculously warm, and the twenty or so wedding guests fitted neatly into Cavan's drawing room that opened into a double-height conservatory. Two sets of French doors opened into the garden with a central water fountain. A canvas canopy had been set up, beneath which were several chairs, sofas and a low table for guests to sit outside.

Cavan's impressive dining table had been co-opted to accommodate the wedding breakfast, laden with more food than Hannah had seen in a year. A whole salmon dressed with transparent slices of cucumber took pride of place on one side of the table, with a whole cooked ham on the other. In between were arranged platters of sandwiches, pork and veal and ham pies, both savoury and sweet pastries, trifles, fruit tarts, fairy cakes and a three-tiered iced wedding cake adorned with sugar novelties and flowers, all spread in a fabulous display.

'Everyone is talking about the minister,' Madeleine said, waylaying Hannah inside the drawing room door. 'I thought he was simply missing?'

'Not any more, Mads. It turns out he was here all the time. Just not alive.' Aunt Violet kept her voice low while nodding and smiling at the arriving guests. 'Hannah hardly needs reminding. She's the one who should be upset. It's her wedding day.'

'Violet, I know perfectly well what day it is,' her mother retorted, a sisterly argument clearly brewing.

'Mama, please don't be difficult. And I'm fine, really.' Hannah pressed her aunt's arm in reassurance. 'I've seen bodies before.' Though her sympathy for the vicar was diluted by disappointment that her long-awaited wedding had included another death. 'If it was an accident, that's something we can be grateful for.'

'Something tells me it wasn't,' Aunt Violet murmured, earning a puzzled smile from Hannah, who would have liked to pursue this idea, but her mother's eager expression showed she was waiting for a reaction to all her efforts.

'This is wonderful, Mama, but there's far too much for just us.' Hannah summoned an appreciative smile, but her aunt's comment repeated in her head. 'Where did it all come from?'

'Don't ask,' her father whispered in her ear. 'Suffice it to say, we'll all be on porridge and pea soup for the next month.'

'Don't exaggerate, Hector!' Madeleine snapped, then lowered her voice. 'Mycroft and Iris supplied most of the fresh meat from his estate. As for the rest, I admit we decimated everyone's ration books, not to mention Cavan's larder.'

'Well, I'm thrilled, and Darius will appreciate all your efforts, I'm sure.' Hannah scanned the room, but her new husband was nowhere to be seen.

'Well, this is a turn up, I must say.' Darius's father elbowed his way into the group. 'Hannah, my dear, allow me to offer my congratulations, and welcome to the family.' His eyes, like Darius's apart from the fine lines at the edges, sparkled.

'Thank you, and I appreciate you making the journey. What

should I call you now? Father-in-law sounds too formal when I've known you most of my life.'

'Joshua will suit quite well, my dear. I'm not old yet,' he said with a slow wink. 'Now what's this about the vicar falling down the steps of the Bentham family tomb? Bit clumsy of him, what?'

Hannah decided this was not the time to enlighten him. 'Will you be staying a while Mr— Joshua? If so, there is always room for you at Ilchester Place.'

'I appreciate your kindness, my dear, but after so many years in the country, London feels foreign to me these days.' He pushed a hank of salt-and-pepper hair that had slipped onto his low forehead, a gesture Norah's husband, Selwyn – bald since his thirties – eyed enviously.

'I went to Green Park yesterday to look for crocuses, but the flowerbeds were all dug up for vegetables,' Joshua said, his irritation evident. 'Couldn't take a stroll on the grass either, what with all those jack-booted soldiers doing drills.'

'I agree.' Madeleine paused to take a sip from her glass. 'The parks have been ruined with those tents all over the place. I'm told the lake in St James's Park has been drained to make way for some ministry or other.'

'It's all very necessary, Mama.' Hannah aimed for a mixture of exasperation at her parent and sympathy for Joshua. 'We need food badly, and the army needs somewhere to train until this dreadful war is over.'

'And when will that be, exactly?' Madeleine sniffed. 'This war has gone on far too long.'

Before Hannah could contrive an answer, her nephew shouldered his way into the group, a fairy cake in his hand.

'Xander!' Iris appeared suddenly and snatched it away. 'Cakes are for after. How many times must I say it?'

'Did Uncle Darius really find a body in the mausoleum?' he

asked with all the candour of an eight-year-old. 'I thought that's where they're kept?'

'Um, well, yes,' Iris replied uneasily. 'No one expected this particular one to be there.'

'Can I see it? I want to tell the boys at school. When I told them I was going to a wedding, they said it would be boring.'

'You're not going to see it!' A look of panic crossed Iris's face. 'Nanny, would you take Xander upstairs? I don't think he should be here at a time like this.'

'Who are you talking to, Iris?' Madeleine stared at her. 'You left your nanny in Surrey in charge of the rest of your brood, remember?'

'Goodness, I completely forgot.' Iris looked nonplussed before she aimed a pleading look at her mother. 'Mama, would you be a dear and take him?'

'Why don't you do it? I gave up child-minding years ago,' her mother snapped. 'Besides, I want to hear what the police think happened to Reverend Aldrich.'

'If Grandma is staying, then so am I.' Xander planted his feet apart, arms crossed and glared at them. 'I want to know how the body got there.'

'So do we all, son,' Mycroft muttered from Madeleine's other side as he joined them. 'But perhaps your mother is right. This isn't the place for—' But he spoke to thin air as Xander was fast disappearing through the open French doors into the garden.

'Oh, good grief, I'd better go after him,' Mycroft said grudgingly. 'He'll be through the back gate and at the church before we know it.' The resigned look on her brother-in-law's face told Hannah it had not been his idea to leave the nanny at home.

'It's unfortunate, but at least they didn't find the body until after the ceremony,' Madeleine said.

'Mother!' Iris snapped. 'Of all the inappropriate things you've said today, that is the worst.'

'The man was already dead, darling, so what difference would it have made to him?' Madeleine shrugged, unapologetic.

'It's still been a lovely wedding, despite the, uh... upset,' Aunt Violet said, possibly to divert the hard look Iris directed at her mother. 'I doubt anyone will want to make any speeches though.'

'Darius will see that as a bonus.' Joshua snorted a laugh. 'My son never took to public speaking. Made a pig's ear of the debating club at school.'

Hannah kept her gaze fixed on the hall door, awaiting Darius's arrival, but he did not appear.

'Let's hope the police don't keep us too long, or you won't be able to leave for your honeymoon.' Selwyn swiped a vol-au-vent from the tray of a passing maid, earning himself a hard nudge in the ribs from his wife.

'We've shelved that idea for the time being, Selwyn.' Hannah tried not to let her disappointment show. 'We cannot leave London in case Darius is called into the War Office. However, he's promised me a trip to Paris when the war is over.'

'I hear Paris has fared no better than London with all the bombings.' Mycroft rejoined the conversation, minus Xander. Hannah wondered how long it would take him or Iris to notice.

'If the French still have control by then,' Aunt Violet murmured darkly. 'The Germans shelled the Tuileries Garden. Such wanton vandalism.'

'Why all the sad faces?' Eliza nudged her way into their close huddle. 'Hannah, darling, you're not allowed to be so glum at your own wedding.' Grabbing Archie's arm as he and Penny passed, she dragged him to a halt. 'Now, Archie, is it? Didn't I hear you say you wanted a chance to play that exquisite piano? Well, now's your chance. Give us a tune we can all dance to.'

'That instrument is a little different from my ma's old upright,' Archie replied, handing his half-full glass to Penny. 'But I'll have a go.'

'No Irving Berlin songs, today, old chap,' Selwyn called, then muttered, 'I think we've all had enough of war songs.'

Silently agreeing with him, Hannah watched Archie slide onto the bench in front of the black, polished Steinbeck and experimented with the opening chords of 'Some of These Days'.

'Is this sort of music suitable for a wedding?' Norah asked, her mouth puckering in mild disgust.

'Nothing wrong with a bit of ragtime,' her husband said. 'And we all could do with a bit of cheer after what has happened.'

'I suppose you're right.' Norah conceded, her eyes narrowing at Eliza, who leaned over the piano and sang along. 'Who is that woman? She's rather, er, theatrical.'

'That's Eliza Soames,' Hannah explained. 'She's Cavan's sister, and a talented actress.'

When Hannah and Aunt Violet had sought Lily-Anne's killer, their search took them to the Strand Theatre. Seated on a hamper of costumes in a tiny dressing room, Eliza had explained she was not Cavan's lover and a murderess as they'd initially thought, but his estranged sister who'd run away from home at fifteen. The pair were reunited over Cavan's grief for his wife, but Eliza had resisted all his pleas for her to live with him, preferring an itinerant life in the theatre.

'An actress?' Norah spluttered on her champagne. 'What do Cavan's patients think about that? Having one in the family won't do much for his reputation.'

'I wouldn't say that.' Selwyn eyed Eliza with an appreciative smile. 'She's rather easy on the eye. Wouldn't mind seeing her on a stage.'

Norah stiffened but kept whatever remark she was prepared to make to herself.

'Eliza is appearing in Ivor Novello's *Tabs* later this month.' Aunt Violet swiped a glass of champagne from a passing waiter. 'Aidan and I have tickets. I could get some for you and Selwyn if you'd like?'

'That would be—' Selwyn had no chance to complete the sentence as Norah grabbed his arm and hauled him towards the food table, muttering, 'Really!'

'You really shouldn't tease her, Aunt Violet.' Hannah sighed. 'You know what she's like.'

'I shouldn't, I know, but it's so easy.' Catching Hannah's expression, she frowned. 'What's the matter, darling? Is something wrong?'

'Of course something's wrong.' A sense of foreboding swept over her, freezing her smile. 'There's a body lying in the church-yard and we're in here eating enough food to feed Brentford for a week and quaffing champagne.' Her throat closed and her voice became a croak. 'Have we been exposed to so much death we don't even feel compassion any more?'

'Death has become all too commonplace, darling.' Her aunt gripped Hannah's forearm and squeezed. 'You're allowed to be happy amongst tragedy, and that man out there cannot be hurt any more. Make today memorable for all the right reasons.'

'I suppose you're right.' Hannah forced a smile, although the lump in her throat persisted. With effort, she turned her attention back to Archie who, it turned out, was a talented pianist for someone self-taught. He reached the end of the piece and lifted both hands from the keyboard to smilingly accept an enthusiastic spontaneous burst of applause led by Eliza.

'Well done, young man.' She wrapped her arm around his

shoulders in a hug. 'That was a nice enough tune for a slow waltz, but not very joyful.' She slid onto the bench beside him, forcing him sideways to make room, and launched into an enthusiastic version of Marie Lloyd's 'A Little Bit of What You Fancy Does You Good.'

Sporting a proud smile, Penny pushed her way to the front of the small crowd of guests who had gathered around the piano and rested her hands on Archie's shoulders. Joshua Clifford leaned an elbow on the grand piano, his other arm around little Xander who had reappeared from somewhere with a cake in each hand. Iris appeared to be involved in a serious discussion with Hannah's schoolgirl friend, Mary Ewell, who had given birth to a son earlier that year, which meant they were most likely discussing the trials of motherhood. Mary's husband, Robson, lounged a few feet away nursing a glass of champagne, his foot tapping along with the tune. Even Reverend Wells, whom they had invited to join the party, swayed in time to the tune, a happy smile on his face.

Hannah's anxious breathing slowed as she relaxed. Aunt Violet was right. There was nothing to be done for Reverend Aldrich now, and whether his death was an accident, from recklessness or a deliberate act, this was the day she married the love of her life and she must remember it with happiness.

She glanced at where she'd last seen Darius, on the other side of the piano, standing head and shoulders above those around him. She was about to join him when Cavan appeared, crossed the room to his side and bent to whisper something. Darius frowned, nodded, and together they left the room.

'Something tells me the local constabulary has arrived,' Aunt Violet said, watching their retreat.

Hannah's stomach knotted and she pasted on a smile. 'Aunt

Violet, would you fetch me another glass of champagne before they come in?'

'Like minds, darling. I was about to suggest the very same thing.'

4

'It's about time they got here,' Madeleine muttered crossly. 'Why did we have to wait for a local constable when Aidan Farrell is a policeman? A high-ranking one at that. He could have sorted this out in minutes.'

'No, he could not, Mama.' Iris rolled her eyes at Hannah, ensuring their mother did not see. 'The police are very territorial, and Chief Inspector Farrell works out of Scotland Yard, so this is outside his area.'

'Semantics,' Madeleine tutted. 'So, what happens now? Are we to be interrogated about our movements since breakfast yesterday? Because if so, I shall protest—'

'Madeleine, dear.' Hannah's father loomed into view over his wife's shoulder, a plate of food in one hand. 'Can you tell if the salmon is fresh or not? I'm quite partial to fish, but we don't want a repeat of the last occasion, do we?'

'Hector, of course the salmon is fresh! I prepared it myself.' Madeleine exhaled a frustrated breath, slammed her empty glass on a nearby table and launched herself towards the food table.

'I'll show you exactly what you can eat without keeping me up at night.'

'Thank you, dear. You know how much I rely on you.' Before following his wife, Hector paused long enough to direct a slow wink at Aunt Violet and his daughters.

'Well done, Papa,' Iris murmured admiringly, making Hannah smile.

'Prepared?' Aunt Violet whispered. 'More likely she carried it to the table so she could take the credit.' Her snigger earned her a sharp nudge to the ribs from Hannah's elbow.

'Attention please, everyone.' Aidan raised his voice above the chatter, holding aloft a wineglass which he tapped with a knife. 'Sergeant Baines would like a word with all of you.' He indicated the police officer at his shoulder, a short man with sparse hair, a double chin and an air of self-importance. 'It's purely a formality and nothing to be concerned about.'

The sergeant stepped forward amidst low murmurs that circled the room, mostly curious rather than disgruntled. 'As you are aware, ladies and gentlemen, there has been a death on church premises which requires investigation. The deceased has been transported to the morgue, and the police surgeon's preliminary examination suggests Reverend Aldrich died from an accidental fall.'

'What I'd like to know is what he was doing there at all?' Cavan said. 'The family mausoleum is only opened for interments, which is definitely not the case here.'

'That, I cannot say at this stage of the investigation, sir. However, it appears the reverend intended to go inside as the key was in the lock.' Sergeant Baines poised his pencil above his notebook. 'May I have your name, sir?'

'Soames, Dr Cavan Soames.' Cavan eased a finger inside his

shirt collar. 'This is my house. I run my medical practice from here.'

Hannah attributed Cavan's clipped tone to the fact his wife's final resting place had been disturbed. Lily-Anne's murder had taken them time to come to terms with, and this morning's events had stirred up old feelings for her, which must be far worse for her widower.

'I questioned Mrs Berry, the reverend's housekeeper, before you arrived, sergeant,' Aidan said, apparently reluctant to hand over the case. 'She informed me the gravedigger and gardener arrived at nine-thirty, and she left soon after to run errands. I suggest you ask him if the tomb was locked and bolted then, and when he last saw the reverend.'

'I'll do that, sir.' The policeman nodded as he scribbled furiously. 'As the mausoleum key was still in the lock when they discovered the reverend's body, we can assume he was alone. Had someone been with him they would have raised the alarm.'

'Unless they pushed him,' Aunt Violet said in an undertone.

Hannah shot her a stern look just as the policeman started speaking again.

'Chief Inspector Farrell informs me most of you are not local, but was anyone here acquainted with the reverend, either before he took up his post or since?'

'Our previous minister retired at Christmas,' Cavan replied, his calm voice lifting the tension in the room. 'Reverend Aldrich arrived in the New Year, so he's been here for four months. To be honest, I hardly knew the man. I'm not a regular churchgoer, but I saw him out and about occasionally. And no, I did not see him this morning.'

'He came here from somewhere near Oxford, I believe,' Hannah interjected. 'He mentioned it when we arranged to post our marriage banns.' She could not remember the name of the place but recalled it was something biblical.

'I'll consult the bishop for details, thank you, miss.' His gaze took in her wedding gown, and he flushed. 'Er, I mean, missus. Did anyone see the minister between ten o'clock this morning and when the ceremony began?'

'I've already questioned the wedding party, and no one appears to have seen him,' Aidan said. 'The guests didn't start arriving until a quarter past one.'

'Ah, yes, of course.' Sergeant Baines crossed out something and peered at the page.

'Get on with it, man,' Darius's father erupted, followed by low mutterings of agreement that went around the room.

'The flower ladies might have seen someone,' Madeleine interjected. 'I was at the church earlier this morning when they were there working. I didn't go anywhere near the mausoleum, so cannot say if it was open or not.'

'The housekeeper will most likely know who they are,' Aidan said in an aside to the policeman, who nodded. 'I assume there's a rota for this sort of thing among the parishioners?'

'I shall certainly be talking to them, sir, once I have their names.' Sergeant Baines tapped his pencil against the notebook.

'He was wearing his cassock and surplice when we found him,' Hannah ventured. 'He couldn't have been killed very early this morning as he was dressed for the ceremony.'

'That seems to be the case, but we'll have to see what the police surgeon says.' He slipped both into his top pocket, the slick movement spoiled when he fumbled securing the button. 'I shan't hold up your celebrations any longer. And might I offer my congratulations on this happy—?'

'Er, yes, thank you, Sergeant,' Aidan interrupted, firmly ushering him from the room.

The sound of the front door closing was followed by low voices in the hall, but the atmosphere had cooled. The room was silent apart from a muffled cough and the odd nervous laugh.

'I'm glad that's over,' Eliza announced, taking centre stage, her arms flung wide to encompass the room. 'Whatever's the matter with everyone? This is supposed to be a party. Get yourselves another drink, and would someone put that gramophone on so we can have some proper dancing?'

The music helped ease the tension as laughter and conversation resumed as guests circulated, descended on the food or drifted into the garden.

'Are you all right, Hannah?' Aunt Violet handed her a glass of champagne, her voice just loud enough to be heard over the gramophone. 'You look worried.'

'I am, a little. As far as I'm aware, no one has opened the tomb for three years, not since Lily-Anne—' She took a swift sip of champagne to avoid completing the thought. 'It must be dusty down there, even if it isn't damp. Why would the reverend go inside wearing his vestments just before he planned to conduct a wedding ceremony? It doesn't make sense.'

'There could be any number of reasons, darling. It was probably a freak accident and no one's fault. This isn't the time to fret over it.'

'I hope you're right, Aunt Violet.' Hannah scanned the room. 'Now, where's my new husband? At the very least, he owes me our first dance at our own wedding.'

* * *

After a protracted farewell to their guests later that afternoon, Hannah and Darius climbed into their Daimler to travel the short distance to Holland Park. Fuelled by unaccustomed alcohol, family and friends gathered on the road in the fading light to wave them off. Madeleine cried happy tears while her father joined the enthusiastic throwing of rose petals, most probably stripped from Cavan's garden.

Hannah twisted in her seat as they set off to wave through the rear window, while Xander, Penny and Archie chased the motor car to the end of Church Street.

'It was a lovely wedding, wasn't it?' Hannah settled back against the leather seat with a contented sigh. 'Even the weather held. And did you see your father dancing with Eliza Soames? I've never seen him so animated. Although Aidan seemed quieter than usual.'

'The responsibilities of a best man seemed to weigh heavily.' Darius chuckled. 'He kept checking the ring and his collar seemed too tight at one point. But we couldn't have asked for a better day, apart from that one unfortunate hitch.'

'Which we won't talk about,' Hannah replied, though she could not help her thoughts going in the same direction. No one had explained the reverend's presence inside the mausoleum, and she couldn't shake the feeling that something was odd about it.

'I'm sorry I couldn't organise even a short honeymoon for us.' Darius turned to check for oncoming traffic at a junction. 'I know I keep making the same excuses but I daren't risk asking my superiors for time off just now.'

'I'm not complaining. I appreciate whatever time we have together.' The crisis talks about the latest German attack on the Western Front seemed to monopolise Darius's time. 'Is it very bad in France?'

'I'm afraid so. The Germans' latest offensive has taken more ground on the Western Front than we managed since the first year of the war. We suspect their intention is to force a negotiation before the full deployment of American forces.' He took his hand from the steering wheel and covered hers on her lap. 'I'm sorry. I didn't mean to worry you with it, especially today. But what happens as a result is going to affect us all.'

'I know, and I appreciate you trusting me with the information.' She gripped his strong fingers in hers and squeezed.

'I promise not to say another word about work, or the war, and will focus entirely on you for as long as possible.' He patted her hand before returning his to the steering wheel.

'That sounds wonderful.' Hannah scooted further along the seat towards him; her cheek pressed against his arm for the rest of the three-mile drive. She found herself nodding off after what had been an eventful day, so it seemed no time at all before Darius pulled the Daimler through the tall wrought-iron gates onto the drive of his elegant Georgian mansion, set in its own grounds, in a leafy part of Holland Park.

The motor car slowed to a crawl as they approached the house where the butler, two footmen, three housemaids and the cook, arranged in order of rank, lined up on the drive in their uniforms, the double doors open behind them.

'You didn't!' Hannah gasped.

'It wasn't my idea.' Darius halted the motor car, his eyes sparkling with mischief that always turned her insides to jelly. Leaning his arm on the back of her seat, he lowered his head to see through the passenger window. 'Travis insisted. He said it was only right the staff should formally receive their new mistress.' He lightly massaged the back of his neck with one hand. 'I'm sorry it's not a more impressive display, but as you know, the two younger footmen enlisted in 1914, and the outside staff are down to two. However, the housemaids and kitchen girls have yet to defect to the armaments factories, so I must be doing something right.'

'That was so sweet of him,' Hannah said, fighting a wave of emotion. 'Now I feel like Queen Mary.' Travis opened the passenger side door, a hand extended to help Hannah out. 'Welcome home, Mrs Clifford.'

'Thank you, Travis. This is a lovely welcome.' He held down her hat against a sudden gust of wind, she reminded herself it was her home now. 'Don't let the staff get cold out here, though.' She recalled when Darius's mother loved to throw extravagant parties for her only child, and after her death, Joshua Clifford signed the house over to Darius.

Summarily dismissed, the staff scurried in all directions like startled blackbirds, coats and aprons billowing.

Darius placed a protective arm around her and together they entered the double front doors into an expansive entrance hall where a lantern ceiling flooded the hallway with evening light and illuminated a curved, cantilevered staircase.

'Lovely,' she whispered, noting the recent addition of brass and glass electric light fixtures. 'No more smelly oil lamps.'

'What did you say, Hannah?' Darius asked.

'Oh, nothing.' She hugged his arm tighter.

'There are a couple of telephone messages for you, sir.' Travis pulled two scraps of paper from his waistcoat pocket. 'One is from the Admiralty. They said it was important.'

'That didn't take the War Office long.' Darius scanned the top page rapidly. 'As I suspected, they want me in the office first thing tomorrow.'

'That's a shame, but not unexpected.' Hannah removed her gloves and hat, placing them in the lobby as she had done a hundred times over the years.

'Hmm.' Darius frowned at a page in his hand. 'This one is for you from your mother.'

'Already? What does she say?' Hannah doubted an emergency had occurred within the last hour.

'It seems Iris experienced some concerning symptoms after we left the reception. Cavan examined her and has advised bed rest.'

'Oh no.' Hannah abandoned tidying her hair in the hall mirror and crossed to his side. 'Does it say how she is?'

'There's nothing else, other than Mycroft returned to the Coach and Horses with the boy, but Norah and Selwyn are staying the night. So are your parents.'

'Trust Mother.' Hannah rolled her eyes. 'Any excuse not to go back to Surrey if there's drama to be had. I hope Iris and her baby aren't in any real danger.'

'With your mother and Norah to fuss over her, not to mention an experienced doctor like Cavan on hand, she'll be well looked after.'

This observation made her feel infinitely better, and she reminded herself this was hardly new ground for her sister, who seemed to positively enjoy being pregnant.

'May I borrow the Swift tomorrow morning? I'll go over to Cavan's and see how Iris is.' She doubted she would ever be confident enough to manoeuvre the more cumbersome Daimler through the London streets.

'Of course you may. And it's yours now too, so you hardly need my permission.' Darius tucked his note into a pocket and handed the other one to Hannah. 'Incidentally, do your parents know you drive? Or is it still your guilty secret?'

'Er... Papa does, but I haven't plucked up the courage to tell Mama yet. She thinks it's most unladylike and still tuts at Aunt Violet, even though she's been driving for years. Promise me you won't reveal my secret?'

'I wouldn't dare. But make sure you park around the corner out of sight of the house.'

'Supper will be in half an hour, sir, madam,' Travis announced, throwing open the double doors to the dining room where a thoughtful arrangement of a small table laden with white china and crystal glasses sparkled in the flickering candle-light from a silver candelabra.

'I assumed you would prefer a simple repast after the day's events, madam, sir?'

'You don't know the half of it, Travis.' Darius laughed.

'Actually, I do, sir. Mrs Clifford's maid, one Miss Ivy Moffatt, arrived with your luggage an hour ago, madam. The kitchen has been in an uproar since.'

'Of course.' Hannah sighed. 'Ivy packed all my things at the house and helped doing food preparation at Cavan's. She's had a front row seat for all the drama.'

'Will soup and sandwiches suffice?' Travis asked, evidently bored with the conversation.

'That sounds wonderful,' Hannah replied, smiling. Trust Ivy to be the bearer of bad news, though it might help her integrate into the servant's hall.

'While we're on the subject of meals, madam.' Travis cleared his throat discreetly. 'Have you chosen the coming week's menus? If so, I'll deliver them to Cook.'

'Goodness, I haven't given them a thought,' Hannah replied, mildly panicked that she might have revealed her inability to be Darius's wife on her first day. 'I suggest Cook serve whatever she can get her hands on, considering the food shortages.'

'As you wish, madam,' he replied sagely. 'But I trust you'll not hold me responsible for what she comes up with. Initiative is not Cook's strong point.'

Hannah was about to thank him, but he had already disappeared through the green baize door. 'I've hardly arrived, and he's asking me about menus?' She widened her eyes. 'Was that deliberate, or should I have been better prepared?'

'Don't let it worry you. He's testing the water to see what sort of mistress you'll be.' Darius shrugged out of his coat, chuckling to himself. 'He's worried you're going to sweep through his routine like a tornado and disrupt the household. Not that he'd really expect for a moment, especially as he's known you since you wore pigtails.'

'Don't remind me. Those, along with the freckles, made me feel doomed at age eleven.'

He crossed the tiled hallway and playfully encircled her waist, making her giggle. 'Your empathy for lame ducks meant you were always lovely to me, even when you fell rear first into that rhododendron bush at my thirteenth birthday party.'

'I didn't fall; you pushed me.' Hannah slapped him lightly on his lapel. 'And you're hardly a lame duck.' She gave the elegant entrance hall a pointed look.

'It is rather grand, isn't it?' He followed her gaze with a self-conscious one of his own. 'But my parents were so happy here and Papa said he wanted the same for me. I didn't have the heart to refuse.' He planted a light kiss on her forehead, laced his fingers with hers and drew her towards the dining room. 'You can do whatever you wish where the staff are concerned.'

Hannah spotted a familiar-looking object on the table – a bottle of Pol Roger, the same brand that had been served at their reception. She assumed her father had obtained them from somewhere, but before she could thank him, the vicar's untimely death had pushed everything else out of her mind.

'This looks familiar.' Hannah lifted the bottle in her free hand. 'Did you filch this from our reception?'

'Ah. Actually, that's from my own cellar. I kept this one back for tonight, the rest I sent to Cavan's for the toasts.'

'*You* brought the champagne for the wedding? I assumed Mycroft brought it.' Her brother-in-law had a reputation for keeping a well-stocked cellar and had boasted that even if the war lasted ten years it would see him through. 'Where did you get it?'

'Um, well, I took an impromptu trip to Rheims last month, and—'

'Rheims?' She gaped at him, horrified, and released the bottle that hit the table with a thump.

'I know.' He winced, but the bottle had only fallen a couple of inches and was undamaged. 'Normally, I'm not required to cross the Channel with my job, but there were extenuating circumstances. And we had excellent protection,' he added, as if that made a difference.

'Oh, Darius!' Her stomach knotted. 'You promised me you would never have to go behind enemy lines!'

He interrupted her protest with raised hands as if warding her off. 'Hush, listen. It wasn't that bad. Rheims itself was being evacuated just as we arrived, so we had to be taken somewhere safer.' He pulled her closer and wrapped his arms tightly around her, his touch welcome, though she took no comfort from it as her breathing quickened. Her throat was suddenly dry with panic.

'We took shelter in some tunnels below a winery stacked with champagne during the air raid. We were quite safe. Well, relatively.' His voice held amusement, as if he were describing an adventure and not a flight to survive. 'The bombing only lasted a couple of hours, after which we were escorted back to our train. My commanding officer was presented with eight cases of champagne, and knowing I was getting married soon, he gave me half.'

An air raid. He never said a word about that!

'I-I wish you had told me.' She stared up at him, but common sense returned. No matter when he had mentioned it, her reaction would have been the same. Blind panic mixed with anger and helplessness. 'Not about the champagne, but the other thing.' The only reason she could accept the nature of his work and his last-minute disappearances was because he always claimed he would never be in danger.

'How could I? You were in the throes of wedding plans and besides, it was a last-minute decision with no advance preparation. I shouldn't have said anything, but I needed to explain the champagne, or you might take me for a gangster or a black-market trader.'

'I could probably cope with that easier,' she replied, making him laugh. 'Will you... will you have to do it again?' All over the country wives and mothers endured far worse, with their menfolk under bombardment in the trenches, so she should be strong enough to overlook a single short trip to France and an air raid when the same thing happened in London.

'I hope not.' He took her hands in his and squeezed them. 'Now stop worrying and let's enjoy our supper. We still have our wedding night before I get summoned back to the chaps at the War Office, so let's forget everything except enjoying our first evening together.'

'What did you have in mind, exactly?' Hannah pulled him to a halt, turned to face him and reached to wrap her arms around his neck. Her body pressed against him from chest to knees; it was the closest she had got to him all day.

'I was talking about soup and sandwiches in front of a roaring fire.' He raised a cynical eyebrow. 'What were *you* thinking?'

Hannah's cheeks felt suddenly hot as she returned his slow smile.

'Hussy.' He chuckled, returning her embrace with one that crushed her ribs until she could barely breathe, but the rush of pleasure that went through her made up for any discomfort.

5

After breakfast the next morning, Hannah found Travis waiting on the front drive beside Darius's compact roadster, its spotless dark green paintwork shining in the morning sunlight.

'How kind of you, Travis, but I would have been happy to fetch it from the mews myself.'

'It's no trouble, madam.' He inclined his head while holding open the driver's door for her. 'I took the liberty of having it cleaned, and the fuel tank filled.' He lowered his voice, adding, 'We keep a supply of petrol here for Mr Clifford's use, which is breaking DORA, I'm afraid, but I'm sure madam will be discreet.'

'You can rely on me, Travis.' Hannah suppressed a smile as she climbed into the driver's seat. 'I won't tell a soul.'

The Defence of the Realm Act, affectionately, and not so much, referred to as DORA, was legislation brought in at the outbreak of the war. This gave the government power to make regulations necessary for the war effort, such as covered street lighting, the no treating order banning the purchase of rounds of drinks in pubs, limiting the use of white flour and making petrol an outrageous 6d a gallon.

Following Darius's advice, on arriving at the four-storey house on the corner of Chiswick Mall, she tucked the motor car into an alley between the church and the garden wall in a spot invisible from the windows before walking around to the front door.

Hannah handed her coat to the maid in the vestibule just as Cavan crossed from the dining room. 'Hannah, what a lovely surprise.' He paused mid-stride and intercepted her, dismissed the maid and drew Hannah into the main hall. 'I thought you and Darius would be too preoccupied to make house calls this soon after the wedding?'

'Darius was called back to the War Office this morning, and when I heard Iris was ill, I came to see how she was.' Hannah smiled back weakly, hoping she would not be fielding innuendos all day.

'Not ill, exactly,' Cavan replied, 'but I didn't like her blood pressure, which was unusually high, so I recommended a couple of days' bed rest.'

'It's generous of you to accommodate my family, especially after the chaos we created yesterday.'

'It's my pleasure. I must admit, this house has been far too quiet lately.' His welcome smile faded as his thoughts took a darker turn. 'In fact, it has been that way since I lost Lily-Anne, so I'm enjoying having house guests again. There's something about female voices and laughter which brings life to the place.'

'It's a shame Eliza's chosen not to live here with you. I'm sure she would have livened things up a bit.'

'My dear sister is torn. She's determined to prevent me becoming a staid old bachelor but is also loath to leave the bright lights of the West End. Not that they are bright just now with the blackout in force, but the theatres are still doing a roaring trade. She's appearing in the musical *Very Good Eddie* at the Palace

Theatre right now. If you want tickets, I am sure she would oblige.'

'I'll bear that in mind, thank you,' Hannah replied. 'Darius and I love the theatre, even if only a matinee.'

Many theatres had changed their schedules to daylight hours to avoid increasing the risk of air raids and curfews made it hard to travel after dark.

The closing of a door overhead brough Hannah's head up to where her mother leaned over the banister rail on the upper landing.

'I thought I heard my darling daughter's voice.' Madeleine descended the stairs and planted a powdery kiss on Hannah's cheek. 'I gather you got my message, but you didn't have to come running over here.'

'It sounded serious, but Cavan has just reassured me,' Hannah said, returning her light hug.

'I admit, we were worried last night, but Iris is much brighter this morning.' Madeleine picked a tiny piece of fluff from Hannah's jacket. 'She's sleeping now, which is the best thing for her. I'm sure she'll be thrilled to see you when she wakes up. In the meantime, why don't you keep Violet company?'

'Aunt Violet is here?' Hannah redirected her mother's hand as she reached to tweak a strand of her hair. 'After living with me, I expected her to be delighted to be in her own home again.'

Her aunt was moving back to her house in Mortlake, that she had abandoned three years before to act as Hannah's chaperone in Chiswick – a condition her parents had insisted upon when Hannah announced her intention to live there alone.

'Violet arrived half an hour ago, ostensibly to ask after Iris, but she seems out of sorts. Not like her at all.'

'She was in the garden a few moments ago,' Cavan said. 'I saw her through my office window.'

'Go and have a chat with her.' Madeleine gave Hannah a gentle shove towards the sitting room where the French doors into the garden stood open. 'I have to check on the men. Your father and Selwyn have commandeered the library where they seem to plan to sit all day reading the war reports and smoking. I suspect they will order coffee at regular intervals too, taking advantage of Cavan's hospitality, not to mention his cigar supply.'

'I only buy them for guests, Madeleine, and Hector qualifies so there's no need to fret.' Laughing, Cavan chose this moment to withdraw, pressing Hannah's shoulder as he retreated to his office.

Hannah found Aunt Violet seated on a peacock-back wicker chair under a gazebo up against the wall at the far end of the lawn, with a tray on a low table in front of her. She looked up as Hannah approached her across the grass.

'Have you left him already, Hannah?' Her aunt smiled at her over the rim of her cup.

'I'm not even going to react to that.' Hannah paused beside her. 'What are you doing here? I thought you'd be up to your elbows in packing cases.'

'I forgot how moving house was so enervating. I was really looking forward to reclaiming my villa in Mortlake, but now it feels like a retrograde step. You'll laugh when I say this, but I miss Ivy. The girl who works for me now is a surly thing with no sense of humour.'

'Have you bothered to get to know this maid? She might have some personal sadness, a relative lost in the fighting, perhaps?'

'Get to know her? Certainly not. She's only been with me two weeks and I don't have time to chat to the staff.'

'Or the inclination,' Hannah said, but only to herself. 'Then feel free to come and see me and Ivy as often as you wish.' Not that her aunt had cultivated a relationship with Ivy, but they maintained mutual respect in which they hurled mild insults at one another without either taking offence.

'I might take you up on that. How is Ivy coping now she's under Travis's supervision?'

'Well, we're still on day one, but Darius anticipated ructions would occur if we got those two together, so he suggested changing her duties to those of my lady's maid to avoid conflict before it started. So far, it appears to be working.'

'Very astute of him, and you're being spoiled already. You haven't had a lady's maid since you lived with your parents. Did you drive by our old house on the river before coming here?' She replaced her cup in the saucer and raised the coffee-pot in enquiry.

'No thank you, I've not long had breakfast.' She eyed the miniature pastries Cavan's cook was famous for. 'But I'll have one of these,' she said, helping herself to one. 'The new tenants are moving in today, and I thought it would depress me seeing other people in my old home when I've decided not to dwell on the past.'

'Nor should you. Your friends are going to cast envious eyes on that mansion in Holland Park you now call home.'

'It has its disadvantages.' Hannah licked icing sugar from her lips, savouring the lightness of the pastry and the hint of lemon. 'I won't have much to do. Travis has run the house since Joshua Clifford's time, so I feel unqualified to criticise or make changes. Not that he needs it, he does a wonderful job. And since Ivy took charge of my wardrobe, I'm practically redundant.'

'Pardon me if I have no sympathy for you, especially with the hours I'm putting in at the bookshop. Although hiring a lady's maid sounds like a plan for me. It might be a little difficult with the current servant problem, but there must be some girls willing to train as domestics. You'll be putting in days at the bookshop, won't you, and continuing with your volunteer work at the hospital library?'

'I could never abandon either, although I'm reluctant to regard my work at Endell Street as war work. It's not like being a nurse, which I'm not brave enough for.'

'If you feel you aren't doing your bit, you could always join me fundraising.'

'Hmm. I'm not very good at badgering people for money. But, changing the subject, have you noticed the change in Cavan? Anyone else having a houseful of uninvited guests would find it a trial, but he says he enjoys it. Or is he simply being polite?'

'I doubt it. He's invited them to stay longer. Are you still feeling guilty for suspecting him of being a wife murderer?'

'Don't remind me.' Hannah winced.

'Aidan says the spouse is always the first to be suspected, so you weren't alone painting Cavan as the villain. But he was exonerated quickly, and, if you remember, for a while Aidan believed even *you* might have killed Lily-Anne.'

'How long a while?' Hannah demanded, having forgotten that small fact.

'Don't look so horrified. He's a policeman, so he suspected everyone who knew her. And it *was* your knife used to kill her, and she was found in your bookshop.'

'*Our* bookshop. And I was the one who found her.'

'Exactly, another reason you were high on the list. Anyway, you weren't a serious suspect. At least, not for long.'

'Though I miss Lily-Anne awfully,' Hannah said. 'And Cavan is a handsome, successful man who should probably find someone else to live his life with.'

'So says the newlywed, but then they say misery loves company.'

'That's a bit cynical.' Hannah then recalled her intimate

supper with Darius the previous evening that had turned into a more intimate night that made her pulse race each time she thought of it.

'Hannah, you're blushing.'

'No, I'm not.' Hannah turned away, recalling how her aunt had sat staring back at the house when she arrived, her thoughts obviously miles away. 'There's something else worrying you, isn't there, Aunt Violet? And don't say it's the house because you've talked about little else since we announced the wedding.'

Her aunt sighed, abandoning the pastry she had been nibbling, and sat back. 'If you must know, it's Aidan. He's become disillusioned with his new post as Detective Chief Inspector.'

'But he worked tirelessly for that promotion.' Hannah eased onto the bench opposite. 'It's a very important job.'

'It is, but according to Aidan it's – what's the word he used – pedestrian. He misses the excitement of embarking on a new case, interviewing witnesses, and searching through evidence. He doesn't get to see anything until it's been collected and reported on by others. He says supervising other detectives isn't the same as finding vital clues and solving problems. He's even toying with the idea of leaving the police force.'

'Leaving?' Hannah asked, shocked. 'And doing what?'

'You'll never guess, but he's thinking of taking over the—'

'Violet! Hannah!' Madeleine's voice carried across the garden as she crossed the grass towards them. 'Both of you, come inside.'

'It's not Iris, is it?' Hannah leapt to her feet, instantly alert.

'No, she's perfectly well and awake now. You can see her later. But Chief Inspector Farrell has just arrived with a colleague and wants to talk to us. I told him you were here too, Violet, and he says to include you. Now come along, you mustn't keep them waiting.' She looked balefully at the messy tray before turning back to the house.

'We've been summoned.' Aunt Violet laughed for the first time since Hannah had arrived, linking their arms. 'I trust you not to repeat what I said about Aidan. He won't thank me for gossiping over a casual remark.'

'As if I would.'

* * *

'Ah, there you are, ladies.' Cavan closed the French doors behind them. 'This is all very mysterious, but Aidan refuses to say anything until we are all assembled.' He settled them on a sofa before returning to the marble fireplace, a foot raised on the fender.

'Good morning, Hannah.' Norah arrived on Selwyn's arm from the door to the hall. 'How are you finding life as a married woman?'

Hannah inwardly groaned, saved from more than a non-committal answer by her father who greeted her as if they had been apart for weeks.

'Have they found out what happened?' Hector released his daughter and took a seat in a wing-back chair, its twin already occupied by Selwyn.

'I expect we're about to find out.' Madeleine paused beside the sofa, one eyebrow raised at Norah who sprawled in the centre, thus preventing anyone occupying the other seats.

'Oh, sorry, Madeleine.' Tutting at the inconvenience, Norah grudgingly slid to one side to make room for her.

'My apologies, everyone, for disrupting your immediate plans.' Aidan announced his entrance. 'But it wasn't possible to recall all the wedding guests from yesterday, so this group will have to suffice.'

'Suffice for what, exactly?' Hector asked.

'This is Detective Inspector Wilson.' Aidan gestured to the presence of a man who hovered in the door to the hall. 'He's in charge of the investigation into the death of Reverend Julian Aldrich.' A younger man in an ill-fitting suit sidled into the room, his clean-shaven face slightly marred by a permanent frown.

'Since when do detectives handle fatal accidents?' Hector huffed, irritated.

'Hush, Papa,' Hannah whispered, though equally baffled.

'That will become clear presently, sir,' Inspector Wilson said, with a nod to Hector. 'A post-mortem was performed last night on the reverend, and the results of the laboratory tests this morning conclude his death was *not* accidental.'

'Not accidental?' Selwyn huffed. 'The chap took a header on some stone steps.'

'The man's skull was damaged, sir, but the fall was not the cause of death.' His bland expression gave nothing else away. 'And you are?'

'Selwyn Atherton.' He waggled his fingers in Norah's direction. 'This is my wife. We're relatives of Mrs Clifford.'

'Thank you, sir.' He scribbled in the ubiquitous notebook every policeman lived by. 'DCI Farrell has already given me a list of wedding guests, but it helps to put faces to names.'

'So how did the man die?' Cavan prompted.

'Ah, yes, sir, I was coming to that. Sometime before his death, Reverend Aldrich apparently ingested a large dose of digitalis.'

'What?' Cavan straightened. 'Are you sure?'

'According to the pathologist, yes, sir,' DI Wilson replied confidently.

'It's Doctor. And digitalis is prescribed for heart conditions. He always seemed like a healthy young man.'

'Was he a patient of yours then, Doctor?' the detective asked.

'Not in a professional capacity, but anyone could see he was fit and exhibited no symptoms.' He thought for a moment. 'Although, defects going undiagnosed is not unheard of. It's a fact there are disappointingly few diseases we can cure with confidence.'

'That's not very encouraging!' Madeleine snapped. At her stunned expression he appeared to realise he had revealed too much, broke off and murmured an apology.

'Of course, he might have become ill after arriving in the parish,' Aidan suggested. 'But the preliminary post-mortem said the damage to his heart suggested a far higher dose than a doctor might prescribe.'

'You mean he was murdered?' Hannah gasped. The room stared to spin before her eyes. An accident on her wedding day was tragedy enough – but a murder! 'Er... could someone fetch me a glass of water?' she asked, her voice strained. 'I would do it myself, but I feel a little faint.' Her vision blurred around the edges, making her nauseous.

'Either that, or he chose an unorthodox method to commit suicide,' Selwyn muttered humourlessly, but just then all the attention remained on Hannah.

'You aren't expecting, are you?' Norah's voice lifted in excitement.

'Don't be ridiculous, Norah.' Madeleine strode to the sideboard. 'It was the shock, that's all.' Returning, she pressed a half-full crystal glass into Hannah's hand. 'Though you do look pale. Are you sure you—?'

Grimacing, Hannah waved her away and took a sip from the glass.

'Why isn't Chief Inspector Farrell leading the investigation?' Madeleine demanded, casting a hard look at Detective Wilson.

'I spend most of my time at a desk these days.' Aidan spoke with a marked lack of enthusiasm, which seemed to confirm what

Aunt Violet had said earlier. 'I shall oversee DI Wilson's investigation, naturally, and he'll submit regular reports. He is an experienced investigator, and I am confident he will bring the guilty party to book. Inspector,' he said, relinquishing the floor to his colleague, 'if you would recap what we currently know about the victim.'

'Sir.' DI Wilson flicked open his notebook, reclaiming their attention. 'Reverend Julian Aldrich was aged twenty-seven and unmarried. He graduated from Merton College in 1916 and ordained a year later. He took a post as curate of St Ethelred's in Jericho before coming here as a minister four months ago.'

'Jericho,' Hannah repeated under her breath, then louder, 'I knew it was something biblical.'

'Did you have something to add, Miss... er?' Inspector Wilson peered at her.

'Er, no, and it's Mrs,' Hannah experienced a small thrill as she corrected him. 'Mrs Hannah Clifford.'

'My apologies, Mrs Clifford. Did you see anything unusual in or around the church yesterday?'

'Apart from Reverend Aldrich's body lying at the bottom of the mausoleum steps, not really,' Hannah replied archly. 'I was getting ready for my wedding and saw no one other than close members of my family.'

'And when did you last see the reverend alive?' the detective asked, gaining confidence.

'My husband and I rehearsed our vows in the church the day before, which took about an hour. My Aunt Violet was there too, as was Dr Soames and Detective Chief Inspector Farrell, but no one else. And besides, who would want to kill a vicar?'

'That's an interesting question, madam.' Inspector Wilson tapped his lower lip with his pencil. 'As the reverend was a newcomer to the district, his associates in Oxford will be questioned to see if anyone had a grudge against the man. The local police there have offered their cooperation,' he added, as if he expected to be challenged. 'Also, his tutors at Merton might be able to tell us more.'

'What form does digitalis take when it is given as a medicine?' Hannah asked.

'What a strange thing to ask, dear.' Madeleine glared at her. 'Does it really matter?'

'Actually, it does, Mrs Merrill,' Cavan interjected. 'It's made from leaves distilled in alcohol and water to make a tincture. Administered in small doses as drops, it tastes bitter and quite unpleasant. In fact the toxic dose of digitalis is only one and a half times a therapeutic one, so it's worryingly easy to make a mistake and take too much. An accidental overdose is more than possible.'

'Do we know when he would have ingested it, Inspector?'

'Er, I'm not, er, madam, if you'd allow me to ask the questions, we could complete this matter more quickly.'

'I wouldn't want to complicate things, Inspector.' Feeling better, Hannah mentally rolled her eyes and placed her empty water glass on the table. However, if the detective had registered her sarcasm, he gave no sign of it.

'I'll need to speak to everyone who knew him during his time here, which I understand was only a few months?'

'Four to be exact, Inspector, and I'm sure we are all eager to help,' Cavan said, taking charge. 'Should you require a room to hold interviews, I'll be happy to put one at your disposal.'

'That's very kind of you, Doctor.' The inspector consulted his pristine-looking notebook again.

'There is something I would like to address,' Wilson said, once the room fell silent again. 'A volunteer who cleaned the church yesterday said another lady she assumed was a member of the wedding party arrived to help arrange the flowers. Can anyone confirm this?'

'That was me.' Madeleine raised her hand as if she was in school, then retracted it again, embarrassed. 'I went to check everything was as it should be.'

'What time would that be, Mrs—?'

'Mrs Merrill. Oh, about eleven, perhaps a little later. I asked after the reverend, but no one had seen him. I thought nothing of it until Darius came to tell us he couldn't be found.'

'I see. Thank you.' The detective made a note in his book before reading from the page. 'I believe Mr Darius Clifford was also at the church?'

'I should think so – he was the groom,' Hector said disdainfully.

'Uh... of course.' DI Wilson flushed unbecomingly, scanning the room. 'I meant at around the same time the reverend went missing. Is the gentleman here?'

'I'm sorry, no,' Hannah said. 'My husband is at the War Office. Although he could make himself available if required.'

'Er, yes, Chief Inspector Farrell informed me he works in intelligence, but if I could talk to him sometime...' He waved his pencil in the air.

'I shall ask him to call you when he can,' Hannah replied.

The door clicked open and a housemaid appeared.

'I'm sorry to interrupt, Dr Soames.' She halted, staring nervously as all eyes turned towards her. 'Um, there's a lady in the hall and I'm not sure what to do with her.'

'*Do* with her?' Cavan regarded the girl with amusement. 'Is she a patient?'

'I don't think so, sir. She went to the vicarage first, and Mrs Berry told her about the vicar and redirected her here. When I told her you were with the police, she insisted I show her in.'

'Then do so, Hetty, I'll speak—' Cavan had barely got the words out before a tall, striking young woman barged past the maid while scanning the room with wide grey eyes.

'I apologise for the intrusion,' the newcomer said in a voice which shook slightly. 'Was what that woman said at the vicarage true?'

'If you mean that the reverend is dead, miss, that is correct.' Inspector Wilson approached her. 'And who might you be?'

'My name is Frances Blackwood,' she said slowly, a small bag gripped in her hands so tightly that her knuckles showed prominently through her gloves. 'That is, I was. Now it's Aldrich. Julian Aldrich was my husband.'

'Oh, my goodness!' Madeleine rose and advanced on the young woman, taking both hands in hers. 'Come and sit down, dear.'

She gestured to Hector to leave his armchair to make room, which he did, slightly hesitantly but with surprising agility.

'Please!' The newcomer ignored the chair, her arm raised to fend off both Madeleine and Hannah. 'Will someone just tell me what's going on? How can Julian be dead? What happened to him?'

'Hetty!' Aunt Violet commanded the still-hovering maid. 'Fetch some tea for this young lady. And make sure it's sweet.'

Madeleine guided the newcomer into Hector's vacated chair while the gentlemen changed positions to make room for the female fussing, though they achieved little. Hannah intercepted Hetty, who had rapidly arrived with a loaded tea tray. Taking it from her, she set it on a low table and poured the tea, handing the newcomer a cup, which she accepted with a grateful smile.

Norah produced some smelling salts from somewhere, and Aunt Violet proffered a lace-edged handkerchief, but the young woman rejected them both with a sharp shake of her head.

'I apologise for intruding,' she spoke calmly, but her gaze darted around the room as if nervous. 'That housekeeper at the vicarage told me the police are here because of Julian. Would someone please explain what's happening?'

'You said you are Mrs Aldrich, is that correct?' Aidan's tone implied disbelief. 'I'm Chief Inspector Farrell, in charge of this investigation. You see, everyone here was under the impression that Reverend Aldrich was single and lived alone. There was no mention of his having a spouse.'

'No, I... I don't live here. At least I was planning to, but not yet.' She took a sip of the tea before continuing. 'I came up on the train this morning from Oxford to see him, but the woman at the vicarage said... Look, I don't understand.' Her hand jumped, threatening to spill the tea, and Hannah reached out a hand to steady it. 'How can he be dead?'

'I'm sorry to have to tell you, but he was found dead in the church grounds yesterday,' Aidan said gently.

'But how? He wasn't ill – well, not as far as I knew.' Frances handed her half-drunk cup back to Hannah and addressed DI Wilson. 'Are you a policeman too? If this one won't explain—' she flicked an impatient hand at Aidan '—could *you* tell me what's going on?'

Unnerved, DI Wilson stared from Mrs Aldrich to Aidan and back again.

'Go on, Wilson,' Aidan nodded. 'Tell the lady what we know thus far.'

'Yes, sir.' DI Wilson cleared his throat, then started to read aloud from his notebook.

'The body of Reverend Julian Aldrich was found inside the Bentham family mausoleum at approximately two-fifteen yesterday when—'

'Detective,' Aidan gestured him to halt, then proceeded to relate the events of the previous day in a gentler tone to which Mrs Aldrich listened without interrupting him, her clear hazel eyes fixed on his face. Her hands had stopped shaking and apart from a heightened colour in her cheeks, she remained composed, possibly, Hannah assumed, because disbelief often greeted news of a loved one's death, and it took time to accept something so shocking.

'Digitalis?' she asked when he reached that part of the story. 'I don't even know what that is.' Her voice rose in anguish and she brought both hands to her face. 'I don't understand what's happening. How did Julian die? Was it an accident?'

'At first, that was a distinct possibility,' Aidan began gently. 'However, certain details have come to light that might suggest otherwise.'

'Might?' Frances' voice rose to a squeak. 'What do you mean by that? Did someone hurt him or not? You're not suggested he did it to himself?'

'No, not at all. But you must appreciate our investigation is in its very early stages.'

'Are you sure no one else knew you and Reverend Aldrich were married?' Hannah scanned the faces in the room in search of reactions but was met with only bewildered shrugs.

'We were careful to keep it secret from everyone,' Frances said, then her expression turned sheepish. 'I know that sounds... underhanded, but we felt it was best. Even his bishop didn't know.'

'May I ask why?' Aidan asked. 'It might be pertinent to the police investigation.'

'Pertinent, how?' Frances held his gaze steadily. 'Are you suggesting someone killed Julian to prevent our marriage? If so, then they were too late. We married a month ago at the registry office in Marylebone.' Her eyes glittered with unshed tears mixed with defiance. 'I have a perfectly legal marriage certificate to prove it.'

'I'm not suggesting otherwise, madam,' Aidan replied. 'Was there some, er... conflict attached to your nuptials?'

'In a way.' She paused before continuing. 'You see, my father disapproved of my seeing Julian because, in his opinion, being a mere vicar's wife was not good enough for me.'

'One can see his point,' Norah observed, drawing all eyes. 'Second sons with private incomes are perfectly acceptable as clergymen, but I assume that doesn't apply here, therefore—'

'That's quite enough, dear,' Selwyn interrupted, nudging her with a well-aimed elbow.

'I was only saying,' Norah replied in her own defence, but grudgingly obeyed.

'Was Reverend Aldrich expecting you, Frances?' Hannah pre-empted Aidan's next question, though he didn't seem to mind the shift of focus from Norah.

'Not exactly,' Frances hesitated. 'Julian felt we should tell Father about our marriage, so I arranged to come and see him to work out exactly what we would say.' She chewed her bottom lip and stared at her lap. 'Father is an expert at twisting words to fit his own perspective, so it was important we presented a united front. When I arrived at the hotel, I telephoned Julian to say I was on my way, but he said to come today instead as he had a wedding to perform.'

Hannah was about to add it was, in fact, her wedding but decided against it.

'What time did you call him?' DI Wilson asked abruptly.

'Just before ten that morning. I got the early train. I usually stay with an old schoolfriend when I come to town, and I allowed Father to assume so on this occasion so as not to arouse his suspicions.' Her cheeks flushed a deeper red. 'I... I realise that makes me sound deceitful, but everything would have been in the open soon.'

'How long have you known Reverend Aldrich?' DI Wilson flicked through his notebook, selected a new page and scribbled something.

'About three years. We met through our parents in Oxford. My father is a Professor of Medieval Studies at Merton College and when Julian wanted to study there, Father wrote a testimonial which helped with his application. We became close in Julian's second year.'

'If your father knew Julian socially, then why the secrecy?' Hannah asked.

'Father never had anything negative to say about Julian before he announced his decision to go into the Church. I told him we were courting, and it was getting serious, which is when he insisted we stop seeing each other. He refused to see reason, so Julian and I decided to elope. Father was bound to come around once we were legally married.'

Aunt Violet gave a low snort, which implied that was an optimistic assumption, but no one said anything.

'Anyway,' Frances continued, 'when he was more accustomed to the idea of our marriage, we planned to have a church ceremony with everyone we knew.' Her face crumpled suddenly, and her bottom lip quivered. 'Now it's all ruined and I don't understand why.'

'Tell us more about the reverend.' Aidan eased onto the arm of the chair next to her, his voice soft.

'He was orphaned young.' Frances's voice cracked and this time when Madeleine offered her a handkerchief, she accepted it gratefully. 'He was raised by an uncle and aunt. But they live in Scotland and as travel is difficult right now, what with troops being given priority, I will make the funeral arrangements.' Her voice cracked on the word, and she pressed the handkerchief to her nose.

'The church will no doubt assist.' Cavan's voice filled a brief but heavy silence that followed. 'And if the vicarage does not appeal, you are welcome to stay here.'

'That's very kind, but unnecessary.' Lowering the handkerchief, she gazed up at Cavan with a shaky smile. 'I'm booked into the Gore Hotel in Kensington.'

'I know it well,' Cavan replied, openly surprised. 'A fine establishment.'

'It is, isn't it?' She crumpled the now soggy square of linen in both hands. 'I've wanted to stay there since I was a girl and always loved Kensington Gardens.' She dabbed her eyes again, swallowing in an effort to compose herself.

'You know London well?' Hannah asked, puzzled. Didn't she say she'd arrived from Oxford?

'I was born here. Father and I moved to Oxford eight years ago after my mother died.' She dabbed at her eyes again. 'In case you're all wondering, my father's protectiveness is not due to my youth and perceived immaturity, but more to the fact my mother left me a considerable inheritance. He sees fortune hunters everywhere, although it didn't occur to me he would include Julian in that category.' She swiped tears from her face and blew her nose noisily.

'I'm sorry to cause you further distress, Mrs Aldrich,' Aidan said carefully. 'But you are certain Mr Blackwood was unaware of your engagement?' Hannah caught his eyes as her thoughts followed the same line.

'Professor,' she corrected him. 'And my father is overly protective, but he is certainly not prone to murder.' Frances raised an eyebrow at him. 'He's an academic and lives among his books. He cares nothing about money and would never hurt anyone.'

Hannah doubted the professor's lack of interest in money was genuine if he was constantly on the lookout for fortune hunters but kept the thought to herself. From the speculative look in Aidan's eye, he had come to the same conclusion.

'Did anyone else know about your plans to come to London

today, miss?' the policeman asked. 'The schoolfriend you mentioned, perhaps?'

She shook her head. 'I'm aware someone should know where I was, so told a friend where I was staying, but she promised not to tell Papa where I was. No one else knows I'm here.'

'Very wise, miss. And does this friend know you and the reverend were married?'

'She does now,' Frances said carefully. 'Esme has always known Julian and I were close, but I only told her we had eloped two days ago.'

'And you know of no one who might have a grudge against Reverend Aldrich?'

'A grudge?' She stared up at Aidan. 'What sort of grudge? He was a minister and, as far as I knew, was liked by everyone.' She hesitated. 'Everyone I knew, at least. He had friends at university I never met, so one of them might have taken against him.' She shook her head. 'But a disagreement among students would never be enough to harm him, surely?'

'You'd be surprised at the reasons people have for murder, miss.' DI Wilson snorted a laugh. 'Er... sorry, Mrs. In my experience it takes little more than a slight and—'

'Yes, thank you, Detective, we get your point,' Aidan interrupted him with a hard look. 'Thank you, Mrs Aldrich. That's all for today, but we— I mean, Inspector Wilson, might wish to speak to you again.'

'Of course.' She rose regally. 'I'll be at the hotel until this matter concludes. But I'm convinced you are wrong, and this was a horrible accident of some kind. I cannot believe someone murdered Julian. Now, if it's not too much trouble, might someone show me where I could refresh myself before I leave?'

'Allow me.' Madeleine extended a hand towards her. 'There's

a charming guest room upstairs you can use. Take as long as you need, my dear.'

'And feel free to return here at any time while you organise the funeral.' Cavan strode to open the door for her. 'I'm sure Mrs Berry at the vicarage will be equally obliging.'

'You've all been very kind.' Frances responded with a watery smile.

'How do you plan to get back to the hotel?' Hannah asked.

'I came in a hackney, so—'

'I have my motor car outside and would be happy to drive you.' Hannah interrupted her, the Gore Hotel being just over a mile away from Holland Park.

'Hannah?' Madeleine snapped as soon as Frances had left the room. 'Since when did you drive motor cars?'

Aunt Violet groaned and Hector suddenly found the clock on the mantelpiece newly absorbing.

'Not now, Mama.' Hannah took in the bemused and puzzled faces around her. 'Mrs Aldrich needs some assistance, and I'm happy to be of service.'

'I won't forget, Hannah, if that's what you're hoping.' Madeleine raked Hannah with a withering gaze as she guided Frances into the hall. 'We'll discuss it later.'

'No, we won't,' Hannah muttered when the door closed on the pair.

'That poor young woman,' Norah said, though with more relish than sympathy. 'Married only a month and now has to return home a widow.'

'She's young, attractive and from what she said, has money of her own,' Cavan observed. 'I've no doubt that in time she will recover, and her life holds plenty of promise.'

Hannah wanted to suggest that was the same for him, but it seemed too forward, so she stayed silent and wandered toward the French doors where her aunt was studying the garden. Her father and Selwyn had commandeered the bench beneath the canopy where she and Aunt Violet had sat earlier, engrossed in deep conversation. 'I'll go up and see how Iris is before I take Frances back to the hotel,' she whispered. 'She'll be mortified to have missed all the gossip.'

'What do you make of all this, Hannah?' her aunt asked, apparently not having heard her.

'About the mysterious Mrs Aldrich?' Hannah thought for a moment. 'That he was married and kept it a secret or that someone killed him?'

'Either or both.' She cocked her head at the closed sitting room door behind them. 'That young woman seemed convinced no one would want to kill him so perhaps it *was* an accident.'

'She was remarkably stoic apart from a few tears, but her shock was convincing.'

'Breeding tells, darling. Properly brought up young ladies do not show their emotions.'

'Even so. Had I received news like that about Darius, I'd be a quivering wreck and unable to ask questions.'

'I've seen far stranger reactions to bereavement. I expect it will hit her later, when she's alone.'

'Possibly. And what about the secret marriage? Do you believe that?'

'Yes. Don't you? I doubt she would have thought that up on the spur of the moment. And why would she?'

'I'm still thinking about it.' Hannah turned from the window, pouting. 'Maybe their liaison wasn't as clandestine as Frances imagined? And what about the inheritance she mentioned?'

'And what better motive for killing someone than money?' Aunt Violet mused.

* * *

'I cannot believe I'm missing everything!' Iris complained once Hannah had apprised her sister of the drama unfolding below stairs. 'Not that I'm glad someone died, but you know what I mean. And that poor girl! Fancy no one knowing they were married?'

Iris resembled a Regency lady of leisure, dressed to receive callers, in a cream broderie anglaise nightgown that complemented her translucent complexion, her fair hair tied in a single braid on one shoulder, in the elaborate canopied bed in Cavan's second-best guest room.

'It seems not.' Hannah perched on the edge of the mattress, trying not to dislodge a pile of magazines and a box of glacé fruit balanced on the counterpane. 'I was quite worried to hear you were ill, but you look quite healthy.'

'It was nothing more than a mild fainting spell, probably brought on by the dancing. But you know Mama. She loves to make a fuss.'

'Indeed, I do.' Hannah scooted further onto the bed, her feet on the coverlet, and hugged her knees through her skirt. 'They both seem to enjoy being here. And Papa and Selwyn are like two piglets in a mud pond. At this rate, Cavan won't ever be able to get rid of them.'

'I'm determined to go home tomorrow, so in the meantime I am doing exactly as Dr Soames recommended and getting plenty of rest.' Iris eased higher up the bed, pummelled a pillow with a fist, and tucked it behind her back. 'I feel a little sorry for Mycroft having to cope alone with Xander. But only a little.' She giggled. 'I imagine he's been run ragged without Nanny to take charge.'

Hannah was about to say it was the least the child's own

father could do, but just then the door clicked open and Hetty's head appeared around the jamb.

'Excuse me, madam, but the lady is feeling better now and wishes to leave.'

'I'd better go.' Hannah rose and planted a kiss on Iris's soft cheek. 'I offered to drive Frances back to the hotel.'

'Which gives you about twenty minutes to interrogate her.' Iris laughed softly.

'Interrogate?' Hannah tried to look offended but failed. 'It's natural to be curious. After all, she didn't know Julian was dead and yet she turned up out of the blue at the perfect time.'

'Or imperfect time. And don't give me that innocent look, Hannah. I know you well enough to know you cannot resist a mystery.' Iris picked up a stray cushion and tossed it in Hannah's direction, which narrowly missed her head, and fell uselessly onto the floor. 'You were just the same that Christmas at Midwinter Manor when Norah's ruby went missing.'

Norah Atherton was the custodian of the Calhoun Ruby, a family heirloom which was meant to pass to her daughter, Millie, on her marriage but went missing that Christmas during a house party.

'And what about when Mycroft's dreadful secretary was selling forged military exemption certificates?' Iris added. 'If the police ever take on women detectives, they'll have to watch out for you.'

'I cannot see that happening. Besides, I'm a married woman now and need to keep up some semblance of respectability.' Returning the cushion to the bed, she blew Iris a kiss. On her way along the hall, she passed an open bedroom door from which came her mother's and Norah's voices. Tiptoeing around a floorboard she knew creaked, she scurried down the stairs to where

Frances took grateful leave of Cavan in the entrance, while Aunt Violet looked on.

'This is so kind of you.' Frances addressed Hannah's reflection in the hall mirror as she adjusted her hat. 'I'm sorry to keep you waiting and hope I'm not taking you out of your way.'

'Not at all, I'm parked just around the corner.'

'Ah, there you are, Hannah.' Norah waylaid her on her way through the hall. 'Madeleine has been looking for you. She wants to talk to you before you go. Shall I fetch her?'

'No!' Hannah grabbed her coat from the hall stand and hauled open the front door. 'Sorry, Norah. No time!'

7

'This is a lovely vehicle. Is it really yours?' Frances ran a hand lovingly over the soft leather upholstery as she climbed into the passenger seat.

'It belongs to my fian— my husband.' Hannah pressed the starter button, and the engine flared into life. 'But then I suppose it's mine now too.'

She had left the tonneau cover of the Swift fastened down, determined to enjoy the mild spring morning after a miserable grey winter. The warmth of a weak sun on her face and the sounds of birdsong lifted her spirits after the oppressive atmosphere of Cavan's drawing room.

'Is it true you were married just yesterday, Mrs Clifford? Right before finding poor Julian.' In response to Hannah's hesitation, Frances added, 'Your mother told me. She also said you had to find someone to perform the ceremony at the last moment.'

'That's true.' Hannah guided the vehicle at a snail's pace around the garden wall, hoping her mother wasn't watching from a window, keeping her gaze fixed on the road ahead.

'I'm sorry. No one wants to go through finding a body on their wedding day. It must have been shocking.'

'It was only a glimpse.' Hannah bit back the urge to add that it wasn't the first time.

'It's very kind of you to take me back to the hotel. After what happened, I wasn't looking forward to having to find another hackney. It took me ages to find one willing to bring me here.'

'They are rarer these days than before the war.' Hannah tried to make conversation. *What does one say to someone who has just lost the most important person in her life?*

'I envy you for having the courage to drive,' Frances said, changing the subject. 'My father would never consider us having a motor car, let alone allowing me to take the wheel.'

'My mother is less enthusiastic and still treats me like a schoolgirl. You know what mothers are like. Oh, I'm sorry!' She silently berated herself, recalling Frances had lost her mother. 'May I ask what happened?'

'She was killed in a carriage accident on Regent Street when I was thirteen.'

Hannah winced, regretting having asked. 'Losing her so young must have been hard.'

'It was. I still miss her sometimes.' Frances stared impassively through the windscreen, as if the event was far enough in the past not to create strong emotions.

'Have you and your father always been close?'

'We were, but he's been... difficult recently. I've been distant with him and I think he senses it. I'm sure you can guess why.'

'Were you close to your mother?' Hannah kept her focus on the road as they approached Hammersmith where the traffic was heavier.

'To be honest, no. I have no doubt she loved me, but she spared me little of her time. She loved to throw lavish parties and was always being escorted to theatres, the opera and every social event London offered. And in case you're wondering, she and Father were not a good match.'

'They weren't happy together?' Hannah had been doing exactly that, but this candid response came as a surprise.

'Not at all, they adored each other. Only they were so... different. Their interests, friends and opposing views on what constituted an enjoyable time.' Hannah felt rather than saw the girl's shrug. 'Which I suppose is what happens in marriages. I asked Mother why she married him once, but all she said was he was her devoted spaniel.' Hannah gave her a bemused look, which made her laugh. 'Not literally. She loved to be loved, and he fulfilled her every whim and desire. Not financially, because Mother had money of her own, but when she was ill, he tended to her with devotion and if she was sad, he would think up things to amuse her. He was always there when she needed him and stayed away when she did not.' Frances fell silent as they bowled along the Cromwell Road.

Hannah did not know how to react to this statement. It didn't sound like any marriage she had experienced, but then people married for all sorts of reasons. Perhaps the Blackwoods made their own happiness?

'Frances, was the reverend expecting you yesterday? I mean, if he knew you were coming it's not likely he would have—'

'Taken that drug on purpose?' Frances finished for her. 'No, Julian wouldn't do that. At least, he never said... Oh, I don't know any more. I telephoned him from the hotel yesterday to tell him I was here. He sounded happy, ecstatic almost, but that he had a wedding to perform so he would come today instead. I wish I had ignored him now and come straight here.'

'Your presence might not have altered the outcome,' Hannah

said, removing self-infliction from her list of possible scenarios. 'Whoever killed him might have harmed you too.'

Frances snapped her head round to face her. 'You really think so?'

'Well, probably not. But don't imagine you could have changed anything. That will only make you feel guilty, which helps no one.'

'But why would anyone want to kill him, and who would do such a thing?'

Hannah had nothing to offer as she accelerated past a horse and cart, and although she was careful not to rev the engine and frighten the horse, the driver still shook his fist at her.

Frances straightened in her seat, a hand on her hat as Hannah turned the Swift into the entrance to Queen's Gate. 'Oh, we're here. Thank you so much, Mrs Clifford. You've been so kind.'

'Do call me Hannah.' She pulled the motor car up to the kerb beside the front steps of the Gore Hotel. 'If you need a ride to the church at any time, I am available.'

'Well...' Frances hesitated, as if wary of asking. 'I need to engage an undertaker and collect Julian's things. I know that sounds hasty, but I'd rather get it over with. Would tomorrow morning be too soon? Around ten o'clock?'

'Not at all.' Hannah looked up as a tall, elderly man in a black suit and top hat approached the motor car, his face twisted in annoyance.

'Oh no!' Frances followed her gaze. 'It was inevitable, I suppose, but I hoped to delay it a while longer.'

'Why, what's wrong?' She followed Frances's look. 'Do you know that gentleman?' Though the question was hardly necessary.

'I'm afraid so. That's my father.'

'Frances?' The man's expression darkened as he advanced on

the motor car and gripped the passenger door-sill with both hands, leaning in so his face was inches from hers. 'Where have you been? I've been waiting for you for hours.' He waved a backward hand at the elegant hotel behind him.

'What are you doing here, Papa?' Frances shoved the passenger door open and alighted onto the pavement, causing him to step smartly backwards to avoid being hit. 'I'm perfectly capable of taking a short trip to London. I've been here alone before.'

'Yes, but on those occasions, you stayed with the Pattersons to chaperone you! Not in a hotel.' He spoke the last word like an insult.

Hannah admired Frances's calmness in the face of his bluster and reddening face.

'It was a last-minute decision, so I didn't want to inconvenience them.' Frances adjusted a glove. 'I assume Esme told you where I was?'

'We had a conversation, yes. Although she was evasive at first, but I insisted she reveal your whereabouts.'

'Bullied her, you mean.' Frances sighed but seemed unsurprised.

'Is it true what she said?' the professor demanded. 'That, despite all my advice, you have affianced yourself to Julian Aldrich!'

'Affianced! Oh Papa, what an antiquated expression!' Frances's scornful laugh turned his cheeks a deeper red. 'I hope you weren't unkind to Esme. She's been a good and genuine friend to me.'

'Genuine friends do not deceive their elders, nor do they conspire in elopements.'

France's smiled dissolved, and he laughed. A harsh, unamused sound. 'That surprised you, didn't it? She told me everything – eventually.' He lowered his voice to a fierce whisper. 'How could you do such a thing, Frances? Have you no respect for my feelings, to marry a man I expressly asked you not to encourage?'

'Julian and I are— were, in love,' she explained with regret rather than apology. 'Your disapproval could not change that. We did what we had to.' She grasped his sleeve and stared up at him pleadingly. 'Your anger is useless now anyway. Julian is dead.'

'Dead! What do you mean?' His face paled and he took a step back, apparently oblivious of the strange looks directed at them from passersby.

Hannah remained seated awkwardly behind the steering wheel as they bickered. Should she offer Frances her support or drive off and leave them to it? Frances didn't appear to need her help, but Hannah's inherent good manners kept her there, wishing she was invisible.

'That is... unfortunate.' Professor Blackwood shook his head as if dislodging an unpleasant thought. 'But if you agree to come home now, Frances, I'm willing to forget this entire matter.'

'How very magnanimous of you,' Hannah muttered, but not low enough for him not to hear.

His gaze snapped to Hannah. 'And who might you be? Another conspirator, I assume?'

'Father!' Frances resisted the arm he attempted to wrap around her shoulders. 'This is Mrs Clifford, who has been very kind to me.'

She turned towards Hannah, her eyes glistening, but her voice remained level. 'Hannah, this rather angry man is my father, Professor Arthur Blackwood.' She wiped a teardrop from her nose with her hand.

'I see.' His face softened. 'In which case, I owe you my grati-tude for your kindness.' He executed a polite if stiff bow. 'However, I'm afraid Frances's judgement is flawed, a result of her sheltered upbringing. For which I take responsibility.'

'Professor.' Hannah nodded in acknowledgement with as much dignity as she could muster while still seated. 'Reverend Aldrich was my local minister,' Hannah said, her brief experience of Frances being the exact opposite to that with her father. 'I knew him only briefly, but he was highly respected.'

'Huh. You haven't the first idea what—'

'Father, please!' Frances held up a hand, silencing him. 'I will come home, but after I've buried Julian. It's the last thing I can do for him.' Frances's composure finally cracked, her face crumpled, and a tear rolled down one cheek. 'We'll discuss this later, but for heaven's sake, Papa, not here on a public street.'

'Um, yes, of course. My apologies.' He stared at the passing traffic as if he had forgotten where he was. 'Now, if you'd kindly excuse me, I need to speak privately with my daughter.'

'Congratulations again on your marriage, Hannah,' Frances said, drawing Hannah's attention. 'I accept your offer of assistance and will see you here tomorrow morning as arranged.'

'You're very welcome, Frances.' Hannah inclined her head at the still angry man beside her, adding, 'Good evening, Professor Blackwood.'

'Er, good evening to you, Mrs... er...' Unable to meet her eye, he placed a firm hand on Frances's back and propelled her up the short flight of steps to be bowed into the hotel by the doorman.

Hannah was about to restart the motor car when she recalled the professor had not asked when or even how Reverend Aldrich had died. His reaction to hearing of their engagement was certainly outrage, but a man was dead. Did he not care, or had he known more than he admitted to?

* * *

Hannah slumped into the leather seat, unsettled by what she had just witnessed, though she couldn't help admiring Frances for standing her ground. Losing Julian had been a shocking blow, but she was not the damsel in distress Hannah had first taken her for.

Hearing her name called, she turned in her seat and frowned, unsure which of the crowd hurrying past had addressed her, just as she saw a tall, slender, young woman in a well-cut suit in dove grey and a pert matching hat with a blue feather attached approach the motor car.

'It's Miss Merrill, isn't it? I thought I recognised you.' Tilly Gilmartin stood cradling her bag with both hands. 'Or should I say Mrs Clifford? I saw the announcement of your forthcoming wedding in *The Times*.'

'Miss Gilmartin, what a coincidence to see you here!' Or was it a coincidence? Tilly was a resourceful, not to mention determined journalist who had almost stalked her during the investigation of the Covent Garden murder the previous year.

'I'm now an editorial writer for the *Hammersmith and Fulham Chronicle*, so I go by Matilda these days.' She paused beside the motor car, her dark eyes sparkling with mischief. 'And pardon me for mentioning it, but for a newly married lady you seem a little down in the dumps.'

'No, not really, just thoughtful. What brings you to Kensington? Are you on the trail of another story?'

'Actually, I'm reporting on the trial of that policeman, Betts, which began this week. I like to follow through on my work. I feel it's the duty of a true investigative journalist.'

'I meant to congratulate you on that. Even Inspector Farrell found your discoveries about Alfred's Gentlemen's Club impressive.'

'Being born with a curious nature pays off sometimes. And how is your intrepid aunt? She must be delighted with the Act.'

Matilda was referring to the Representation of the People Act, which had been passed in February.

'She is, although I feel she's disappointed it didn't come about because of the militant actions of the Women's Social and Political Union.'

'I'm sure they can take some credit, although it might have more to do with women taking on factory jobs and running hospitals that clinched it.'

'You're probably right.' Hannah glanced back at the elegant facade of the hotel, wondering what, if anything, she ought to confide to Miss Gilmartin. Their previous encounters had been, if not hostile, then certainly confrontational. But then who better than a keen journalist for finding out things?

Her conversation with Frances also required looking into, as her rapid switch from distraught fiancée to chatting about her childhood and motor cars seemed too fast to be authentic. Although maybe Julian's death had not yet sunk in, and the grief and tears would come later?

'Is something bothering you, Mrs Clifford?' Curiosity entered the young woman's eyes, a look Hannah had seen before.

'You could say that. I appear to have stumbled into another case of murder.'

'Oh, do tell.' The journalist's eager smile appeared, then faded. 'Er... the victim was no one close to you, I hope?'

'No, but we were acquainted – sort of. He was the minister at my local church in Chiswick.'

'Now, that *is* interesting.' Matilda leaned a hip against the motor car and bent closer. 'You don't get many cases of aggression towards vicars. What happened?'

'Perhaps we shouldn't talk about this on the street. Or at all. This is a police case, and I should leave it to them.'

'Don't pretend you won't do some snooping of your own.'

Matilda looked sceptical. 'You, the woman who dressed as a street girl and crept into Alfred's club looking for evidence of that Belgian jeweller's murder.'

'It wasn't quite like that,' Hannah said, wishing Matilda would keep her voice down as she was drawing stares. But the reporter was nearer the mark than Hannah liked to admit. 'No one was aware of it, but the minister had married in secret. His wife turned up as the police were announcing his death was murder, not an accident.'

'Sounds delightfully intriguing. How was he killed?'

'He was— Never mind. Look, if I hear anything of interest that is suitable to put in your newspaper, I could call you. Will that do?'

'As long as you promise. The murder of a vicar is unusual enough to get into the papers, and reporting crime is what I do. Why don't we meet and discuss it?'

'I suppose we could.' Hannah regretted her impulse, but Matilda was right in that she could not stay away, if only to help Frances.

'Wonderful.' Matilda dragged the word out enthusiastically. 'Do you have time now?'

'Um, well, not really.' The last thing Hannah needed was to be spotted by Frances talking to a journalist. 'Is there somewhere I could contact you?'

'There is, indeed.' Matilda pulled her bag up to her chest and delved inside, handing Hannah a business card of thick paper stock. 'This is my office number. If I'm not there, you can leave a message with our secretary, Miss Buzby. She's about eighty years old and is horrified that I was taken on. She thinks young women should be waiting at home for suitors to call, not running around town interviewing people. She considers writing a man's job. However, I do my own typing, so she tolerates me. Just.' She leaned an elbow on the door-sill and leaned closer. 'What was that encounter about a few minutes ago with that stern-looking gentlemen and the girl? Anything which might interest me?'

'Er, I doubt it, Tilly. Their particular issue should be resolved quickly, so I wouldn't want to waste your time with trivia,' Hannah began, then she had an idea. 'However, I might have some research work for you if you're interested.'

'I told you, it's Matilda now – it looks much better on a byline. And research is something I could definitely handle. Incidentally, is your Aunt Violet still seeing that attractive Inspector Farrell?'

'Detective Chief Inspector now. I'm surprised you don't already know, what with your sources in the police.'

'I did,' she smiled coyly. 'But it never hurts to have confirmation.'

'Thank you for this, Tilly, er, sorry, Matilda.' Hannah tucked the card into her bag and started the engine. 'And it was lovely to see you again,' she added warmly.

With Aidan no longer the leading officer in the case, perhaps Matilda Gilmartin could be of help after all.

Matilda swung her bag onto one shoulder, narrowly missing a man on his way into the hotel. 'I must go. I want to get to the Old Bailey early to secure a seat for the afternoon session. The public like nothing better than seeing a policeman in the dock, so it's bound to be crowded.'

8

Hannah spent the evening alone before weariness drove her to retire to bed. Some hours later, her new husband's attempt to enter the bedroom undetected failed when he dropped a shoe onto the wooden floor, followed by the other a few seconds later. After he mumbled an apology for waking her, he treated her to a rambling monologue about losing his way twice on his way home beneath shrouded streetlights that had been turned off before falling asleep minutes later.

Being prematurely awakened meant sleep eluded her as she conducted an internal debate about the restrictions of his secret work. Finally accepting he had no choice, she hoped things would settle into a proper routine when this war was over, although when that was likely to be rested on other's shoulders.

Or did all husbands live their lives apart from their wives and have different interests? She compared it to her parents' marriage and her childhood, when her father would walk through the front door at six o'clock every evening without fail, patted each of his daughters' heads before settling in his favourite chair with a newspaper until the butler announced supper.

'Did you at least enjoy the dinner?' Hannah asked when Darius joined her for breakfast the following morning.

'Hardly. I would much rather have spent the evening at home with you. However, there's no such thing as forward planning in a crisis.'

'You're forgiven.' The word 'crisis' sent her heart into freefall. 'Was anything resolved or is everything top secret?' She eagerly awaited time together after such a long engagement, but he looked dressed for the office, handsome in his dark suit and crisp white shirt, his damp hair slicked back and curling at the ends, so it took effort not to let her disappointment show.

'We're working through the logistics for the amalgamation of the Flying Corps and the Naval Air Service into the Royal Air Force, so I doubt you'd be interested anyway,' he said, confirming her fear. 'With von Richthofen dead, the recruiting for pilots has increased tenfold.'

The infamous Red Baron had been shot down in France during a dogfight with a Canadian pilot the previous April. The news was welcomed with much celebration by both countries.

'How did your visit go with the family yesterday?' Darius waved his knife in the air before applying it to the butter dish. 'Has Iris recovered from her indisposition?'

'The early months of pregnancy can be fraught, or so I've been told.' Hannah forked up a bite of scrambled egg without looking at him.

'Ah, did that sound insensitive?' He glanced up, genuine regret in his eyes.

'A little, but a few days of bed rest is all she needs. A respite from Mother's fussing might help too, but that's not likely.'

'Is your family still staying at Cavan's? I imagine he's sick of the disruption and will be glad to see the back of them.' He took a bite of the toast and chewed.

'It seems not. He's enjoying having company after so long.' She studied him over the rim of her cup, one eyebrow raised. 'And I'll remember you said that when I invite my family to stay with us.'

'I'm sorry, I didn't mean—' Darius looked up again sharply, the slight hunch of his shoulders showing his remorse.

'I know you didn't,' she assured him, regretting her sharpness. Maybe their marriage was too new for banter if he took her words at face value. 'They planned to leave today, but soon after I got there, Aidan arrived to tell us more about Reverend Aldrich.'

'Oh, yes? I almost forgot about him, the poor chap. Was it a fall which killed him, as they thought?' Darius stabbed a piece of tomato with his fork and brought it to his mouth.

'Not exactly.' She formed the words carefully. 'Someone murdered him.'

'What?' Darius's fork clattered onto his plate, sending tomato flying across the table to land a foot away from hers.

Retrieving the offending fruit from the tablecloth she placed it on her side plate.

'Good grief.' He stared at the table as several disparate emotions flitted across his face. 'I admit I wasn't expecting that.'

'No one did. Aidan has assigned a detective inspector named Wilson to investigate. But more was to come when the housekeeper arrived and announced Reverend Aldrich's wife had arrived.'

'Wife?' Darius's fork halted in mid-air. 'But he wasn't married. At least as far as I know there was no lady living with him at the vicarage.'

'She's very real. Her name is Frances, and her father is a Professor of Medieval Studies at Merton College.' Hannah picked at her food but was unwilling to complain about her aversion to fried sausages first thing in the morning when every household in London would have jumped at the treat. In contrast, the speed with which Darius consumed his portion made her smile with wifely pride.

'Strange.' Darius frowned. 'We had several meetings with Reverend Aldrich and he never mentioned a wife.' He plucked his glass from beside his plate and took a mouthful. 'What's she like?'

'Very pretty and quite charming. Naturally, she was shocked to hear he had been murdered.'

Darius's attention strayed to the folded newspaper at the side of his plate.

'I met her father when I drove her back to the hotel where she's staying,' Hannah said, hoping to get his attention again. 'Strange man. Not only did he disapprove of their relationship, but his reaction to the reverend's death was rather odd.'

'Odd how?' Darius put down his cutlery and eased the paper closer, his gaze flicking to it and then back to Hannah.

'Shocked. I'd say genuinely so, but he wasn't upset by it. It was almost lukewarm, considering he had known Julian for several years.'

'Really? Did his reaction suggest to you he might be involved in his death?' Darius mopped up his fried egg with a piece of toast, still darting the odd glance to the newspaper.

'It did not,' she said, knowing he was teasing. 'I don't think so, anyway. Not without further investigation.' Hannah spread blackcurrant jam on a bread roll. 'Oh, and you'll never guess who I ran into outside the hotel.' She paused, waiting for his full attention, and when he gave it, said, 'Matilda Gilmartin.'

He frowned and stared at the ceiling, his lips forming the name. Then it came to him.

'I remember now.' He pointed his knife at her briefly. 'That journalist who reported on what she termed the "Covent Garden Killer" last year?'

'The same. I might have made a glaring error telling her about Reverend Aldrich's murder, but it was on my mind, so it just popped out.'

'Be careful, Hannah. With my job, we don't want our name in the papers.'

'I trust her to be discreet.' *Sort of.* Hannah liked his use of 'our name'; it sounded permanent. 'I thought she could help me with some research.'

'What sort of research?' He pushed the newspaper away, giving up on reading it. 'The number of vicars murdered in the last twenty years? I doubt there have been many.'

'No.' She mirrored his mischievous grin. 'Frances told me she used to live in London, but after her mother's death they went to live in Oxford.'

'You appear to have found out quite a lot about them in a short time.' He raised an enquiring eyebrow at her over his coffee cup.

'It was a twenty-minute drive, so naturally we'd strike up a conversation. His death happened on our wedding day, so naturally I'm interested.'

'I expect Aidan will tell us the outcome when he, or this DI Wilson, has completed the investigation.'

'And there's another thing. Aunt Violet said Aidan is not enjoying his new job.' Hannah picked the remains of her bread roll into crumbs on her plate.

'Really?' Darius topped up his coffee from the silver pot, replacing it carefully onto the paraffin burner. 'He worked hard for that promotion to chief inspector and has only been in post a year.'

'That's what *I* said. His duties now involve supervising the work of more junior detectives, but little or no actual investigation work, which he finds disappointing. Aunt Violet told me he's considering leaving the force.'

'To do what? What else is he qualified for, but the police?'

'Aunt Violet mentioned something do with research into shell shock, but we didn't get into details.' Hannah recalled her mother had interrupted their conversation at that point. 'I'll ask more when I next see her.'

'Is that the time?' Darius glanced at his watch, started, then tossed back the rest of his coffee, and rose. 'I had better get going.' He looked down at her from his impressive height. 'I'm sorry to do this to you, but I might be late again tonight.'

Hannah's heart sank. 'I've agreed to take Frances to Chiswick this morning to avoid her having to take taxis everywhere. I imagine she hasn't mastered the Tube, although...' She paused, thinking. 'She said she'd lived in London until she was thirteen, so I might be wrong about that. I also thought I might visit the bookshop later.'

'I'm really sorry about all this.' He laid a hand on the back of her chair, his head bent towards her close enough for his warm breath to stir the hair at her temple. 'You appear to have a busy day planned. Is this going to be a regular occurrence?'

'My doing things without you, or requisitioning your motor car?' She leaned into his lingering farewell kiss on her cheek, his Floris cologne stirring remembered sensations from their first night together.

'Either, or both.' Darius remained looming above her, one eyebrow raised in knowing enquiry.

'That depends on how much you neglect me.' Hannah ran a hand across his shaven cheek, the feel of his soft skin and firm jaw that was familiar and yet not. Being confident enough to instigate touching him whenever she felt like it was still new and exciting.

'I'll try not to.' He planted a soft but brief kiss on her mouth. 'In the meantime, give DI Wilson a chance to do his job.'

'I will.' She nodded, but his low chuckle that accompanied footsteps into the hall intimated he doubted it. Travis's voice wished him a good day and then the front door closed with a dull thud.

Hannah set her coffee cup into the saucer and sat back in her chair, listening to the sound of Darius's Rover as he roared through the front gates followed by the sound of hoofbeats moving past on the road outside. An oppressive silence descended, and she shivered, feeling if not lonely, then decidedly alone.

* * *

Frances was already waiting for her on the pavement when Hannah pulled the Swift up in front of the Gore Hotel. She was wearing a layered dress of pale green crepe with a matching straw hat – what some might deem an inappropriate outfit for mourning – and anticipated the journey in the open-top vehicle by securing her hat with a wide yellow scarf tied under her chin.

'I hope you haven't been waiting long.' Hannah moved her jacket from the passenger seat to make room, feeling guilty for thinking badly of her. After all, Frances had only discovered her fiancé was dead the day before; there was hardly time to go shopping for black dresses.

'Not long, but I needed to get out of that oppressive hotel room. I've been in such a fug since yesterday. When it hit me that Julian was really dead and it was not a horrible dream, I couldn't stop crying.'

'I should have offered to stay with you.' Hannah's guilt surged again for being uncharitable, although she couldn't imagine describing the rooms at the Gore as oppressive. 'Is your father not staying at the hotel?'

'He wanted to, but I'm afraid we exchanged more cross words.' At Hannah's shocked look, she added, 'Mostly a rehash of what you witnessed yesterday, but I would rather not talk about it. He wasn't at breakfast this morning, so I assume he's returned home, but he's agreed to come back for the funeral once I've arranged it.'

'It's odd that he disapproved of your fiancé so strongly,' Hannah said. 'I thought the reverend was a self-assured young man, and quite charming.'

'He was both those things. Everyone liked him.' Frances blinked away welling tears. 'I was confident we could have smoothed things over with Papa, but now it will always be a shadow hanging between us.'

At a loss as to how to respond, Hannah kept her focus on the road, careful to keep a distance behind anything being pulled by a horse. The silence between them continued for the next two miles, giving her curiosity free rein until she couldn't contain it any longer.

'I hope you don't mind me asking, Frances,' Hannah began, 'but something is bothering me. You said your father used to think well of Reverend Aldrich, but yesterday I witnessed how strongly he disapproved of your relationship. Did something specific happen to make him change his opinion?'

'I wondered that myself, since we socialised with the Aldriches a good deal when I was younger, and often had them to dine with us.' She grew thoughtful. 'But that was before.'

'Before what?' Hannah briefly turned her head to look at her before returning her attention to the road. Frances looked torn, as if unsure whether she ought to say any more.

Hannah waited, and then Frances inhaled a slow breath before continuing. 'Julian grew up with his younger cousin, Benjamin, known as Benji, who was almost six years younger. He was a good-looking, charming boy but difficult in some ways. The two boys were very different.

'Julian's parents put funds into a trust to pay for Julian's living expenses and education, whereas Benji depended entirely on his father's small business. He resented the fact Julian could afford more of the finer things in life, like music lessons and better clothes. The disparity also meant he didn't have the resources or the intellect to be accepted into university. The worst bone of contention was that as a student, Julian was exempt from conscription whereas Benji would have to join the army and fight when he turned eighteen.'

'That must have been hard for Benjamin,' Hannah said sympathetically. 'From your tone, I assume something awful happened to him. Was he killed overseas?'

'Benji never got to join the army. He drowned in the river a mile away from his home in Oxford.'

'Oh, I'm so sorry.' The slight shock of her answer made Hannah ease her foot off the accelerator, then speed up again to join a line of traffic on the edge of the Cromwell Road. 'I understand if you don't want to talk about it.'

'I don't mind, not really.' The end of Frances's scarf fluttered over her face as they slowed, and she tugged it over her shoulder. 'That day was so fast and chaotic, I still cannot recall every detail. Benji insisted on jumping from a bridge and Julian telling him he was foolish to even contemplate it made him even more determined. He must have got tangled in the reeds, or maybe it was cramp. I'm not sure. Anyway, Julian tried to save him, but he reached him too late. The Aldriches moved away after that. I suppose they couldn't live with all the memories. Julian was about to start his final year at university, and we had only just begun courting, so we were still a bit shy with each other. After the accident, he changed his course to theology and intended to go into the Church. He didn't say, but everyone assumed Benji's death must have affected him.'

'I can see how he might take Benji's death personally, even though he was not at fault,' Hannah said.

'That's the odd thing. Mrs Aldrich was broken by it – he was her only child, after all – but my father was too. I know he was fond of Benji and, like his parents, made excuses for his boyish recklessness, but it was almost as if he blamed Julian for not saving him. When I spoke to him about Julian's decision to study theology, he didn't want to know.'

'How long had your father known the Aldriches?' The line of traffic ahead sped up again and Hannah pressed the accelerator down a little.

'Since we came to Oxford after Mama died. Benji was a year older than me, and Julian was almost sixteen, far too grown up to take an interest in me then.' She laughed softly at the memory.

'I imagine your father's disapproval made you want to see him all the more?'

'I suppose you could say that.' Her cheeks flushed a becoming pink. 'Julian often sought me out. I was flattered to receive his attention. What girl could resist that?' She smiled as the church came into view. 'Oh, we're almost there,' Frances said as Hannah turned the motor car into Church Street and pulled up in front of the vicarage.

'I've been thinking about his death all night.' Frances turned in her seat to face Hannah. 'I can only think that Julian was prescribed this digitalis – or whatever it was – by a doctor and he took too much.'

'Was he worried about his health?' Hannah was unwilling to

repeat Darius's speculation about an accident so as not to offer her false hope. And why would he be taking digitalis? *Unless he was a hypochondriac, and no one knew.*

'He never seemed to be. But who would want to hurt him, let alone kill him? And to do it in such a way. It seems so... calculated.'

'You're right. It does.' Hannah had no time to reflect on this comment as the door to the vicarage opened so quickly to reveal Mrs Berry that Hannah wondered if she had been looking out for them.

9

'Please, do come in, ladies.' The housekeeper greeted them at the door of the tidy villa which served as the St Nicholas Vicarage located behind Cavan Soames's house in Church Street. 'I've left everything as it was,' she said over one shoulder as she ushered them through the hall and up the dog-leg oak staircase. 'To be honest, I'm surprised the reverend had so few belongings, but then he hadn't been here long.'

'He liked to travel light,' Frances explained. 'We planned to move everything from his house in Jericho and from mine here after we were married.' Frances's voice remained level, but Hannah saw her hands shook, halted by a tight grip on her bag.

'Oh, I see. Well, that explains it.' Mrs Berry showed them into a bedroom which, though of good size, resembled a monk's cell. A brass bed occupied the centre of the room, with an ancient mahogany wardrobe to one side and a matching desk. A porcelain bowl and pitcher sat atop an ancient chest of drawers; a rectangular mirror balanced against the wall behind it dotted with silver spots, which made Hannah's reflection blurry. A watercolour landscape hung on one wall and a pen-and-ink drawing of a fox on the other, but the room contained few personal effects.

'It's quite bare,' Hannah pointed out. 'I assume he worked elsewhere. Writing sermons and so on?'

'He did all that in the vestry,' Mrs Berry replied. 'But I've packed his papers away in there and left this room upstairs for you to empty. There's a suitcase beneath the bed and a portmanteau on top of the wardrobe. It was all he brought with him, so I assume everything will fit.' The bemused look Hannah exchanged with Frances seemed to unsettle her. Swallowing, she stared at her feet then up again.

'Look, excuse me if I'm speaking out of turn,' Mrs Berry continued, 'and I'm truly sorry about what happened to Reverend Aldrich, only the bishop called yesterday and asked me clear out the vestry as the temporary minister is due in a day or two. He said it would take a while to appoint a new one so we're a bit up in arms around here.'

'That certainly didn't take long,' Hannah said, feeling sorry for Frances. 'The poor man isn't even buried yet.'

'Yes, well, as I said. It's right unsettling, what with Reverend Aldrich being so young and dying the way he did.' Her pebble eyes locked on Frances. 'Then there's you, who we never even heard of.'

Hannah raised an eyebrow and, seeing she had gone too far, the housekeeper muttered, 'Anyway, if you need me, I'll be in the kitchen.' Wiping her work-reddened hands on her apron, she eased between them.

'Thank you, Mrs Berry,' Hannah answered for both of them and closed the door firmly on the housekeeper.

'I thought I could do this.' Frances eased backwards onto the bed, one arm wrapped around the bottom post. 'But I... I'm not so sure now.'

'Let me help you.' Hannah pulled the suitcase from the bed, into which she began piling items of underwear, socks and shaving implements from the chest of drawers. 'The sooner it's done, the better.'

'You're right. I mustn't be a weakling.' Frances pushed off the bed and joined her. She brought a neatly folded shirt to her nose and sobbed quietly into the fabric before placing it on top of others until the drawer was almost empty.

'Oh, I forgot about this.' Frances held up a black leather-covered Bible. 'It was my mother's. I gave it to Julian when he first came here.'

'What was she like? Your mother?' Hannah used it as a distraction 'You must remember a lot about her.' Despite Madeleine Merrill's foibles, Hannah could never imagine growing up without her.

'I have only pleasant memories of her.' Frances flicked open the front cover and smiled. 'Look, it has her name inside. She had beautiful handwriting.' She tilted the book so Hannah could read the words *Lydia Fortescue* written in copperplate script, the ink slightly faded to a brownish colour, before she placed it lovingly inside the suitcase.

'Even at such a young age, I was aware she was spoiled and indulged by her family. I was about eleven when she told me to marry for love, because boredom was worse than hatred.' In response to Hannah's surprised glance, she smiled. 'I know. It wasn't an appropriate thing to say to a child, but she could be impulsive at times. There was no malice in her, she just said what she thought.' Frances continued talking as she moved to another drawer that gave a shriek as she tugged it free.

'Mother loved to dance and throw parties. The house was always full of people or friends calling at the house to whisk her away on an outing or other. I was devastated when she was killed, and within weeks, Papa moved us to Oxford because he had been offered the post at Merton College. I convinced myself it was because he didn't want me to have contact with any of Mother's friends, which made me resent him for a while. Poor Papa, he was only doing what he thought best.'

She spoke without resentment, which told Hannah she loved her father a good deal. 'I think he believed it would make me forget about Mama, but it didn't work. Any more than his attempt to separate me from Julian. But then he'd likely disapprove of any young man interested in me.'

'Fathers are like that,' Hannah said. 'Although fortunately, mine isn't. He always approved of Darius – who was a childhood friend of mine – and was ecstatic, almost relieved, when we finally announced our engagement.' Hannah surveyed the now empty room, the wardrobe doors standing open and each drawer pulled out. 'That's about everything.' Hannah hefted the portmanteau in one hand and the suitcase in the other, dragging them into the hall. 'There's just the vestry to clear now.'

Frances started to follow her out, then lingered at the door and gave the now bare room a long, mournful glance. Mrs Berry called up from the hallway below to instruct them to leave the luggage on the landing, and that she would get the gardener to transfer it to Hannah's vehicle.

Hannah thanked her, grateful she would not have to manhandle bulky objects down the stairs and led Frances into the rear hall. 'I brought you this way around,' Hannah said, guiding her though the rear door where a path wound around the church to the vestry, 'because the ladies of the parish will be cleaning the church at this time of day. They all know what happened, so I thought you would prefer some privacy.'

'That was thoughtful of you.' Frances's gaze went to the tomb that stood alone in a patch of grassland opposite the vestry door, a few low gravestones dotted here and there, mostly old and lopsided. 'Is that where—?'

'Yes. It's been locked up since... well, you know, and the gate is secure so you cannot get inside. Did you want to take a closer look?'

'No. No I don't think so, I...' Her voice tailed off and she swayed slightly. Had Hannah not moved forward to steady her, she might have fallen.

'Frances, why don't I collect the reverend's papers and meet you back at the motor car?'

'That's a good idea. Let's do that.' She nodded, though she continued to stare at the mausoleum for long seconds before moving away.

Hannah pushed open the arched door to the vestry that contained a large desk with an oxblood leather inlay and an upright chair. A row of uniform cupboards took up one side of the room, one of which was open to reveal shelves with piles of church linens in neat piles and what looked like books of church records and a box of candles.

She scooped up a pile of random documents, including several letters, a notebook and three books laid out neatly on the desk. She was about to leave when the housekeeper entered from the church.

'Finished up, have you?' she asked, looking relieved.

'We have, and we won't bother you again, Mrs Berry.' *Until the funeral.* The woman's apparent hurry to be rid of them rankled. Then a thought occurred to Hannah. 'Incidentally, did Reverend Aldrich ever show interest in the Bentham family mausoleum? Was he curious enough to venture inside, perhaps?'

'Not that I know of, dear.' Both of the woman's eyebrows rose in surprise. 'That's the key to it there.' She pointed to an oversized wrought-iron key that hung from a hook beside the rear door.

'Why he would want to, I don't know with nothing but coffins and dust in there.' She gave an exaggerated shudder at the suggestion.

'I was just curious. And thank you as well for your help with his belongings.' Hannah turned to leave through the rear door.

'Is... is the young lady all right?' Mrs Berry brushed her hands down her skirt and took a tentative step closer. 'I'm sorry if I seemed abrupt earlier, but I had no idea Reverend Aldrich was married.' The affront in her voice at his having kept secrets from her was obvious. 'But then he was a private young man. Although...'

'Although what?' Hannah cradled the papers in both arms and experienced a sense she was about to hear something unpleasant.

'Well, um... He was an unusually handsome man and quite young to be put in a position of power over impressionable minds, don't you agree?'

'What are you trying to say, Mrs Berry?' Hannah's hackles rose at the gleeful tone in her voice.

'His coming created quite a stir among the ladies of the parish, especially the young girls who would hang around him after service. And, well, he didn't do much to discourage them, if you get what I mean. He took at least one of them out to tea that I know about.' Hannah regarded her in stoic silence until the other woman dropped her gaze. 'I kept it to myself, of course. I'm no gossip. But had I known he was a married man, then perhaps I—'

'You might have reminded him?' Hannah replied, deciding she didn't like this woman much. Was she implying Julian Aldrich was a womaniser?

His intentions could have been perfectly innocent – a distressed girl having conflict with a sweetheart or her parents, who came to him for advice?

'Only I thought...' The housekeeper hesitated, as if unsure she should continue, but could not resist. 'Might a jealous beau or even an angry husband be goaded enough to kill him?'

'Which would imply some degree of violence, Mrs Berry. And if you recall, the reverend was poisoned. But if you have a list of possible candidates, I'm sure DI Wilson would like to see it.'

'Oh no, dear, nothing like that,' she simpered. 'It was only a thought.'

'Hmm. Is that what it was?' Hannah shifted the papers from one arm to the other. 'Thank you for your help with the reverend's things, Mrs Berry. I'm sure his widow appreciates it.' She emphasised the word 'widow'.

Without looking back, Hannah clamped her lips together and stomped back to the motor car, which stood empty, but a quick search located Frances by the river on the other side of the road. A slight breeze lifted her long, fair hair away from her face as she stared at the ribbon of blue-green water, her eyes dry, and a distant look on her face.

Leaving her to her thoughts, Hannah circled the motor car intending to stack the letters and books behind the driver's seat, when she noticed the jump seat was closed tight.

Frances looked up at that moment and spotting Hannah, she crossed the road and hurried towards her.

'How did you manage to get both bags in?' Hannah asked.

'I didn't. I asked the gardener to store the bags for me while I go to the undertakers.'

'In which case I'm happy to—'

'No, really,' Frances interrupted. 'You've been more than helpful, so I won't impose on you further. Besides, the walk to the High Street will do me good and give me time to think. I'll get a hackney back to the hotel later.' She reached out and took the papers and books from Hannah's arms.

'Helping you is no imposition,' Hannah assured her, releasing them. 'If there's anything you need between now and the funeral, please let me know.' She delved into her bag and handed Frances a crisp new visiting card that had arrived from the printers the day before, her married name in elegant script above the house telephone number.

'Thank you for bringing me here today.' Frances tucked the card into her bag and leaned against the driver's door once Hannah was seated. 'Seeing where Julian lived and worked has helped me, somehow. And please accept my belated congratulations on your marriage.'

'Thank you, and I meant it when I said to call me if you need anything.' Hannah pressed the starter button and giving a final wave she pulled away, with thoughts of Lydia Blackwood, formerly Fortescue, occupying her thoughts all the way to the bookshop.

10

'Hannah!' Aunt Violet greeted her with open arms at the door of the bookshop. 'I didn't expect to see you today. I thought you'd still be playing newlyweds with the delicious Darius.'

'He has important work to do, or we definitely would be.' Hannah strolled the rows of shelves heavy with books and inhaled the comforting smells of leather and furniture polish. 'Are you having a quiet morning?'

'You should have been here an hour ago,' her aunt said with a sigh. 'It was positively heaving. But you've arrived at a fortuitous time as I'm about to close for luncheon.' She turned the 'Open' sign to 'Closed' on the shop door and flicked up the door latch, drawing Hannah to the back of the shop where they could talk without being heard.

'The new manager arrives tomorrow to take over while Archie is away.' Aunt Violet relaxed into the wing-back chair where she resembled a young Queen Mary posing for a royal photograph.

'Of course. He's leaving for France soon, isn't he?' Hannah took the upright chair opposite, unable to bring herself to sit where she had discovered her murdered friend three years before. The original chair had been replaced some time ago, but the memories persisted.

'This afternoon, but don't let's talk about it – Penny's been in tears all morning.' She lowered her voice, even though there was no sign of Penny, who had a habit of hiding behind bookshelves to eavesdrop. 'How did it go when you took Frances back to the Gore yesterday?'

'You won't believe this, but her father was waiting for her outside.' Hannah proceeded to repeat everything she had told Darius earlier, embellishing it with the odd detail or two. 'Frances said the professor disapproved, but you'd think he could at least pretend to be sympathetic now.'

'I agree. I got the impression it was more than him thinking she was too good to be a clergyman's wife. Anyway, we returned to Chiswick this morning to fetch the reverend's belongings and I had an unpleasant conversation with the reverend's housekeeper.'

'Mrs Berry? Ugh, malicious woman.' Aunt Violet grimaced. 'I wouldn't believe anything she had to say. I've heard she's not a widow at all but calls herself a missus to give her more status.'

'How come you know her well enough to fling insults, Aunt Violet? You rarely attend church.'

'I get all my parish gossip from Ivy. Or I did. According to her, Mrs B put it about that she and the previous minister had an understanding. That the poor man expired before she could drag him to the altar, literally, was probably what saved him. The arrival of Reverend Aldrich was a serious setback to her plan, since he was too young and attractive to be interested in her.'

'Hmmm.' Hannah dismissed this but resolved to pay more attention to Ivy in future. It also threw doubt on whether Julian Aldrich had exhibited inappropriate behaviour towards his female parishioners.

'Maybe she poisoned him, hoping he would be replaced by a more mature man? I found out something though. Frances's mother was a Fortescue. I saw it written in a Bible Frances gave Julian.'

'Fortescue,' Aunt Violet repeated, tapping her lower lip with a finger, frowning slightly. 'What was her mother's given name?'

'Letitia?' Hannah thought for a moment. 'No, Lydia. Why do you ask?'

'Goodness, I knew her!' Aunt Violet straightened. 'We weren't close but certainly acquainted enough to be invited to the same parties – the Henley Regatta and suchlike. An attractive, fair-haired girl with unusually light blue eyes. Almost icy blue. She was rather notorious, if I recall, and smitten with some lord's son. When she married someone else, it surprised everyone.'

'Strange you should mention that.' Hannah became thoughtful. 'Frances was very candid about her mother being a social butterfly with a host of friends.'

'I'd say she was a little fast, if that's not too uncharitable, and her friends were mostly male admirers. But then daughters of wealthy families get away with more than most.' Aunt Violet raised a sardonic eyebrow as if that explained everything. 'I lost track of Lydia for years. The last I heard she had died.' She stared off as she went back in time in her head. 'She had a friend, a shy girl she treated like a minor servant. I mistook her for a paid companion once, but it turned out she was the daughter of Lydia's godmother.'

'I knew girls like that at school,' Hannah said. 'They latched on to the prettiest and most popular girl in class to avoid being ignored. Perhaps that's what I was to Lily-Anne?' She laughed lightly, but then instantly regretted it in case her aunt agreed.

'Nonsense. You were every bit as beautiful and talented as Lily-Anne. No one could ever call you a wallflower.'

Hannah relaxed, her attention caught by voices that floated up from the office downstairs, one of which she recognised. 'Is Aidan here?'

'Ah yes, I forgot to mention, he and Inspector Wilson are comparing notes downstairs, although why they don't use Aidan's office at the Yard, I don't know. I tried to eavesdrop, but they simply glared at me until I left.'

'I thought he wasn't leading the investigation?'

'He isn't, officially, but he's eager to keep his hands in, as they say. They want to interview Penny when she gets back from the bookbinders.' In response to Hannah's enquiring look, she added, 'We've been commissioned to do some custom work for a private library, which is rare, but highly lucrative.'

As if on cue, Aidan's measured tread sounded on the stairs and his head appeared above the floor level. Catching sight of Hannah, he beamed. 'Vi didn't tell me you were coming in today.'

'An impulse visit. With Darius busy, I thought I would be a tourist. I also drove Mrs Aldrich to St Nicholas this morning.'

'Really? Is she with you now?' Aidan gave the front window a swift look, as if he expected Frances to be waiting outside.

'No, but she'll be at the hotel later if you need to speak to her again.'

'Inspector Wilson shall, no doubt, but it can wait. He's in that rather impressive basement room compiling his notes from yesterday. I must say, you've done a remarkable job down there.'

'Thank you, we're both very proud of it.' Hannah's idea of turning a dark, nondescript storage area into a reading space resembling a gentleman's club had proved even more of a success than her reading corner.

Framed Art Deco posters of vogue fashion plates and theatre productions in bright, almost garish colours adorned the wall, each illuminated from above with individual electric lights.

A long, narrow window set high in the wall of the basement room depicted a grapevine set in stained glass with clusters of purple grapes and dark green foliage threw distorted shapes of coloured light into the room; the street beyond visible with passing feet, wheels and tyres.

Bookshelves at waist height to make the space less crowded filled the gaps between leather chesterfields arranged around low tables, where customers could meet friends and chat. Hannah had toyed with offering tea and biscuits to customers, but thus far Aunt Violet had commented it was not Lyons Corner House and refused to entertain the idea.

'How is the investigation going?' Hannah asked.

'As expected.' Aidan's reply was non-committal, his face revealing nothing. 'Wilson had a long, tiring day in Oxford questioning Reverend Aldrich's former acquaintances. Well, those he could find. Everyone they spoke to said much the same thing. That he was an amiable young man with no obvious enemies. His tutor had to be reminded of who he was, and another retired to the West Country last year so he's not of much use. The gate porter had a different perspective of him, though. Seems he mixed with the rowdier contingent in his first years and was popular with the ladies. He appears to have got involved in the normal student pranks during his first year but had settled down by graduation.'

Hannah expressed slight surprise but stayed silent, debating whether to pass on what Mrs Berry had told her, ultimately deciding against it just as Inspector Wilson's head appeared above the basement steps.

'Chief Inspector Farrell was just keeping us informed about the Aldrich case.' Hannah acknowledged him with a nod and a smile.

'Was he?' DC Wilson exchanged a disapproving look with his

superior. 'I understood we were here to interview Miss Wells, the bookshop assistant?'

'Oh, come on, Wilson.' Aidan crossed his arms and smiled. 'Mrs Clifford found the body and her entire family were witnesses, so what harm can it do?'

This reaction was so unlike Aidan that both Hannah and Aunt Violet turned to stare at him in surprise.

'I suppose not, sir.' The policeman scratched his left ear, putting emphasis on the *sir*. Before he could say more, they were interrupted by a sharp, repetitive tap and Penny's face, contorted by the bullseye glass, appeared in the front door panel.

'Ah, here's Penny now.' Aunt Violet rose from her chair to unlock the front door for her. 'Penny, dear, the police would like to talk to you, but there's nothing to be concerned about.'

'Really?' Penny stared up at Inspector Wilson, who was several inches taller. 'I've never been questioned by the police before.' She pushed her spectacles further up her nose, giving her an owlish appearance. 'Do I have to swear to tell the truth or anything?'

'No, Miss Wells,' DI Wilson replied. 'But the truth is not optional.' His tone was that of a headmaster berating a student. 'Miss Edwards, would it be possible to use your office again?'

'Whatever for?' Aunt Violet lifted her hands to illustrate the empty shop. 'There's only us here and we all have a vested interest in this case. And Penny is young, true, but she's sensible and – more importantly – she's honest.'

Wilson turned to Aidan. 'It's most irregular, to conduct witness interviews in public, sir.' This attempt to enlist Aidan's support elicited no reaction, and accepting defeat he sighed and removed his notebook from a jacket pocket. 'Miss Wells.' He cleared his throat. 'Kindly tell me what time you arrived at St

Nicholas Church and your movements between then and the wedding ceremony.'

'I got to Miss Merrill's house at around nine-thirty to help Ivy with preparing the food,' Penny explained with confidence. 'We didn't have to cook anything as Ivy had already done what was necessary, just arrange it in the baskets and take it along to Dr Soames's house. That's where the party was being held after the ceremony.' She paused, and he gestured with his pencil for her to continue. 'Ivy and I were about to return to the house when the flowers arrived, so we helped carry them inside the church.'

'What time was this?'

'Um, about half past ten, or maybe a bit later. One of the ladies complained they were late so they would have to work quickly, so me and Ivy stayed for a while to give them a hand.'

'When did the housekeeper' – he consulted a page in his notebook – 'Mrs Berry return?'

'Not sure.' Penny scowled. 'But she came to Dr Soames's house while I was there and asked if we had seen the reverend.'

'And had you?'

'Not then, but I did earlier,' Penny said sheepishly.

'Earlier, when?' Wilson snapped.

'After we dropped off the food, I popped over to the church and peeked inside. It was a warm day, and both front and rear vestry doors were open. I could see the churchyard from there. Reverend Aldrich was at his desk.'

'Sorry to interrupt,' Hannah said. 'Penny, it's not possible to see the vestry from the porch as it's on the right side of the church. You must have walked as far as the altar to see through the vestry into the churchyard.'

Aidan aimed a look of mild enquiry at Penny, while DI Wilson's sigh showed irritation.

'Which suggests you did more than peek, Miss Wells. What were you doing inside the church?'

Penny's shoulders slumped. 'All right, I walked down the aisle. You know, pretending a bit. The reverend looked up and saw me and smiled. I was a bit embarrassed as it was obvious what I was doing, so I ran out.'

Hannah conjured an image of Penny performing a slow march towards the altar and smiled, one which Aunt Violet mirrored as she imagined the same thing.

'Was he alone in the vestry?' Aidan cut off DI Wilson before he could speak.

'I thought so, at first. But the door closed when he was sitting at his desk.'

'Then who was with him?' Inspector Wilson asked. 'I imagine the door didn't close by itself?'

'Er, I suppose not, but I didn't see who it was.' Penny split a look between the two policemen, her brow furrowed in thought. 'Mrs Berry was coming back from her errands and saw me come out of the church. She demanded to know what I was doing inside, quite rudely, I thought.'

'Did Mrs Berry go inside the church?'

'No. She had shopping bags and took them to the vicarage.'

'And you didn't see Reverend Aldrich after that?' the inspector asked.

Penny shook her head. 'Not when I was there, no. The flower ladies arrived soon after and we went back to Dr Soames's house to arrange the food. The drawing room is like a palace, all that gold and crystal, and he lives there all by himself. Such a waste, it is.'

'Yes, thank you, Miss Wells.' DI Wilson pinched the bridge of his nose with his free hand. 'And you're certain you didn't see the reverend leave the church while you were there?'

'No.' She frowned and stared at the floor. 'He might have gone through the rear door that leads into the churchyard. There's a path to the vicarage from there.'

'And what time was this?'

'Um.' She pursed her lips and stared at the ceiling. 'I'm not sure. Around eleven-thirty, or maybe later. I wasn't wearing a watch. And I never hear the church bells.' She grinned up at the policeman. 'I've lived in a vicarage all my life, so you just don't notice them, do you? Not when they are going every hour of every day and all through—'

'Yes, thank you, Miss Wells. Can you recall what Reverend Aldrich was wearing when you saw him in the vestry?'

'I only caught a quick look, but he had on his cassock and surplice, but not his stole,' Penny answered confidently. In response to his sharp look, she added, 'I'm a vicar's daughter. I know what vestments are. He would have added the stole just before the ceremony.'

'Um, yes, of course. And where did you go after Dr Soames's house?'

'To Miss Merrill's house. I had been there about half an hour when Mr Clifford came to tell us no one could find the minister.' Her eyes widened, and she gasped. 'Does that mean I was the last person to see the reverend alive?'

'Apart from his killer, we assume so,' Aidan said.

'Goodness!' Penny gaped, more delighted than shocked.

DI Wilson snapped his notebook shut, showing the interview was at an end. 'That will be all for now, Miss Wells. Thank you. I trust you won't be leaving the area in case I wish to speak to you again?'

'That's not likely, is it?' Penny gave him a look. 'There's a war on.'

Hannah turned her laugh into a cough and stared at the

floor, while Aunt Violet directed Penny towards the rear store-room. 'I need those books unwrapped and the packing cases stacked outside before we leave tonight, so I suggest you get started.'

'Yes, Miss Edwards.' Penny's shoulders slumped as she left, her moment of fame over.

* * *

'Inspector Wilson.' Hannah waited until the storeroom door closed on Penny. 'Have you discovered anything new about the reverend's death?'

The inspector's gaze flicked to Aidan before answering, but on receiving no response other than a raised eyebrow, he sighed resignedly. 'The coroner said it was impossible to tell how much digitalis he had ingested but what he had would likely have made him dizzy and his speech would have become slurred. Mrs Berry claimed he appeared quite normal at breakfast, if a little curt with her. Between you and me, the woman has an attitude which would make anyone sharp.'

Hannah silently agreed, wondering if Mrs Berry would have mentioned a change in the reverend's behaviour to her when they talked that morning. Perhaps she had not noticed?

'Could the reverend have taken the drug himself, Inspector?' Aunt Violet rejoined the conversation. 'Some people have an unorthodox attitude to medication and like to dose themselves.'

'Possibly. But the pathologist said he would have had no reason to for his heart was sound. It's possible he would have started to feel the effects within an hour depending on how much he had taken. Also, no drugs were found in the vicarage or the church, and no residual traces on the teapot or cups used at breakfast either.' Inspector Wilson tugged his nose. 'We're trying to trace any other visitors Reverend Aldrich might have had that morning, but it's proving difficult.'

'Mr and Mrs Clifford found him at around two forty-five that afternoon, so he could have been poisoned any time before that.'

'Well, obviously.' Hannah inserted a hint of sarcasm to her voice. 'Was he in the vestry from breakfast onwards, or did he return to the vicarage to change into his vestments when Mrs Berry was out?'

'Er, I'm not sure on either count.' Inspector Wilson flushed beneath Aidan's speculative gaze. 'However, I shall be sure to find out.'

'Sooner rather than later, Inspector,' Aidan said levelly, his head cocked towards the door, a gesture to which the policeman responded.

'I'll see you back at the Yard then, sir.' He inclined his head. 'Miss Edwards, madam.'

'I hate being called madam,' Hannah said when he had gone. 'Are you all right, Aidan? You're looking rather pensive.' Hannah wondered if his job was getting him down but didn't want to repeat what Aunt Violet had told her in confidence.

'This case is a challenge, certainly.' He dropped his arms to his sides and sighed. 'However, I'm more concerned about my mother right now.'

'Oh dear. Is Mrs Farrell ill?' Hannah had met Aidan's formidable mother on several occasions when they had entertained her and Darius for dinner at the family hotel. A small but fierce woman, with a smile that lit the room, who ruled her staff with a no-nonsense attitude she delivered in a musical Irish brogue.

'I had to call the doctor last night, who diagnosed influenza and admitted her. I'm only here to get Wilson on the right track, and then I'm going to the Brunswick Hotel to ensure everything is running smoothly there. With Mother out of action, the hotel has probably devolved into chaos by now.'

'How awful for her. Influenza can be very debilitating,' Hannah said sympathetically. 'Do you know how she contracted it?'

'I have my suspicions. The hotel is full of army officers returning from overseas, and who knows what they might have picked up from places like Turkey and North Africa? Mother is strong, though, so I'm not too worried. If only she would do what the doctors tell her and rest, but she can be stubborn.' He patted Hannah affectionately on the shoulder. 'Well, I'd best be off.'

Aunt Violet saw him to the door and as they said their farewells, Hannah turned tactfully away and returned to her desk, only to swing around again at her aunt's cheerful call of, 'Look who's here!'

A young soldier had entered the shop on Aunt Violet's arm.

'Archie!' Hannah left her chair and went to greet him but was beaten by a yard as Penny flew across the floor and threw her arms around his neck.

'Steady on there, old girl. You'll have me over.' Archie ducked his head and slung one arm around Penny, who clung to him, her eyes alight with pride.

Hannah took in his soft flat-peaked cap above a khaki tunic and trousers of thick wool, which looked as if they might be itchy in warm weather. He wore a webbing pack fastened around his waist and expertly wound puttees up to his knees. He had only been a boy when they first met, and the thought of him going off to war made her chest hurt.

'I didn't recognise you for a moment.' Hannah fought to keep her surging emotions from her voice. Penny clung to his arm, having spared a second to remove her spectacles.

'My train leaves in a couple of hours.' He dropped his canvas kit bag on the floor at his feet. The tin Brodie helmet tied to the back clunked as it hit the floorboards. 'I couldn't leave without saying goodbye to you all.'

'I'm so glad you didn't.' Hannah removed a brown-paper-wrapped parcel from a drawer in the bureau that had been there for a week. 'I was going to ask Aunt Violet to give you this, but now I can do so personally.'

'That's so kind, Miss Merr— Mrs Clifford.' He took it with such care it might have been the only gift he had ever received. 'And so unexpected.'

'It's not much. Some socks, a couple of bars of soap, three bars of Five Boys chocolate and a packet of Woodbines.' Archie protested that he did not smoke, but she interrupted him. 'I know that, but Captain Ellis once told me that cigarettes are useful for gaining favours.'

'That's so thoughtful, the socks especially. Our training officer warned us we'll have trouble keeping them dry in the trenches. Now I have spares. Thank you so much.'

'You'll have to thank Ivy for those, as she knitted them. But I'll convey your appreciation to her.' Hannah retrieved a brown-paper-wrapped parcel from the bottom of her bag. 'And there's this.'

'A book?' Archie accepted it thoughtfully; one eyebrow raised in puzzlement. 'That's so thoughtful of you.'

'Not much of one, we're surrounded by the things,' Penny muttered good-naturedly.

'Hush.' Archie nudged her. 'I'm sure it was very well-chosen as Mrs Clifford is a great reader and knows what I like.' He untied the string that held the package together and placed it in his pocket; the act of someone brought up to be frugal and avoid waste. He stripped off the brown paper to reveal a thin red leather-bound volume with the words, *The Collected Poems of Rupert Brooke* embossed in gold on the front.

'This is so kind of you, Mrs Clifford.' Archie held the book in both hands. 'Brooke was a soldier too, wasn't he?'

'He was. My favourite is entitled *The Soldier*. I think you'll appreciate it.'

'It came with a standard linen cover,' Penny said, eager to be involved. 'But Mrs Clifford took it to the bookbinders to have it replaced with this leather one.'

'I'll treasure it.' Archie's eyes gleamed as he gave the book a final pat and stowed it carefully in his knapsack. He straightened and scanned the floor slowly with a frown.

'He's on that chair,' Aunt Violet said, giving Hannah a bemused look.

'Ah, so he is!' Archie crossed to the wing-back chair and swept Bartleby into his arms, burying his nose in the thick black pelt. He was rewarded by the animal's contented purr. 'I'll miss you, old chap.'

'He'll have sardines once a week, I promise.' Penny swiped a hand across her wet cheek.

'Is it true you're on the trail of another murderer, Mrs Clifford?' Archie continued to stroke the cat that had settled happily against his chest.

'I have, but you won't be involved this time, Archie. Besides, you'll be busy keeping the country safe.'

'I'd like to think that's true, Mrs Clifford. And I'm sure you'll find out who did it.' Reluctantly, he handed Bartleby to Penny. 'Now I must go. If I miss the train, my sour-faced sergeant will put me on a charge.' He hefted his bag onto one shoulder with a broad smile that betrayed a grudging respect for his superior officer.

Penny watched him reach the door before turning pleading eyes on Aunt Violet.

'Go on then, you might as well wave him off at the station.' Aunt Violet sighed and took Bartleby from her. 'We'll unpack those books together tomorrow.' She patted the girl's shoulder and whispered, 'But no more tears. Let him take your smile with him.'

Penny's lip trembled and, nodding, she grabbed her coat from the hook and followed Archie out.

'You're getting soft in your maturity, Aunt Violet,' Hannah said as she and her aunt watched them go, neither daring to express aloud the hope he would come back, and in one piece, as if to say it aloud would tempt fate.

'How dare you!' Her aunt threw her a shrivelling look, which softened immediately. 'I meant to ask, how is Iris? Are she and Norah still staying at Cavan's?'

'If Cavan had anything to do with it, they probably would be, but no, they've gone home. It seems it was nothing serious. Iris is fine, and the baby is growing well.' Hannah retrieved her coat and started to pull on her gloves. 'I had better be off too. Although it seems so strange not to be going home to Chiswick Mall.'

'It does for me too,' her aunt mused. 'I was so looking forward to moving back into my villa in Mortlake, but I miss not being woken every morning by Ivy.'

Hannah chuckled. 'What, even when she'd deliberately bang the door to wake you after you came home late the night before?'

'Even that.' She sighed. 'I wonder how she always knew when she didn't live in? It always baffled me.'

'It could have been something to do with your clothes being scattered across the floor and all the way up the stairs.'

'Not *all* of them.' Aunt Violet pulled a face. 'But admittedly, she did trip over my shoes occasionally.'

'I must go.' Hannah patted her aunt's arm on the way to the door. 'I hope Aidan's mother is feeling better soon.'

'I'll give her your best wishes when I next see her, although she really doesn't like hospitals. And don't tell Aidan this, but it's those nurses I feel sorry for. Mrs Farrell has a way of conveying her displeasure which could leave a sergeant major speechless.'

Hannah smiled at this image, but her steps dragged as she made her way back to the motor car she had parked around the corner. Mrs Farrell must be quite seriously ill and Aidan was understandably distracted.

She climbed into the driving seat and slumped behind the steering wheel, contemplating her next move. With Darius away, the thought of returning to Ilchester Place and a large empty house held no appeal. It wasn't as if she had much to do there either, as Travis had the household running like clockwork.

Conscious she had begun to attract strange looks from passersby, she stabbed a finger at the starter button. As the engine rumbled into life, she chastised herself. 'You have everything you've ever wanted, Hannah, so stop this self-pity,' she said aloud as she steered into afternoon traffic.

Hannah arrived home to find a telephone message from Matilda Gilmartin written in Travis's precise sloping script, with a request to call her at the newspaper offices.

Once the connection was established, Matilda said, 'Since I ran into you outside the Gore Hotel, I've been thinking about your murdered vicar. If you have time, I would appreciate a chat.'

'Um...' Mildly panicked, Hannah sought a way to redirect her.

When Matilda got a whiff of a story, she was ruthless. 'I may have been premature in broaching that particular subject. Perhaps I should allow the police to investigate first? For all I know, they might already have a suspect.'

'With no insult to your aunt's beau, it's only been two days. It takes the police that long to sharpen their pencils.' Matilda snorted a laugh. 'My digging into the victim's background wouldn't hurt, and if I find anything significant, they might even be grateful.'

'Look, Tilly – sorry, Matilda – I might have been a little hasty the other day and I wouldn't want to tread on Aidan's toes.'

'You said he wasn't in charge of this case.'

'He isn't. But I doubt he'll be pleased if he finds out I've talked to the press. Thank you for calling—'

'No, Hannah, please don't hang up.' Matilda's urgent plea caused Hannah to pause in replacing the earpiece. 'Actually, I've been asking around to see what anyone knows about it. I have a friend...' The clatter of typewriters in the background muffled the rest of Matilda's words. Hannah jammed a finger into her other ear in an attempt to hear her. 'What friend? What have you asked them to do?'

'...in the police who lives in Brentford. Another works at *The Times*, you know how these things get out.'

'What exactly have you heard?' Hannah insisted.

'Not much so far. Just that Reverend Julian Aldrich was poisoned with digitalis after eloping with an Oxford don's daughter.'

'Matilda! That makes it sound as if the second action precipitated the first.'

'Can you assure me it did not?'

'Um, well, no. But really, you cannot print supposition as fact. DI Wilson is going to blame me for—'

'Is that the name of the investigating officer?' Matilda interrupted.

Hannah imagined her scribbling the name down for future reference. Her next question followed quickly. 'I don't suppose you know the bishop? I'd like to get his views on the dangers presented by proselytizing to soldiers in times of war.'

'What?' Matilda's fast change of subject caught her off guard for a moment. 'Are you suggesting soldiers might hold God responsible for the war?'

She heard rather than saw the reporter's shrug at the end of the line. 'Hannah, last year in the Covent Garden case, you were the one who told me that the sale of Bibles has dropped since the war began, and—'

'All right, I see this has sparked your interest.' Hannah closed her eyes and exhaled. 'I'll meet you as long as you promise not to put anything into your newspaper without talking to the police first?'

'I always double-check my facts with at least two sources before I write my articles,' Matilda replied, though without answering her question. 'Have you talked to the reverend's widow since we spoke?'

'I have, but unless Frances's keeping a dark secret, she's as baffled as anyone about who would kill him.'

'She's our best starting point. Look, why don't we meet soon? You can tell me what you know about the former Miss Frances Blackwood and her family, and we'll form a strategy.'

Hannah wasn't sure she liked the sound of that. When Matilda Gilmartin was on the trail of a new story, she evidently wasn't easily dissuaded. But then, in her profession she most likely had more resources to call upon than Hannah did, and this case was an enigma. 'When and where do you suggest?'

'This afternoon? Say four o'clock at Maison Lyons in Marble Arch?'

'That's less than an hour from now,' Hannah said, glancing towards the grandfather clock inside the front door.

'Is it too soon?' Matilda's voice took on a plaintive tone.

'Er, no, I can make that – just. I'll see you there.' She completed a brief goodbye and rang off; thankful she had Darius's motor car to call on for such emergencies.

Once she'd tidied her hair and swapped her jacket and handbag for more suitable attire for an afternoon excursion,

Hannah descended the stairs into the hall and was almost at the front door when the telephone rang. Travis crossed the tiled floor, lifted the earpiece and announced, 'Clifford residence'.

'Whoever it is, would you let them know I'm on my way out?' Hannah called over her shoulder.

'It's Miss Violet Edwards, madam.' Travis emphasised her aunt's name, the earpiece pointed toward her.

Sighing, Hannah stowed her bag and hat on the hall stand and retraced her steps to accept the receiver.

'Did I leave something behind at the bookshop?' she asked as Travis retreated. Her aunt rarely telephoned, but then there had never been much need when they lived together.

'No, but I've been thinking about Lydia.'

'Lydia? Oh, you mean Frances's mother. Have you remembered anything else from your wilder days?'

'Goodness, you make me sound like I was a flapper.'

'My apologies, I didn't mean to.' Hannah sighed, noting her aunt seemed unusually prickly today.

'You're forgiven. Actually, I have remembered something—'

'Aunt Violet,' Hannah interrupted. 'Could we talk about this another time? I've arranged to meet Matilda Gilmartin at four, and I don't want to be late.'

'Who? Oh, that reporter? Whatever will Aidan say? Remember what happened the last time we had dealings with that girl?'

During the hunt for a murderer the year before, Miss Gilmartin had given the killer an epithet that panicked the public into believing there were more killings to come.

'I do, but Matilda offered to use her contacts to do some research, and I thought it might help.'

'What sort of research?'

'I'm not sure.' Hannah frowned at her aunt's snappish tone.

'But I agreed to listen to her suggestions. Anyway, what was it you remembered?'

'Never mind. I wouldn't want to interfere where I'm not wanted. However, would be convenient to call in on you tomorrow morning.'

'Of course, and you don't have to make an appointment. But won't you be busy with the bookshop?'

'Normally, yes, but my new manager is proving not only highly efficient, but he has a comprehensive list of suggestions to make the administrative processes not only simpler but more productive. And I'm quoting him here.'

'He sounds like a real asset.'

'He's an interfering martinet, and don't get me started on his views about votes for women. I doubt he'll last the week.'

'You cannot sack him for his personal views, Aunt Violet.' Hannah suppressed a laugh.

'I'll see about that. Now I'll see you tomorrow. You can compare your reporter friend to your aunt and see what kind of investigator each is. I still have some ideas left in my ageing repertoire.'

'Aunt Violet, please don't think I'm—' But the line had disconnected, leaving an ominous hum in Hannah's ear. 'Blast!' She cursed under her breath, annoyed at having upset her aunt, and the fact she would be late for Matilda.

The sky hung low when she left the house, so she used up her precious time enlisting a footman to raise the tonneau on the Swift and arrived in the middle of a brief but heavy spring downpour. The rain had stopped by the time she found a suitable parking spot alongside Hyde Park, but she had to splash through puddles on her way into the imposing building occupied by Maison Lyons.

The vast department store had opened almost ten years

before, with each of its four floors featuring a different thematic restaurant and its own orchestra that performed all day for patrons. Conscious Matilda was already waiting, she quickly crossed the grand entrance that resembled a luxury hotel, with its curved polished wood staircase and long hallways lined with counters offering every item the discerning – and not so discerning – shopper would want. She hurried past the ground-floor food hall, with its impressive display of meat, bakery prod-ucts, wine and cheese, and a large flower stall, although these days many shelves stood empty, as almost four years of war had reduced the number of both ordinary and luxury goods as they became harder to obtain.

She assumed, correctly, that Matilda would choose the tearoom on the first floor where waitresses in black and white uniforms scurried between small tables set out for couples and parties of four. A three-piece orchestra sat on a raised platform at the far end. Couples and families occupied most of the cafe; ladies in afternoon dresses wearing artistic hats, some men in khaki uniforms, and a couple of small boys on too-high chairs in plus fours and shiny shoes, kicking their feet above the floor. The uniforms apart, the room felt a long way from the war with the tinkle of crockery, low chatter and the subtle notes of a Mozart concerto on the piano.

'Did you get wet?' Matilda grinned at her. 'It was pouring a few moments ago.'

'No, I missed it, but my shoes and stockings got a thorough soaking.' Hannah hung her coat on a row of hooks on the wall behind their table.

'I hope you don't mind, but I ordered for us.' Matilda, in her professional costume of crisp white blouse over a navy-blue skirt and matching boater, half rose from her seat and waved her over to where she occupied a table for two. It was far enough from the musicians to allow a private conversation. 'I hope you like the famous Lyons Battenberg, as I've ordered for both of us.' Matilda poured the still hot, fragrant tea from the metal pot on a tiny blue flame of a paraffin trestle into two cups. 'If marzipan isn't to your taste, I'll order something else for you.'

'That sounds perfect.' Hannah reeled from the girl's rapid and cheerful bombardment and settled into the chair opposite.

'Thanks for coming.' Matilda handed her a cup and pushed the milk jug towards her. 'I have something to ask you about your aunt.'

'Go on.' Hannah waited as the waitress returned with a plate containing four perfect squares of pink and yellow checkerboard cakes wrapped in marzipan.

'This new Act of Parliament will come into law in the next few months, and I would like to interview Miss Edwards about her views on it.'

The Representation of the People Act that had passed in February gave women over thirty who met the prescribed property qualifications the right to vote.

'My aunt isn't a leading light in the WSPU any more. As you know, they suspended activities for the duration of the war – although Aunt Violet always made her views on Women's Suffrage abundantly clear.' Hannah laughed. 'If you read the Bow Street Court records, you will find a glowing account of her actions and how far she went.'

'I'm more interested in her personal viewpoint and how her passion for the cause helped bring about a change in attitude towards women in general.'

'I'll ask her if you like, although these days she's not quite the firebrand who threw bricks through the House of Commons windows and fired post boxes. Her principles are the same, but she's less strident. Don't misunderstand me, I'm proud of my aunt and delighted to have the option to choose who governs us, even if it means waiting another five years to take part. This act is equally important for all those men who were denied the vote because they weren't wealthy enough.'

'After that speech, perhaps I should interview you, Hannah.' She chuckled. 'And I haven't forgotten male suffrage either, only I *do* think your aunt's perspective will interest my readers.' She placed her cup down and seemed to gear up for her next question. 'Have you made any progress on your murdered vicar?'

'As far as I know,' Hannah replied carefully, 'the police have found no suspects or even a motive for the reverend's death.'

'Don't worry, I always check my facts with the police in criminal cases, but surely there's *something* you can tell me. A vicar brutally murdered with poison at a wedding and a secret wife with a disapproving father has all the elements of a Gothic novel. My readers will love it.'

'Who told you he was poisoned?' Hannah frowned. Who else had Matilda been talking to?

'Wasn't he?' Matilda gazed innocently at her over the rim of her cup.

'I keep forgetting all your useful contacts.' Hannah forked up a miniscule piece of cake and brought it to her mouth, conscious of Matilda's expectant expression. 'Oh, all right. But you're not to print any articles yet. Do you promise?'

'Of course.' Matilda shrugged, though Hannah could not tell if she had her fingers crossed or not.

Over cups of tea and cake, Hannah recounted the events surrounding her wedding to Darius, the panic over the missing reverend, and even her mother's drama with her grandmother's veil, while Matilda peppered her with questions.

'And you actually stumbled over the man's body while wearing your wedding dress?'

'Not stumbled, but, yes, I spotted him first.' She shuddered as the memory returned and distracted herself by topping up her tea and stirred in milk. The Battenberg cake had been reduced to crumbs on both of their plates. 'All I know about Reverend Julian Aldrich is that he was orphaned young and studied theology at Oxford University. He was something of an enigma.'

Matilda made discreet but copious notes as Hannah talked, and once she had finished, set down her pencil long enough to hold the teapot over her cup. When no more than a few drops trickled out, she waved to attract a waitress, but there appeared to be only one on duty, so it took a few minutes for her to notice.

Finally, the girl rushed over to their table. 'I'm so sorry for keeping you waiting, miss. But we're short-handed here today as half our Nippies are up on the roof doing rifle practice. It's compulsory, you see.'

'Could we have some more tea, please?' Matilda asked. 'And Battenberg too. What about you, Hannah?'

'No more cake for me, thank you.' Hannah tried to imagine what a German would feel about being shot by a waitress in a cap and apron.

'Rifle practice sounds interesting,' Matilda said when the waitress had disappeared with the empty teapot. 'I wouldn't mind having a go at that.' She took up her pencil again. 'Now what was I saying? Ah, here we are.' She read aloud from her notes. 'Frances's father turned up at the hotel and insisted she leave with him, even though he had just learned the reverend was dead.' She looked up from the page, still frowning. 'That was an unusual reaction, don't you think?'

'I do. His disappointment at their elopement is understandable, but he regarded the whole affair as done, dusted and best forgotten. When Frances said she was staying for the funeral, he seemed put out. And when I spoke to her next, she told me he had returned to Oxford.'

'Hmm. Interesting.' Matilda greeted the returning waitress with a fresh teapot with a wide smile, which endured until she left again, when her professional demeanour returned. 'Perhaps the engagement wasn't as much of a surprise as the professor claimed?'

'That occurred to me, too,' Hannah replied, beginning to feel like she was being formally interviewed. 'Is there anything I've said so far which concentrates your thoughts on a motive?'

'No, not really, but this is how I do things – I choose a starting point and follow it through until something interesting turns up.' Matilda refilled her cup, then held the teapot over Hannah's cup.

Hannah halted her when it was half full. 'Oh, that's enough for me.' At this rate, she'd need to visit the ladies' conveniences, but at least Lyons had one.

'You've given me plenty to work with.' Matilda furrowed her brow in thought. 'I'll see what I can find out, but don't worry,' she added in response to Hannah's nervous look. 'I'll be discreet.'

Matilda glanced at the wall clock. 'Oh, gosh, is that the time? I had better be off. I'm having supper with my father tonight and he's bound to harass me again about why I haven't yet found a husband. He's threatened that if I don't apply myself, he'll find one for me. I dread to think who he'll come up with.'

'I'm sure you'll be able to distract him.' Hannah laughed.

'Huh. You don't know Father. He's ruthless. And can you believe my mother claims I'm just like him?'

'No!' Hannah feigned shock. 'How unjust of her.'

Either ignoring or not registering the sarcasm in Hannah's tone, Matilda gathered her bag and tossed a ten-shilling note from her pocket onto a saucer. 'It's my pleasure,' she said, waving off Hannah's protest. 'Next time, you can treat me.'

Hannah sat alone for a while after she had gone, her mixed thoughts accompanied by mournful yet stirring cello music from the three-piece orchestra. She hoped she had not made a serious mistake revealing details of the case to a newspaper reporter, and one she had had previous run-ins with at that. However, she couldn't help liking Matilda Gilmartin, whose analytical nature made her look forward to their cooperation.

12

The following morning, Hannah and Darius were halfway through breakfast when Travis interrupted to announce the arrival of Miss Violet Edwards.

'Goodness, she's early,' Hannah exclaimed. 'You'd better show her in, Travis. And perhaps you'll bring more coffee for us all. I'm sure she won't refuse one.'

'With pleasure, madam.' Travis retreated, looking delighted with himself. He had always admired her Aunt Violet, who treated every man she met as if he was the only one in existence, servant or lord.

'Were you expecting her?' Darius asked, forking scrambled egg into his mouth as if it was his last chance.

'I was, but certainly not for breakfast.' Hannah pushed back her chair just as her aunt sailed into the room.

'Don't get up, Hannah,' Aunt Violet said, too late as Hannah was already on her feet. 'My apologies to you both for interrupting your early meal,' she said, joining them at the table, 'but I'm worried about Aidan, and I need some advice.' She turned a beaming smile on the butler. 'Thank you, Travis. You're looking very dapper this morning.'

'It's so nice to see you again, Miss Edwards.' The butler hovered a moment before retreating, his cheeks turning a distinct pink.

'You've made his day, Aunt Violet,' Hannah said as the door closed on the butler.

'Nonsense.' Aunt Violet's hand fluttered to her throat. 'He has a beautiful new mistress now, so doesn't need me to cheer him up.'

'Oh dear,' Darius looked up from his plate. 'Shouldn't I, as a new husband, have said that?'

Hannah pouted in feigned disappointment, then showed she was not offended by blowing him a kiss. 'Is that what you wanted to discuss with me yesterday, Aunt Violet? If so, I'm sorry if I was dismissive, but I was in a rush to—'

'Get to your meeting with Miss Gilmartin, yes, you mentioned that.' Aunt Violet concentrated on removing her gloves as if the task required her full attention. 'I assume your reporter friend wanted to know about our murdered vicar?'

'She did, but it wasn't the entire purpose of our meeting. Matilda also wished to ask if you would be willing to be interviewed.'

'Me?' Aunt Violet's thoughtful expression cleared. 'Whatever for?'

'She wants to write an article about your time in the WSPU and how you feel their activities contributed to the vote being granted to women.'

'Only *some* women, darling.' Her aunt preened. 'But how flattering. Will she require a photograph? I haven't had one done for ages.'

'Possibly, and I assume that means you aren't averse to the idea?' Hannah winked at Darius, who smiled.

'I'll think about it.' Though her look of triumph showed she had already made up her mind. 'Anyway, the reason I'm here is because I had luncheon with Aidan yesterday and he made me think.'

'How is Aidan?' Darius glanced up in enquiry. 'I haven't seen much of him since he was promoted to Detective Chief Inspector.'

Aunt Violet was about to answer but paused as Travis returned and advanced on them with a bone china cup and saucer in one hand, the coffee-pot in the other.

'Thank you, Travis.' She pressed his arm flirtatiously, then waited for the door to close on him before speaking again. 'Aidan rarely shares details of his cases, but Inspector Wilson doesn't seem to be making any headway. Aidan thinks the man lacks imagination when questioning witnesses and he doesn't pick up on visual clues or mannerisms either.'

'That doesn't sound like the makings of a good detective,' Darius observed.

'I agree.' She propped her elbows on the table and cradled her cup in both hands. 'Aidan fears he won't discover who killed Reverend Aldrich, which would then reflect badly on him.'

Aunt Violet's troubled expression transformed into delighted surprise when she sipped her coffee. 'Goodness! This is the best I've tasted since before the war. Where *did* you get it?'

'I have no idea, and I'm loath to ask.' Darius grinned. 'I'll see if Travis has some spare you can take home with you.'

'I won't say no.' Aunt Violet licked her lips, her mood considerably improved. 'As I was saying, DI Wilson questioned Julian's associates in Oxford, but predictably, those he studied with have graduated and are now scattered to the winds. Even Julian's old landlord had nothing to say about him other than he paid his rent on time.'

'I'd be interested to know why Professor Blackwood forbade Frances to associate with him,' Hannah said between mouthfuls of pastry. Her meals had become more elaborate recently, with a full-time cook in the kitchen, so she would have to take care not to overindulge.

'You don't go along with the "A vicar isn't good enough for my daughter?" explanation, then?' Her aunt raised a sceptical eyebrow.

'It seems odd, or why would Professor Blackwood help Julian get into Merton by writing a reference to the Dean?' Hannah said, frowning.

'An interesting question.' Her aunt nodded slowly. 'Inspector Wilson regarded the professor's disapproval as being unrelated to the case, since he was not in town when Julian was killed.'

'Which is true.' Hannah turned this over in her head. 'But surely the fact Julian and Frances kept their relationship a secret has some relevance? Perhaps someone else objected to their marriage?'

'Inspector Wilson appears to have taken everything at face value.' Aunt Violet's tone conveyed the frustration Aidan must have felt with his colleague's lack of progress.

'Witnesses rarely tell the whole truth,' Darius pointed out. 'Either deliberately, or because they feel the information is irrelevant. Which is why Aidan is a great believer in repeat interviews. However, if he conducts them himself, it will undermine Inspector Wilson.'

'Precisely what Aidan said.' Aunt Violet waved her spoon at him in emphasis. 'The Oxfordshire police have been more than obliging, but Wilson dismissed a second visit as a wasted journey.'

'Perhaps he doesn't like trains?' Hannah said into her cup, but when her aunt asked her to repeat it, she waved her off.

'I must have more of this coffee,' Aunt Violet announced. Choosing not to summon the butler, she crossed to the sideboard to retrieve the replenished coffee-pot, topping up her cup before offering the pot around the table.

Hannah declined, although Darius held his cup towards her. 'What's the betting Wilson's "I'm from the Met" attitude did him no favours with the Oxford police either.'

'Possibly.' Aunt Violet set the pot down on the table with a thump. 'In fact, I thought I might make the drive to Oxford myself today.'

'Aunt Violet,' Darius began, exercising his right to address her as a relative by marriage. 'I understand your wish to help, but you have no authority to ask questions during an ongoing police investigation.'

'I don't intend to masquerade as a policeman, Darius, dear.' Aunt Violet's low, attractive laugh filled the room. 'But it occurred to me that Professor Blackwood might be more amenable to a lady who has befriended his daughter and has her interests at heart.' She turned to look at Hannah.

'You want *me* to go with you?' Hannah perked up at the appealing prospect.

'What do you think?' Her aunt leaned an elbow on the table and eased closer. 'Didn't you say Frances's closest friend knew Julian as well?'

Hannah nodded. 'Esme, I think she said her name was. The professor went to see her when Frances left for London. Do you think someone knows more than they are letting on?'

'Only one way to find out.' Aunt Violet wiped her lips on a napkin which she then slapped on the table. 'Are you game?'

'Absolutely, I wouldn't miss—' Hannah hesitated, her gaze

split between her aunt and her husband. 'That is, if you agree, Darius. I wouldn't go if you disapprove?'

'You don't have to ask *my* permission before going off on one of your jaunts.' Darius raised a sardonic eyebrow.

'Not as a rule, but, um, things are different – now we're married, I mean.'

'Of course you must go.' Darius relaxed back in his chair. 'Aidan might even appreciate the help.' He turned towards Aunt Violet. 'How's his mother, by the way?'

'That's another thing,' Aunt Violet said when she resumed her seat. 'They've transferred her to an isolation ward in Euston Road hospital, making it harder for Aidan to visit her.'

'Oh dear, that must mean she's worse?' Hannah said.

'I'm afraid so. Aidan has taken the day off to sort out problems at the hotel. Three soldiers on leave staying there and a bellboy have fallen ill this week. He intends to insist the staff refuse entry to anyone who appears unwell.'

'That's rather harsh,' Hannah said, frowning. 'Those chaps returning from France are all going to look pasty and thin because of what they've been through. Some of them are likely recovering from injuries.'

'Maybe, but he's acting in everyone's interest.' Darius reached for a slice of toast, peered into the butter dish, which was depleted, so pushed it aside and instead spread a thick layer of preserve on the slice. 'There's been an outbreak of influenza in army camps in Northern France because of the conditions and overcrowding. It's not too serious as there have been few deaths, and the army hopes to get it under control quickly.'

'I hope you're right about it not being serious,' Aunt Violet said. 'Aidan is convinced that one of his mother's guests infected her.'

'He could be right, but I hope Mrs Farrell recovers soon.'

Darius rose and nodded to where spring sunshine flooded through the window. 'It certainly looks like a nice day for an excursion.' Circling the table, he bussed Aunt Violet lightly on the cheek before approaching Hannah, bent and pressed his lips to hers in a soft, lingering kiss, his breath warm in her ear, and whispered, 'I'll do my best to be home for supper, but I cannot make any promises.'

* * *

'Are you sure you want to drive all the way to Oxford?' Hannah settled into the passenger seat of her aunt's roadster. 'The train is probably quicker.'

'Not necessarily.' Aunt Violet started the engine and let it idle on the drive. 'The last time I was at Paddington, I couldn't move for the crowds waiting to gawp at the hospital trains. Ghouls. Then the guards ordered us off as they needed the carriage for troops. We had to wait a full hour for the next one.' She barely paused for breath before continuing. 'And who knows what the taxi situation is like in Oxford these days, so having our own transport will be more convenient.'

'You don't mean that, Aunt Violet.' Hannah wished she had not mentioned trains at all. Even four years on since the beginning of the war, crowds still gathered outside Charing Cross Hospital to watch in silence as the injured were driven in. Hannah regarded their vigil as an acknowledgement of the soldiers' bravery rather than simply to satisfy morbid curiosity.

'Perhaps that was harsh, but it seems so disrespectful.' Aunt Violet guided the motor car along the drive towards a pair of wrought-iron gates. 'Anyway, who shall we talk to in Oxford?'

'Professor Blackwood? And that friend of Frances's, Esme?

They both knew Julian Aldrich well, but how do we find them in a city?'

'Our first call will be at the porter's lodge at Merton College. My guess is they will know everything there is to know about the dons and their families.'

'That's assuming they will part with such information,' Hannah observed. 'It's a long way to go for a wasted journey.'

'Don't be a defeatist, darling. If they are close-mouthed, I'll think of something.' Her aunt glanced at the red leather-covered book Hannah held in her lap. 'What have you got there?'

'It's a new pocket companion for Oxford.' Hannah read out from a much thumbed and ragged title page. 'Well, I'm calling it new, but the publication date is 1810.'

'Where on earth did you find that? Not in the bookshop, I trust? It's almost a relic.'

'In Darius's library last night. Or maybe it's mine now too.' She patted the cover possessively. 'I assume it once belonged to his father.'

'More like his great-grandfather,' Aunt Violet scoffed, manoeuvring the motor car around a horse and cart so aggressively that Hannah squeezed her eyes shut and held her breath until they slowed down to a more comfortable pace. 'It might be old but it features all the colleges which have existed since medieval times. I doubt the city layout has changed that much.' She flipped to the last page and held up a folded sheet of thick paper. 'I discovered this street map inside, which is more recent, so that might come in useful. But we have a long way to go, so I hope you have at least a vague idea of our direction.'

'Well, west, obviously, but as far as locations are concerned, we'll have to play it by ear. Keep a lookout for signposts as we go, would you?'

Hannah's smile hinted at a fraught day. The way her aunt

drove meant they weren't likely to see any signposts other than in the rear-view mirror.

'Darius was very obliging this morning,' Aunt Violet commented as they drove through Greenford; the tang of manure and exhaust fumes gave way to clear air and birdsong. 'Despite his impeccable manners, I hope he doesn't resent me for taking you away for the whole day?'

'He said he'd do his best to be home for supper, but he's working late again tonight at the Admiralty at a crisis meeting or something similar, so I doubt he'll notice.' Hannah settled back in her seat as the motor car headed through the suburbs. 'I was thinking about coming back to the bookshop for a couple of days next week. What do you think?'

'If you're at a loose end, you're welcome anytime. I could do with someone to talk to, what with Mr Hendry constantly ordering me to sit down or have a cup of tea and he will handle everything. Anyone would think I'm in failing health. I'm also trying to keep Penny occupied to take her mind off Archie. I shall have to keep her away from the newspapers or she'll spend her working day going through the casualty lists, which will do nothing for her peace of mind.'

Did Aunt Violet regret her choice of manager? The last one was also a failure, having been involved with a spying ring, passing messages to German agents through the bookshop.

'Are you all right, Hannah?' Her aunt's eyebrows scrunched together as she shot a brief glance at her before turning back to the road. 'For a newlywed, you seem a little despondent.'

'I suppose I am, a little.' Hannah sighed. 'I thought things would be, well, different. I hardly see Darius, and we've been married less than a week.'

'Poor you. I know it's disappointing, him being so busy.' Aunt Violet took her hand off the wheel long enough to pat her knee.

'But the war isn't something one can predict. He'd be home with you if he could, I'm sure.'

'I know, and now I feel churlish for making a fuss when there are wives with much more to cope with than me.'

A comfortable silence settled on them, accompanied by the rhythmic distinct huffs and putts of the cylinders firing as the engine ate up the miles through picturesque country towns and villages like Beaconsfield, High Wycombe and Tetsworth. They stopped for refreshments at a public house in the riverside town of Henley before resuming their journey through the Chiltern Hills to Stokenchurch and on to rural Oxfordshire and Wheatley, a few miles outside Oxford.

'I'm glad I filled up before we left.' Aunt Violet peered at the petrol gauge, frowning. 'And at sixpence a gallon, I don't intend to do that too often.'

'As long as we have enough to get back to London.' Hannah unfolded the street map onto her lap, squinting at the street names. 'Merton College is located a mile away at the end of this road. My ancient guidebook says the university was founded in the thirteenth century with an outer crenelated wall like a castle.' With her finger held in place on the page; she twisted in her seat to face her aunt. 'Were you aware that noblemen had to obtain a licence from the monarch to add battlements to their property?'

'I did not, but it doesn't surprise me you do, what with all the time you spend in the reading corner at the bookshop.' Her aunt halted outside a long grey stone building with the promised battlements above and a massive arched entrance covered by a wall of thick oak with a wicket gate on the left side.

'This is Merton Street, so I assume we have arrived.'

'This looks like the main entrance.' Aunt Violet peered at a plaque attached to the wall beside the gate. 'What does that sign say?'

'It says the Porter's Lodge is through there. It also lists the quadrangles. There's Front Quad, Fellows' Quad, St Alban's Quad, Mob Quad, Grove Buildings, and Fellows' Gard—'

'That's enough. You don't need to recite the entire thing. We aren't on a tour.'

'I was trying to be helpful.' Hannah suppressed a smile, adding, 'Have you considered getting spectacles, Aunt Violet?'

'Now you're being impertinent. Have more respect for your senior relatives.'

'You're forty-four, hardly *senior*.' Hannah tutted as she exited the motor car onto the path. 'That man in a grey bowler and dark blazer beside the gate is wearing a badge that says—'

'I can see it perfectly well, thank you,' her aunt snapped. Leaving the motor car, she slung her bag over her shoulder and set off towards the porter, who greeted her with an ingratiating smile and lifted his bowler an inch.

Following, Hannah hovered as Aunt Violet launched into a story about a phantom nephew on whose behalf she sought an old friend he once studied with.

'Julian Aldrich, eh? Aye, I remember him.' The porter nodded his head. 'Handsome lad, and one for the ladies. But then most of them are when they first get away from home. Liked a drink too, as I recall, and walked out with the Webb girl from the Bookbinders.'

The jangle of an insistent bicycle interrupted his last words as a student rode past them at speed, his ankle-length black coat flapping behind him.

'Oy! Mind where you're going, sir!' the porter yelled after him, but the cyclist paid no heed and disappeared around a corner.

'Did you say Mr Aldrich's lady friend was a bookmaker?' Hannah asked, puzzled.

'Naw, miss. The Bookbinders.' He chuckled. 'It's a pub in Jericho near the canal.'

'Oh, I see. Sorry, I must have misheard.' Mildly embarrassed, Hannah wandered back to wait beside the motor car, leaving them to their conversation.

Aunt Violet rejoined Hannah a few minutes later. 'Well, that was an interesting interaction, despite costing me ten shillings.'

'Ten shillings!' Hannah's voice rose in indignation as she slammed the passenger door behind her. 'The man's an extortionist.'

'He's enterprising, I'll say that for him.' Chuckling, Aunt Violet tucked her bag behind the driver's seat and climbed inside. 'I doubt he earns much, and with his eyes and ears on all the comings and goings, he's bound to be tempted to share it with those willing to pay. But in return for that, I got Professor Blackwood's address, not to mention the name of Julian's former girlfriend, a Miss Ruby Webb. We'll make her our first call.'

Hannah tugged her skirt from under her where it had caught on the edge of the leather seat and spread the now crumpled map over her lap where she located the canal before working backwards to find the public houses. 'Ah, here it is!' she announced triumphantly, a finger held to the page. 'The Bookbinders is in Canal Street near St Ethelred's Church. Wasn't that where Julian worked as a verger before he came to St Nicholas?'

'I believe so.' Aunt Violet revved the engine and swerved widely past a grocer's van, much to the startled annoyance of some passersby. 'Now, which way?'

'Keep going straight ahead along the High Street then onto Queen Street, and I'll navigate from there.'

'I'd forgotten what an attractive town this is.' Aunt Violet kept to a sedate speed as she followed Hannah's instructions, her head turning from side to side to view the variety of old buildings that jostled for prominence in the ancient thoroughfare.

'You've been here before?' Hannah's voice held an edge. 'Then why did you make me handle all the directions?'

'Silly, we came down in Tommy Rutherford's Rolls-Royce, which was packed to the gills with champagne, so I paid no attention to the road. And talking of the road, I feel as if we have been driving for hours. Is it time for a sherry yet?'

'It's still only mid-morning, so no.' Hannah gritted her teeth. 'I think we must turn left here. Or do we?'

'Well, make up your mind. There's a coal truck behind me and the driver doesn't seem to be a patient man.'

'Try it, and we'll backtrack if I'm mistaken.'

After a couple of false turns, they found The Bookbinders public house in a narrow side street not far from the canal. On their first run, Aunt Violet drove straight past it into an even narrower road, which required a tricky manoeuvre to turn full circle without scraping the paintwork.

'That was a mission.' Aunt Violet sighed and leaned back in her seat as she pulled up beside an ancient half-timbered building hunched between two larger ones, its low lintels and leaded windows set at waist height.

'It wasn't *that* hard to find!' Hannah climbed out onto the pavement, refusing to take responsibility for her navigation. 'And I still think that porter is a crook!'

'Do stop complaining, Hannah. We'd never have known about this place without him.' Aunt Violet alighted onto the uneven pavement and slammed the driver's door behind her.

'You're being very cavalier about it.' Hannah increased her stride to catch up as Aunt Violet raised a fist to the wooden door. 'Aren't maiden aunts meant to be morally scrupulous?'

'Now I know you're joking. And if I recall, darling, you paid the barman at the Priest's Hole the same amount to put you in touch with a fence named Nell Grogan.'

'That was totally different. I was incognito and on a hunt for stolen jewellery, so it was a business transaction.'

Another minute passed, then a disembodied female voice called through the door. 'We aren't open yet.' Undeterred, Aunt Violet knocked again, harder this time. She was rewarded by the dull click of a latch and a girl in her twenties with red hair and freckles yanked the door open. She wore a faded cotton dress beneath an apron that had once been white, but was now a pale grey with the shadows of old stains on it.

'I've just told you, the law says we can't open until noon— Oh! Pardon me, madam. How can I help you?'

'Miss Webb?' Aunt Violet summoned her most ingratiating smile. 'Could you spare us a moment or two?'

'What for?' A pair of greenish-brown eyes shifted to Hannah then back to Aunt Violet. 'You aren't selling anything, are you? Because if you are—'

'We want to speak to you about Mr Julian Aldrich,' Aunt Violet interrupted her before she could slam the door shut on them.

'Oh.' She gave the street behind them a swift glance before jerking her chin. 'You'd better come in then.' She pulled the door wider, then closed it so quickly that Hannah leaped over the sill, fearful the door was about to remove the skin on her heel. Halting, she eyed the dim interior of the public bar, with its mismatched wooden bench seats and captain's chairs. The low-ceilinged room smelled of stale beer and cigarettes, and from the windows slanted beams of spring sunlight in which dust motes danced onto scarred tables and the uneven flagstone floor.

'What do you want to know?' The girl regarded them both

with suspicious eyes but did not invite them to sit. 'You do know he's dead, don't you?'

'Indeed, he is,' Aunt Violet replied. 'More importantly, it looks like someone killed him. We're trying to find out who the murderer is.'

'Murdered?' She pulled in her chin, eyes rounded. 'No one told me that. The police came to ask Dad if Julian was a regular customer, which he was.' This seemed to have unnerved her. 'No need for me to get involved though, was there?' So she hadn't revealed her historic relationship with the victim. Interesting, Hannah thought.

'But you knew Julian?' Hannah pressed. 'I believe you were close at one time.'

'We were. Sort of. But that was a while ago. I haven't seen him since he went into the Church. Big surprise, that was 'n all. He never mentioned it while we were together.' She wrinkled her rather flat nose, which made her attractive face almost comical. 'But then he seemed to like those medieval paintings of sad-eyed saints, angels and cherubs and whatnot.'

'Did he have any enemies when you were, uh, walking out?' Hannah asked.

'Only me, when he dropped me without a word.' She rolled her eyes and crossed her arms over her chest. 'But I didn't kill him, if that's what you're asking.'

'Did he make promises to you?' Aunt Violet's voice softened in sympathy, which appeared to have an effect as the girl dropped her arms to her sides and shrugged.

'Not in so many words. But I... I had expectations. I heard he was going out with that Toliver girl.'

'Would her name be Esme, by any chance?' Hannah recalled Frances mentioning the name outside the Gore.

'That's her.' She sniffed and Hannah sensed the hurt that lay behind her curt nod. 'She was more Julian's style, I suppose. Her father's a don and Julian liked to think he belonged among that sort.' She cast a swift look at the rear of the bar and sighed. 'If you must know, Julian broke up with me just before his cousin, Benjamin, died. He claimed it was for my own good as much as his. He was probably right. I never saw myself in that world in any case.' She shrugged resignedly, though her eyes held a trace of bitterness.

'Did you know Benjamin?' Hannah asked, suspecting Julian was probably fond of Ruby and his reasons for ending their liaison were genuine, although she still felt slighted.

Ruby nodded. 'Good-looking lad, but very different to Julian. He came into the pub sometimes with two other local lads, mostly to scrounge drinks off Julian for him and his friends. Arrogant, he was, and sure of himself. Julian only gave in to stop him spreading around to his university friends that he was courting a barmaid. One of them – Andrew Bowles, I think his name is – has been home on leave a couple of times and popped in here to show off his uniform. He looked right 'andsome in it too, but we barely spoke.'

'Have you seen the other youth, Jack Friar, since the accident?' Hannah asked, hoping to be able to contact the lad and get his perspective.

'Come to think of it, no. I heard he joined the army too.' Ruby frowned thoughtfully. 'He was conscripted too, probably. He was about the right age.'

'Heard from whom?' Aunt Violet asked.

'Dunno, word just gets round. I don't think he had any family around here, but I think he was apprenticed to a bookbinder. There are a lot of those hereabouts, but I couldn't tell you which one he worked for.'

'Maybe he simply doesn't want to return here after losing a

friend in such circumstances,' Aunt Violet suggested. 'This place might hold too many memories for him.'

'Yeah. I s'pose that's it. Though for all I know his body could be lying in a trench somewhere. A few lads round here have been reported missing but haven't been found. Sad that.'

'Yes, it is. Very sad,' Hannah agreed.

'Or,' Ruby said brightly, 'if he's smart, he could be living in France now, holed up in a remote mountain farm with some mademoo'selle.'

Hannah smiled, hoping this was true. Better that, than being shot, forgotten and left to rot in some mud-filled trench somewhere.

Ruby might have carried a grudge, but Hannah could not imagine she possessed enough cunning to plan a murder. And where would the daughter of an innkeeper get digitalis, even if she knew what it was?

'Do you work every day?' Aunt Violet asked, probably her diplomatic way of discovering if the girl was in town when Julian was killed.

'Here in the pub?' Her shrug implied agreement. 'Dad can't afford anyone else and most of the chaps who'd want the job have enlisted. Pay's better in the army than bar work, and the uniform is included. I get one day a week off, though. Why do you ask?'

'Was your day off last Saturday, by any chance?' Hannah asked.

'How did you know?' She pulled back her chin and glared at each of them.

'Would you mind telling us how you spent it?' Hannah asked.

'As a matter of fact, I would mind. My time's my own, and I don't answer to anyone.'

The rattle of a door behind the counter was accompanied by a harsh male shout of 'Ruby!'

Sighing, the girl cast an annoyed look over her shoulder. 'I have to go. Dad needs me to help prime the pumps before we open.'

'I don't think there's anything else to learn here,' Aunt Violet lowered her voice, then spoke louder. 'Well, thank you for your help, Miss Webb – Ruby. And we sympathise. Some men have no regard for the finer female character. I'm sure you'll find someone more worthy of you.'

'Yes, well.' Ruby looked contrite. 'I didn't mean to sound disrespectful to the dead, and I'm truly sorry Julian's gone.'

The pub door shut behind them with a thump, and Hannah placed a hand on Aunt Violet's arm, her chin cocked behind her. 'It appears Ruby does answer to someone.'

13

'Which number did the porter say the house was?' Hannah asked, as Aunt Violet slowed the motor car to a crawl and crept past a row of handsome Georgian properties with wrought-iron railings across the front, each three storeys high with steps up from the street.

'Twenty-five,' Aunt Violet replied, looking at the buildings. 'Or was it twenty-seven?'

Hannah peered over the windshield to read the numbers on the doors. 'There, the one with the black iron lantern hanging from the porch.'

She flapped her hand to signal to her aunt to stop.

Aunt Violet climbed out onto the pavement and leaned back to collect her bag from behind her seat. She approached the house and, with a foot on the bottom step, looked back to where Hannah still sat in the car. 'Aren't you coming?'

'I suppose so,' Hannah replied, not moving. 'To be honest, I don't relish meeting the professor again. He wasn't exactly welcoming the first time.'

'Then let me do the talking.' Her aunt made a hurry-up gesture with one hand. 'Come on. Isn't this why we came?'

Hannah sighed and dragged herself from the seat, making sure she was standing behind her aunt when she reached the front door. The professor opened the door to her aunt's knock wearing shirtsleeves beneath a tweed waistcoat, a pair of spectacles balanced on top of his slicked-back hair and an expression of mild enquiry.

'Professor Blackwood?' Aunt Violet asked in her low, seductive voice 'My name is Violet Edwards. We're sorry if we're disturbing you, but would you spare us a few moments?' The man gaped slightly, obviously taken unaware as Aunt Violet had not paused for breath. 'I believe you know my niece, Mrs Hannah Clifford?' She eased to one side where Hannah was cowering on the second step down.

'Ah, yes.' His wary stance relaxed, his eyes sliding from Aunt Violet to Hannah, widening in recognition. 'I remember well, and fear I owe you an apology. You were kind to Frances at the hotel and I was less than cordial to both of you. Please accept my apology.' His expression sharpened as a thought occurred to him. 'Frances is all right, I hope?'

'We didn't mean to alarm you, and yes, Frances is quite well,' Hannah replied, experiencing a pang of guilt she had not called on her in the last couple of days. 'She's distressed naturally, and confused.'

'We hoped that by talking to those who knew you both we could learn more about the reverend,' Aunt Violet added.

'Reverend!' He snorted the word. 'I find that word incongruous when applied to Julian. I could never see him in that role. Though one cannot judge what others choose to do with their lives. Not that it matters now what *I* think.'

'We would be interested in your perspective, Professor,' Aunt

Violet said. 'It might give an insight into who might want him dead.'

'Isn't that the duty of the constabulary?' His air of friendliness persisted, though his eyes grew wary. 'They've already questioned me about my movements before and after his murder.'

'We have a special interest in this case,' Hannah attempted to explain. 'Reverend Aldrich was my parish priest. He was not with us for long, so I cannot claim to have known him well, but he was a capable and popular minister.' She omitted having attended only four of his services, three of which were to hear their marriage banns read.

'That doesn't surprise me.' Professor Blackwood repositioned his glasses on his nose. 'Julian could make an impression. But then, I suppose we all conceal part of our true character to some extent.' His eyes narrowed slightly but he recovered quickly. 'I might not be as helpful as you imagine, but I'll do my best. Please, ladies, do come in.'

He stepped back to allow them to enter a hallway with a high ceiling, decorated with intricate egg-and-dart coving. At the far end he threw open a door to a bright but cluttered space that seemed to serve as both sitting room and study, for the walls were crammed with bookshelves. Papers and books covered every surface; they lay open and stacked at all angles, and yet the room appeared clean, its predominant smells of old leather and paper.

'I hope we haven't interrupted your work?' Hannah viewed the disarray.

'Not at all. I needed a break anyway. Too much small print.' He swept a thin pile of pamphlets from a settle that might easily have come from a church. Giving the upholstered seat a swipe with a handkerchief, he gestured for them to sit. 'I'm compiling a history of obscure churches in Oxfordshire villages, which has rather absorbed my attention.'

'It's kind of you to tolerate our intrusion.' Aunt Violet summoned her most gracious smile. 'This room is delightful. It's not unlike our bookshop in Covent Garden, if smaller.'

'You own a bookshop?' His eyebrows lifted in delighted surprise. 'How interesting. I assume you are also avid readers?'

'I am,' Hannah replied. 'Obscure medieval churches sound like a fascinating subject. Do you—?'

'We won't waste too much of your time, Professor,' Aunt Violet interrupted, shooting a stern look at Hannah.

The professor waited until both women were seated before he flicked up the back of his jacket and eased into a faded leather chair behind the desk. He stared at Aunt Violet for a moment, and something passed across his expression. 'Pardon me, Miss Edwards, but haven't we met? I feel I know your face from somewhere.'

Hannah mentally rolled her eyes as she had seen this reaction before from men of all ages, most of whom turned out to be mistaken or hopeful.

'I wondered if you would remember me,' Aunt Violet replied, her head tilted. 'We knew one another in London, oh twenty or so years ago. I was a friend of your late wife. And I was so sorry to hear about her premature death.'

'Now I remember. Of course!' He slapped his knee with his hand, a smile revealing he was still a handsome man and must have been striking in his youth. 'Miss Edwards, how uncanny. And thank you for your condolences. It was a long time ago now, but the memories linger.'

'I sympathise. Lydia and I weren't close, but we were part of the same circle.'

'You know, Violet – I may call you Violet, might I? You haven't changed at all.'

Hannah could feel a yawn coming but quickly smothered it.

'Actually, you might not remember, Professor, but you and I parted on bad terms,' Aunt Violet replied coyly. 'I invited your wife to a suffrage meeting and as I recall you were extremely angry about it.'

'Goodness, so you did!' He stared off as if recalling the memory. 'In my favour, I'm not averse to women's rights, however Lydia was... let me say *fickle* in her loyalties. I objected because after that outing, she insisted on making our entire household vegetarian. Even our infant daughter. An innovation I insisted she abandon when our housekeeper threatened to give notice.'

'For which I'm sure Frances will always be grateful.' Aunt Violet laughed. 'I've never embraced those particular principles myself. They always baffled me.'

'I quite agree. How one can live entirely on cabbage and potatoes escapes me, I—'

'Er, might we get to the matter in hand?' Hannah cleared her throat pointedly. 'Professor, Frances told me you were close friends of Julian's family, though you disapproved of their attachment?'

'That's true. We occasionally socialised with his aunt and uncle. In fact, as a favour to Hugh Aldrich, I supplied Julian with a reference which assisted his application to Merton to study Art History. It's not my field as I'm a Medieval Studies Professor, so our academic contact was minimal. He never attended my lectures.'

'Yet he maintained contact with Frances during his studies and for some time afterwards?' Hannah studied his face for a reaction.

'Apparently.' His jaw clenched. 'I knew they were acquainted but I was unaware of the depth of their association until a few days ago, when Esme Toliver told me. Under duress, I might add.'

'Might we ask why? You see, my niece said Reverend Aldrich

was a charming young man and seemed the type who would make an agreeable partner for any woman.'

'My reasons were entirely personal. I wanted better for my daughter than marriage to a country vicar. Frances has talents which could take her far in society. Oh, I don't mean academically, although she's no fool. But she's beautiful, poised and wealthy. It would have been sacrilege for her to moulder away as a clergyman's wife.' He smiled wryly. 'If you would excuse the pun. Anyway, that's all irrelevant now as he's no longer with us.'

'Did you suspect Frances's wealth was the reason Julian courted her?' Hannah asked.

'You're very direct, Mrs Clifford.' He dragged his gaze from Aunt Violet's face and stared at Hannah. 'But I'll respond in kind. I had my suspicions. You see, at one time he also expressed a romantic interest in Miss Toliver.'

'The fickleness of youth, Professor.' Aunt Violet's voice held an impatient edge. 'Not all friendships are successful, or long-lasting. Which doesn't cast him as a bad character.'

'Perhaps.' His voice was guarded. 'Although their association ended abruptly, with no explanation, which was hardly the actions of a gentleman. I warned Frances to guard her emotions, but it's clear now she disregarded my advice.'

'Was your objection because of religious differences?' Hannah took in the room, which was devoid of religious items, only a bland landscape and the occasional animal print.

'Religion had nothing to do with it,' he snapped. 'I just didn't think he was a suitable young man for my daughter.' Several emotions crossed his face as he debated with himself. 'Look, I told the police all this, and they didn't appear to think it was relevant.'

'Pardon me, Professor,' Hannah asked, 'but you don't seem overly distressed about his death.'

'On the contrary; I abhor the unnecessary loss of a young life. However, I cannot pretend to regret his death as it means my daughter is now free to marry again one day. When that happens, I hope she will consider my opinion regarding her choice.'

He removed his glasses, folded them and placed them on the desk in front of him as if he needed time to compose what he was going to say next. 'The Aldriches are a perfectly respectable family, and I would never disparage them, but Julian was a complicated character.'

'Would you care to elaborate?' Aunt Violet prompted.

He considered for a moment, then nodded as if making up his mind. 'Julian lost his parents at a young age, but they left enough funds to see him through a first-class education. An education which, to my mind, he did not make the best use of. But don't take my word for it. Talk to any of his lecturers and they'll confirm he was work-shy. Only doing what was necessary to get passing marks. He did not... excel.'

'Perhaps he wasn't as academically gifted as yourself?' Aunt Violet offered, earning a 'don't overdo it' look from Hannah.

'He was intelligent enough, but indolent.' He appeared not to register this by-play between them, staring at his feet as he spoke. 'Julian had a sullen, resentful quality about him.' He inhaled a slow breath as if composing himself while Hannah waited, hoping he would continue. When he did, he sounded resigned, even tired. 'Then there was the tragedy which took a long time for everyone to recover from.' He dragged in a slow, resigned breath, as if trying to decide how much to reveal.

'Tragedy?' Hannah asked. Was he referring to the death of Julian's cousin, which Frances had touched on?

He nodded again. 'It was two years ago, on an unusually hot day at the end of May. We, that is the Aldriches and I, arranged a picnic at Angel Meadow on the bank of the Cherwell. Being low-lying, it's prone to floods in the first two months of the year but is a popular spot in the summer. Julian and Benjamin, their young son, were present, as were Frances and Mr and Mrs Toliver, who are also friends of ours, with their daughter, Esme. Benjamin had arrived in the company of two working class lads he hung around with. I suspect, and Hugh Aldrich agreed with me, he did so to embarrass his parents.'

'Why would he do that?' Hannah asked.

'Why does any youth on the verge of manhood act outrageously?' He raised both hands from the desk in a gesture of frustration. 'Benjamin was rather spoiled by his parents, who always made excuses for him. He was also jealous of his cousin. At Merton, Julian mixed with the sons of society and Benjamin lacked the intellectual ability to compete.

'At the picnic, the boys lounged on the grass with their shirt-sleeves rolled up and talked loudly. They teased the girls; ate food they didn't provide or pay for. Mostly youthful bravado, annoying but not malicious. Benjamin issued a challenge to jump into the river from Magdalen Bridge; an unwise, even dangerous decision, what with the water being shallow in that area. But the boys were in high spirits and determined to show off and refused to listen. They had been gone for a short while – around half an hour perhaps, maybe less – when we heard shouts from the direction of the bridge. Julian was the first to react, followed by the rest of the picnic goers. At the bridge, we saw Andrew Bowles had made it to the bank, but he was done in. Poor chap was gasping for breath. It appeared Benjamin had jumped off the bridge from a standing position and hadn't resurfaced. The smaller boy, Jack Friar, was in the water searching, but had failed to find him.

'The boys were tiring, and Julian took over, finally locating Benjamin and hauled him to the shore. It was a relief for everyone to see, but he had been submerged for too long and by which time...' He closed his eyes as if reliving the moment, then reached for his glasses and balanced them on his nose.

'How awful,' Hannah said. 'For everyone. Especially Julian.'

'That must have been terrible,' Hannah murmured.

'It was. Hugh was distraught and kept asking me how he was going to tell Louise.'

'What happened to the other two boys?' Aunt Violet asked.

'They were admitted to the hospital overnight, and from what I was told, were interviewed by the police there.'

'You were told?' Hannah frowned. 'You didn't speak to them yourself?'

He looked sheepish. 'To be honest, I was so upset about Benjamin, I couldn't bring myself to talk to them. I suppose that was cowardly.'

Hannah offered no comment, but privately she thought it was unkind. Both boys must have been equally affected.

'Anyway.' He slapped his thighs noisily 'There was an inquest, naturally, where Benjamin's death was declared a misadventure.'

'Did you speak to the boys at the inquest?' Aunt Violet asked.

'No, not really. I passed the time of day with Bowles, but it was somewhat awkward as I'm sure you can imagine. I didn't see young Friar. By the time the inquest was held, the police said he had left for training camp. I was told he had been sent to Belgium. I've no idea where he is now.'

'And Julian? How was he after it happened?'

'He seemed quieter, more reflective. When he returned to university for the Michaelmas term, I was told he changed his course to theology. He gave his reason as wanting to carve a more community-based path through life as opposed to an artistic one.'

'You didn't believe him?' Aunt Violet asked.

'Not entirely.' He rocked forward in his chair, his eyes cast down. 'Oh, he trotted out all the sentiments of a man in conflict, but I felt he lacked sincerity. I said as much to Frances, but she dismissed me as being too critical and unwilling to accept any man she chose.' He snatched off his glasses again, placed them on the desk and massaged his forehead with a thumb and forefinger before replacing them, like they were never far from his hand.

'The boy's parents couldn't bear to look at Julian again,' the professor went on without prompting. 'They packed up and left the county. I haven't seen them since.'

'Do you know where they went?' Hannah asked.

'I-I'm not sure. Hugh was Scottish so I assume they went to live among family. I assume the police will locate them to inform them of Julian's death.'

'You said Julian once courted Esme Toliver,' Hannah said. 'I assume Frances was aware of that, because the way you talked, they seemed to be friends.'

'Oh, they are. Esme is a couple of years older, but she's an intelligent young woman who shares Frances's interests.'

Especially in men, Hannah thought.

'Why are you so interested in Benjamin Aldrich, anyway?' He frowned as if the thought had just occurred to him. 'He died two years ago. Surely that incident could have nothing to do with Julian's murder?'

'You're probably right, but thus far no one in Julian Aldrich's past or present appears to have any reason to want him dead. But didn't you say the two boys who were with him both went into the army? That makes them difficult to question, if not impossible.'

'I suppose it's possible one or other of them could have blamed Julian for Benjamin's death, but then they couldn't save him either. I doubt the answer is in that direction.'

'And with the Aldriches in Scotland, I doubt we'll be able to talk to them either.' Hannah directed this question at her aunt. 'Do you think Esme Toliver would talk to us? If she and Frances were friends, she might know more about Julian and what happened to Benjamin.'

'I don't see as it would do any harm.' Professor Blackwood stroked his chin. 'She lives with her parents in Orchard House, on Radcliffe Street, which is within walking distance.'

Aunt Violet motioned to Hannah that they should leave. 'Thank you for agreeing to talk to us, Professor. We're sorry to have opened old wounds.'

'I cannot say I have been much help,' he said, as he escorted them back to the front door. 'But perhaps Esme will be able to tell you more?'

With a warm, if brittle, smile, he saluted them from the top step as they walked back to the motor car, his glasses swinging from his other hand.

* * *

'Professor Blackwood is quite good-looking for his age, although I always think of professors as white-haired, wearing horn-rimmed spectacles and walking with a stoop,' Hannah said over the bonnet of the vehicle, as she tossed her bag onto the front seat. 'And when were you planning to tell me you had met him before?'

'Don't sound so surprised, he's only a couple of years older than me.' Her aunt sniffed. 'I was going to mention it on the telephone yesterday, but I didn't think he'd remember me, but now you know.' Her aunt slid behind the wheel. 'Anyway, it was a brief association at various social events. I doubt we even had a proper conversation.'

'Barring your attempt to convert his wife to vegetarianism?' Hannah hid a smile and busied herself arranging her skirt around her knees. More likely her aunt was peeved at her eagerness to end the call and meet Matilda.

'It wasn't quite like that.' Aunt Violet adjusted the rear-view mirror and tweaked stray hair back beneath her hat. 'I took Lydia to the suffrage cafe once to meet the other members. I had no idea she would then want to become a champion to non-meat eaters.'

'You aren't even a vegetarian.'

'Of course not.' She wrinkled her nose in distaste. 'No one's going to deny me a decent steak. I only went there because there were only a few places lone women could go in public without a male escort.' She started the engine, letting it idle for a moment. 'He didn't say much about it, but I sensed he still carries a lot of anger that Julian and Frances eloped. I doubt he's forgiven her.'

'I got that impression too. Could he have already discovered their marriage and only feigned his ignorance?'

'What? You think he killed Julian, making his daughter a widow? That's a bit drastic.'

'Hmm, maybe.' Hannah stared up at the house from the kerb where the windows stared back at her blankly, and there was no sign of the professor.

The Tolivers lived in a house built some years after that of the professor, set back from the road on a wide street lined with mature trees over thirty feet tall.

'Miss Esme is in the garden. Reading,' the maid who answered the door informed them in a tone which said she regarded the pastime as a luxury not available to her, which she found vexing. 'I'd announce you, but I'm up to my ears with the laundry and Cook is out.' Without waiting for a response, she hooked a thumb towards the side gate before closing the door again.

'That baggage wouldn't last a day in my house.' Aunt Violet directed a fierce glare at the closed door.

'Nor mine,' Hannah giggled. 'At least she didn't see us off.' She pushed open the full-sized gate and beckoned her aunt through into a well-ordered garden, with geometrical flowerbeds filled with spring flowers and early blooming roses in a riot of pastel shades. A young woman in a flowing dress of pastel blue that swung as she walked approached them as they came through the gate.

'Miss Toliver?' Aunt Violet ventured gently. 'I hope you don't mind us coming through, but your maid said you were here.'

'Who made no attempt to either escort or announce you?' Esme Toliver's wide smile on an open, attractive face endeared her to Hannah. 'She's dreadful, isn't she? But I'm sure you are aware of the servant problem, so I'm in no position to let her go.' She gestured to a set of wicker chairs below a pergola from which hung frothy pendants of mauve wisteria, and a white blossom Hannah could not recall the name of. 'Do come and sit down, as it's warm enough. Or would you rather go inside?'

'Here would be perfect, although we haven't even told you who we are or why we have called.' Aunt Violet claimed a peacock-backed chair, leaving the wrought iron one to Hannah, which, without a cushion, proved more uncomfortable than it first appeared.

'No need.' Esme lowered herself onto a chair opposite them. 'Professor Blackwood telephoned a few minutes ago to tell me he had spoken to you. He said you've come to talk about Julian's death?'

'As long as you agree.' Hannah introduced herself. 'This is my aunt, Violet Edwards, but you're not obliged to tell us anything.'

'The police have already been here to question us. A detective from Scotland Yard. An Inspector Parson, or Palmer. Something like that.'

'Wilson,' Hannah corrected her.

'That's it, yes. He was very formal, trotted out questions like bullets from a gun, and barely listened to my answers. May I ask how you are connected to Julian Aldrich?'

'He was engaged to officiate at my wedding, but we had to enlist a replacement at the last minute.' Hannah stopped short of saying how she and Darius discovered the body, which struck her as too ghoulish for a first meeting.

'Goodness!' Esme's hands flew to her cheeks. 'How awful for you! But the wedding went ahead, or is Clifford your maiden name?'

'No, it went ahead,' Hannah replied, hiding a smile.

'That's some consolation then. Not that I could tell that detective much.' Esme sighed. 'Poor, dear Frances. I cannot believe someone murdered Julian. Who would do such a thing?'

'Who, indeed,' Hannah murmured. 'Have you known Frances long?'

'We first met when she and her father moved down from London after her mother died, which was oh, about eight or nine years ago, when Professor Blackwood accepted a post at Merton College. Frances always regretted leaving London as she loved the city, but her father wanted to leave behind the life he had with his wife. Frances said they were devoted.'

'I knew Lydia Blackwood in London when we were girls,' Aunt Violet said.

'Really?' Esme's eyes lit up with genuine delight. 'She was a beautiful woman. We never met, but Frances keeps her photograph in her room.'

'I apologise for asking, but how did you feel when Frances began a liaison with Julian?' Aunt Violet asked gently. 'As it must have been a difficult time for you?'

'Why would it be?' Esme lifted her chin defiantly. 'I wasn't jealous, if that's what you think. Only I thought he was unsuitable for Frances.' Suddenly flustered, she rose. 'I'm being so inhospitable. I haven't offered you any refreshment. Would you like tea or maybe some lemonade? Cook always makes a fresh batch when the sun comes out.'

'No, thank you, we shan't keep you long,' Hannah answered for both of them and waved Esme back down. 'Frances told us she kept her relationship with Julian a secret. But not from you?'

'We were close friends, so of course she told me.' Esme resumed her seat slowly, her gaze sliding away towards the trees at the end of the garden.

'Even though you and Julian were romantically involved at one time?' Aunt Violet said.

Hannah shot her aunt a look which held a warning.

'I'm not sure you could call it that.' Esme flinched, but she recovered in an instant, which could be the sun had been in her eyes. 'My father and Professor Blackwood are tutors at Merton, and we socialised with them and the Aldriches. I had known Julian since we were young. I thought we might be closer at one time, but it didn't turn out that way.'

'Frances mentioned Julian's parents died when he was a child,' Hannah said.

'That's true.' Esme stared at her lap. 'Julian always felt like a cuckoo in the nest. Tolerated but not wanted. His father had put aside funds in trust for his education and living expenses until he reached his majority. His aunt and uncle had their own business and were comfortable, but Benjamin resented the fact Julian had more money than he did.'

'Professor Blackwood told us about the accident.' Hannah took this comment to imply Julian wasn't particularly generous towards his family.

'The accident, yes,' Esme murmured. She kept her head down, the hanging plants in the canopy overhead throwing her face in shadow, obscuring her expression. 'It was a terrible thing. Benjamin was such a bright, handsome boy. A little brash and reckless, perhaps, but we all loved him. Except Julian. He didn't have much time for Benji.'

'Even if they weren't close, the circumstances of his death must have been hard for Julian,' Hannah said.

'It was hard for all of us.' Esme's eyes flew open. 'Are you suggesting Julian's death was linked to Benjamin's?'

'And I'm sorry if I gave the wrong impression. Frances told us she kept her relationship with Julian a secret.'

'We were friends, so of course she told me.' Esme resumed her seat, her chin lifting, though her lip trembled a little. 'And I wasn't jealous, if that's what you think.'

'Did you know why Professor Blackwood suddenly took against Julian?' Aunt Violet asked.

'His attitude changed before the accident.' Esme twisted a frill on her sleeve around her fingers, only stopping when the stitches unravelled. 'Julian, well let's say he embraced the life of a student. You know the sort of thing. Frequenting public houses, courting unsuitable young women when so many young men his age were enlisting. It made him look... callous. Professor Blackwood thought his behaviour was an insult to the young men dying for their country.'

'Surely he was exempt from having to enlist?' Aunt Violet pointed out.

'That's true, but many students deferred their studies so they could do their duty. And as for the girls Julian associated with—'

'Like Ruby Webb?' Hannah said.

'Oh, you know about her?' Esme's upper lip curled. 'There were others, or so I've been told. But Frances was convinced he had changed. But then, everything is different now what with khaki-clad soldiers and girls in nurses' uniforms everywhere. One wonders when it will all end.'

Hannah could not help agreeing with that.

'Did Julian explain why he changed his course from a Bachelor of Arts degree to theology in this third year?' Hannah asked.

'He didn't, not to me anyway. Then his decision to enter the

Church surprised us all. But my mother was ill by then, so I had other things to think about.'

'Your mother is unwell?' Aunt Violet asked with sympathy.

'Rheumatic fever. She's virtually bedridden now, so my father and I share her care, which keeps me busy.'

'I'm sorry to hear that,' Hannah said sincerely. 'Were you shocked when Frances confided in you that she and Julian were married?'

'Of course I was.' Esme frowned. 'I didn't understand why she would agree to go ahead with it. I knew Professor Blackwood would be crushed to be excluded from his only child's wedding. Not that he would have given his blessing.'

'Perhaps that's why she took the course she did,' Aunt Violet suggested. 'She couldn't risk him sabotaging her plans.'

'Probably, but it was still a mean-spirited thing to do. Professor Blackwood would have come around eventually. They only had to give him time. I don't know why they were in such a hurry.'

'Could the fact Frances had come into her inheritance be a factor?' Aunt Violet asked. 'Her father might have dissuaded her had he known in advance.'

'I'm sure he would have.'

'I thought Professor Blackwood wasn't interested in wealth,' Hannah pointed out.

'That's what he tells everyone.' Esme's voice sharpened. 'He's hardly likely to say he covets his own daughter's money, is he?' Hannah's sympathy rose as she imagined what life must be like for Esme, watching Frances live her dream while confined at home caring for a sick parent and with so many young men her own age being lost on foreign battlefields.

'What were you doing on the fourth of May, Esme?' Aunt Violet asked. 'The day Julian died.'

'I know what day it was,' she snapped. 'When Mother can spare me, I help at Somerville College. Saturday was one of my days.' This was not a complete answer, but Hannah had the impression it was the best they were going to get.

'Are you studying at Somerville?' Hannah asked, impressed she might be among her own generation of women who were determined to make the best of themselves.

'No, but I would like to. Not that I could ever be awarded a degree like my male counterparts.'

'Perhaps not, but that might change now, so don't lose heart,' Aunt Violet said encouragingly.

'I'm so glad you said that, Miss Edwards.' Esme's polite smile widened into real pleasure. 'Father thinks I should be content not having to compete with men in this world, but he doesn't understand that domesticity isn't enough for me. Whether it's for Mother or a husband, I want to do more.'

'You were saying?' Hannah prompted, unwilling to get into a discussion about women's rights at this juncture.

'The college is being used as a convalescent hospital for officers. I serve the teas and wheel the patients into the gardens for some fresh air, read to those who have sight problems and so on. Not dissimilar to what I do for Mother the rest of the time.' Her eyes took on a faraway look, but she recovered quickly. 'Frances was waiting for me the day before. She said she was leaving for London the next morning for a few days to see Julian but not to tell Professor Blackwood.'

'Was it usual for Frances to take off like that with no advance notice?' Hannah asked.

'It was not. I asked her why she didn't tell him herself, but she didn't want him to know until after she left. She knew he would come after her and she wanted some time alone with Julian.' She tugged at the button on her sleeve again, this time detaching it completely. 'I fretted about it all that night and when Professor Blackwood called the following morning saying Frances had not been home all night, I panicked, and it all came tumbling out. Their elopement, where Julian was and everything.' She inhaled a long, shuddering breath. 'He left saying he was going to have the marriage annulled and bring her home.'

'We all know how that worked out,' Aunt Violet muttered under her breath.

'How did you find out Julian had been murdered?' Aunt Violet asked. 'Frances didn't know he was dead when she left, and Professor Blackwood had no way of knowing.'

Unless he was the murderer, Hannah thought.

'Father spoke to him on the telephone when he returned from London. He was much calmer and even apologised for losing his temper.'

'Probably because Julian Aldrich was no longer a threat,' Hannah said.

'I suppose that's one way of putting it.' Esme turned pleading eyes on Hannah. 'How is Frances?'

'She is well, if distraught by what happened. She's staying in London to plan Julian's funeral.'

'I'm glad she's not entirely alone, although Frances is stronger than most people think. She knows her own mind.' She twisted her hands together. 'If Professor Blackwood has forgiven me for deceiving him, I'll ask him if I can attend. I want to be there to support her.'

'I'm sure she'll appreciate that.' Hannah changed the subject. 'Were Julian and Benjamin close?'

'Not so you would notice. There was an age gap, and Julian was intended for great things after university, so it was a surprise when he went into the Church. But then Benjamin was always jealous of Julian, who had advantages his cousin did not.

Although I'm sure Julian would have preferred to have his parents alive more than having a new wardrobe every year. Benjamin also resented Julian for being careful with his finances, whereas money slipped through his fingers.'

'Are you saying that Julian was selfish with his money? Even though the family weren't affluent, surely he wouldn't let them go without if he could help? They lived in the same house.'

'That isn't what I meant.' Esme held up a hand to halt her. 'Julian wasn't rich. His parents left enough to feed and clothe him, send him to a good school and to university when the time came. Julian gave them what he could, but Benjamin squandered his allowance and always wanted more. Julian wasn't going to hand over funds to a youth who would waste it. He even told me once that after graduation it would be gone, and he would have to make his own way in the world.'

'And he chose to go into the Church,' Aunt Violet repeated Esme's words from earlier. 'Which isn't exactly well-paid.'

'Maybe not, but it's a secure profession, and very respectable. Those things meant a lot to Julian.' She licked her lips slowly as if debating her next words. 'His life was about to become a lot more comfortable when he married Frances.' Hannah looked up sharply and Esme flushed. 'I don't mean he was marrying her for money. But, well, he couldn't ignore it, could he?'

'I suppose not.' Julian evidently had an eye on the long term and saw the Church as a safe bet. Until he realised Frances had an inheritance coming and his life could be very different to what he imagined. Did he truly love Frances or was his courtship of her simply a means to an end?

'Benjamin's death must have affected the whole family.'

'You know about that?' Esme's features sharpened then softened again. 'Of course you do. You've spoken to Professor Blackwood.'

'Why don't you tell us your version?' Aunt Violet asked gently.

'I don't have a version.' Esme emphasised the last word. She clenched her hands in her lap and stared over their heads into the branches of an ash tree as her thoughts drifted to the past. 'It was such an awful thing to happen.' Her eyes fluttered closed then suddenly flew open again. 'Are you suggesting Julian's death was linked to Benjamin's?'

'Not directly, but his death must have affected you all,' Hannah said gently.

'It did.' Esme sighed resignedly. 'The picnic was enjoyable until Benjamin arrived with those two boys. They made everything awkward with their ridiculous horseplay. They were boasting that they would soon be soldiers as their conscription papers had arrived. Frances and I tried to ignore them and stayed talking to Julian. Benjamin didn't like being ignored and teased the three of us until Julian snapped at him to behave like a gentleman, but that only made things worse. Mr Aldrich joined in, and his wife told him not to be so unkind. That Benjamin was only having fun. That's when Julian...'

'When Julian what?' Aunt Violet prompted when Esme fell silent.

'He said that it might make a man of Benjamin to be conscripted, then he could stop wasting his time. Benjamin didn't like that. He threw a punch at Julian which he reacted to by shoving him. Benjamin hit his head against a tree and Mrs Aldrich rushed to his side and fussed over him like a baby, which made Julian laugh. This infuriated Benjamin, who launched at Julian and there ensued a brief scuffle. They had to be separated by Professor Blackwood and Mr Aldrich. It wasn't pleasant.'

'Was Benjamin badly hurt?' Hannah asked.

Esme shrugged. 'He was rubbing his head a little.' She raised a finger to her left temple. 'He blinked and seemed off balance but not exactly hurt. He recovered quickly and got loud again, challenging the others to jump into the river from Magdalen Bridge. Andrew and Jack were eager, but then they always did what Benjamin suggested. Julian refused, which came as no surprise to anyone. He said the water wasn't deep enough and that students were always being told not to try it. Benjamin just scoffed at him and made some remark about students being pampered idiots. That it had rained heavily during the past two weeks, and the river was swollen higher than usual. Anyway, it was just a jump, they weren't trying to swim the Channel.'

'Didn't anyone else agree with Julian?'

'Mrs Aldrich warned Benjamin to be careful, but she overdid it. After the fourth time Mr Aldrich was embarrassed and told her to stop fussing; that Benjamin was not a child and he wouldn't do anything stupid.'

Hannah groaned inwardly, conscious that everything leading up to the accident made it almost inevitable.

'Frances and I stayed chatting to Julian to make him feel better,' Esme continued. 'Not that he seemed to need it. He was quite jocular and dismissed Benjamin's behaviour as high-jinks.

'It was about twenty minutes later that we heard a shout, and Andrew came running towards us, gasping for breath and gabbling they couldn't find Benjamin.

'Julian didn't hesitate. He reached the bridge first, kicked off his shoes and was in the water by the time the rest of us got there. Frances tried to comfort Andrew who explained Benjamin made two jumps with no problem but on the third, he dived further out where the water was deeper but he didn't surface again. We went up onto the bridge to see from there but the water was murky green, and it was difficult to see anything. Then Jack's head appeared about ten feet away, and he yelled he hadn't found him.

Frances stared to cry, and Mrs Aldrich was pale and silent as if in shock.

'Julian dived several times in different places looking for him and at last, he came up holding Benjamin under his arms. Mr Aldrich and Professor Blackwood waded in and helped drag him out, but Benjamin looked awful – his skin was blueish white, and he wasn't breathing.

'Mrs Aldrich screamed and clawed at Benjamin until her husband pulled her away to let the ambulance men deal with him. I don't know who called them. My clearest memory was Andrew in tears saying he had to get home. He kept repeating that his clothes and bicycle were still at the picnic and he needed to get them. Professor Blackwood said he was in shock and should see a doctor first and made him go in the ambulance. By this time Mrs Aldrich was hysterical, and Father told Frances and me to bring her back here to wait for news. She kept insisting she wanted to go in the ambulance with Benjamin, but there was no room.'

There was little Hannah could say, other than repeat her aunt's low sigh and add 'I'm so sorry.'

'Julian tried, you know. He really did.' Esme's voice was pleading. 'But there was nothing anyone could have done. A policeman arrived here later and told us Benjamin must have landed hard on something when he hit the water and lost consciousness. During the time it took to find him, he drowned.'

'Have you spoken to Andrew or Jack since then?' Hannah asked.

'Not since the inquest.' Esme shook her head, visibly emotional and wiped her nose with her handkerchief. 'Jack Friar didn't turn up, but Andrew arrived with his parents, who didn't want anyone to talk to him. Perhaps they thought he would be blamed, I'm not sure. He was in uniform, and I heard someone say he was leaving for France in a few weeks. Not that I made any effort to contact him again. I mean, he's not the sort of young man I normally associate with. He was a runner in a bank, and the Friar boy was an apprentice and an orphan.' She lowered her voice to whisper as if afraid to be heard. 'Anyway, Benjamin probably only invited the boys to embarrass his parents.'

Hannah made no comment as this was close to Professor Blackwood's opinion.

'The funeral at Holywell Cemetery was awful. Mrs Aldrich was in a state of near collapse, unable to stop crying. Mr Aldrich was the opposite. He didn't say a word and looked as if he was in a daze the whole time. It didn't help matters that the funeral had to be delayed.'

'Why was that?' Hannah asked.

'Since the war began, burial plots are being taken up by soldiers brought into the hospitals who don't survive their injuries. Added to the normal number of deaths in town, the undertakers are particularly busy.'

'Of course, I should have known that.' Hannah regretted having asked the question.

'Julian must have been upset at not being able to save his cousin,' Aunt Violet said gently.

'Of course he was. He was inconsolable.' Esme blinked away tears at the memory returned. 'We all were.' Esme locked eyes with Hannah to emphasise her point. 'Benjamin could be irritating but he was part of our lives. Julian changed his course because he felt guilty and it was his way to make amends. The Aldriches couldn't bear to stay where Benjamin died, so they left Oxfordshire altogether. Papa writes to them sometimes, Christmas cards and things, but they've never been to visit.'

'Thank you for speaking to us when you didn't have to.' Hannah brushed a trailing branch that hung from the pergola from her face as she stood. 'We'll leave you to your lovely garden.' She cocked her chin in her aunt's direction.

'Oh, yes, of course.' Aunt Violet started from her somnolent doze in the sunshine and gathered her things together. 'It was a pleasure to meet you, Miss Toliver.' They headed to the gate.

'You rushed us away quickly.' Aunt Violet pulled the front gate closed behind her, almost running to catch up with Hannah. 'Did I miss something?'

'Only that Miss Toliver wasn't being entirely truthful.'

'Which part?' Aunt Violet suppressed a yawn.

'For one thing, I doubt that young woman is intimidated by anyone. Panicked, indeed. She revealed the elopement to Professor Blackwood out of spite. She could have waited for Frances and Julian to announce their news in their own time, but she wanted him to go running after Frances and cause a scene.'

'You believe she was jealous and carried a torch for Julian despite her protests?'

'Don't you?'

Aunt Violet shifted her bag from one arm to the other and flung open the driver's side door and slid into the driving seat. 'Perhaps seeing her former suitor find happiness with another woman was hard for her, especially when that woman is her best friend.'

'More than one person has said Julian was something of a ladies' man.' Hannah skirted the motor car and eased into the passenger seat. 'Esme might have imagined she meant more to Julian than she did. Like Ruby. Perhaps Matilda Gilmartin could look into the newspaper reports of Benjamin Aldrich's death?' Hannah suggested. 'There might be something there no one has yet mentioned.'

'Quite the paragon, is our Miss Gilmartin.' Aunt Violet

stabbed the starter button with a finger while yawning. 'You know, I almost fell asleep in that garden.'

'I noticed.' Hannah raised an eyebrow at her. 'Is that why you suggested we come here today? To steal a march on Matilda Gilmartin?' This wasn't the only time her aunt had disparaged Matilda. Their first meeting had been somewhat confrontational, after all.

'Nonsense. Actually, I like her. She reminds me of myself at the same age, together with some of my own inherent foibles. I wonder how many governesses Matilda sent packing when she was a child?'

'How many did you?' Smiling, Hannah turned to stare at her.

'Four. Not counting my dancing master,' Aunt Violet answered without looking at her. 'Which was for an entirely different reason.'

'What reason?'

'Never you mind.' Her aunt yawned again as the engine flared briefly, spluttered and died. 'Oh bother.' Her shoulders slumped. 'I don't suppose you'd like to drive for a bit?'

Hannah didn't need a second invitation. Her aunt was barely out of the driver's seat before Hannah shifted across and settled behind the wheel. 'And just so you know, you are irreplaceable. Our adventures wouldn't be anywhere near as exciting without you.' She pressed the accelerator, relishing the low roar as the engine responded. 'Now, where shall we go for some lunch?'

15

Hannah relished her all too brief turn behind the wheel as they headed back towards the High Street, a thoroughfare the porter had referred to as The High, which contained a wide a variety of ancient timber-fronted buildings that jostled side by side with more modern structures. Hannah pulled the motor car alongside multiple rows of stacked bicycles, although there were few motor cars in evidence. After a brief scout of the area, Aunt Violet chose an ancient four-storey rendered building with the words The Angel Cafe painted in gold lettering on a blue-grey background above a plate-glass window.

The interior was not large but cosy, decorated with sage-green paint and gilt mirrors, and pristine white tablecloths on small tables for intimate dining. Several patrons appeared to be enjoying a savoury-smelling repast.

A girl in a crisp white apron and cap over a flowered dress, who looked to be too young to be working, showed them to a table by the front window with a view of the street.

'Have you still got your nose in that guidebook?' Aunt Violet smirked as she stowed her bag beneath her chair.

'I have,' Hannah replied unapologetically, while running a finger along the page. 'I thought so. The Angel was a coaching inn, established in 1650,' she read aloud. 'It says here, Queen Henrietta Maria and her entourage lodged at Merton College.' She looked up at her aunt. 'Did you know the King set up the court here after losing the Battle of Edgehill in 1642?'

'I did not know that, but it's no surprise that you do, since on our quieter days in the bookshop you can invariably be found in the history section.' She turned to smile at the girl who appeared at her shoulder, order book in hand. 'I'll have the mushroom soup and an egg mayonnaise sandwich.'

'Mayonnaise with egg?' Hannah asked, frowning.

'I ate it all the time in New York, it's quite delicious.' Aunt Violet pulled at each finger of her left glove, laid it on the table and did the same for the right. 'They serve it at Fortnum's now.'

'Then I'll have the same.' Hannah would have preferred chicken soup, but suspected that in these rationing times, the carcass would have been boiled too long to extract all the flavour, whereas locally grown mushrooms were more likely to be fresh.

'Aunt Violet,' Hannah began when the girl had retreated. 'Which of those we spoke to this morning do you feel might have killed Julian Aldrich?'

'That depends on whether we can place any of them in Chiswick on the day of the murder. And how did Julian's murderer persuade him to go inside the tomb? There were only coffins inside, and—'

'Please, Aunt Violet.' Hannah winced. 'Lily-Anne's was one of them, remember?' She pushed away the gruesome image that floated into her head.

'I'm sorry, darling. I don't mean to be insensitive. I keep forgetting you were the one who found Lily-Anne that day.' She gave the pristine white tablecloth her full attention, moved her cutlery an inch then moved it back again.

'What about Ruby Webb?' Hannah dropped the subject not wishing to make her feel worse, and after three years, perhaps she ought to be less touchy when Lily-Anne's name came up. 'Was Ruby angry enough at being dumped by Julian to want to kill him?'

'She didn't like it when we mentioned Esme, did she?' her aunt mused. 'But she struck me as more the type to lash out in the heat of the moment, not wait that long to exact her revenge.'

'I wish I had pushed harder to discover where she was the day Julian was killed, but I was afraid she would refuse to cooperate.'

Aunt Violet shrugged out of her jacket and draped it over an empty chair. 'It's rather warm in here, don't you agree?'

'I'm perfectly comfortable,' Hannah said, determined to be distracted. 'When Inspector Wilson spoke to her father, Ruby did not admit to knowing Julian. Could that be significant?'

'In her position, would you volunteer to be added to a suspect list for a relationship that had finished so long ago?' Her aunt raised a cynical eyebrow. 'I doubt it. Besides, no one in Oxford knew his whereabouts, apart from Frances. How would Ruby know where to find him, let alone plot to kill him?'

'That's true. Julian rejected Esme too eventually, so maybe they collaborated and planned it together?'

'Now, there's an idea.' Her aunt chuckled, apparently not taking the suggestion seriously. 'And Esme works at Somerville, which could be where she got the digitalis?'

'A neat theory, but how would we prove it? Esme isn't a nurse; she just helps out. And isn't Somerville more a convalescent home?'

'Hmm, shoot me down why don't you?' Her aunt shrugged. 'But you're probably right. Ruby Webb was too pragmatic to be a killer. She even admitted Julian wasn't right for her.' She propped her chin in one hand. 'The timing has been bothering me though.'

'Timing of what? In what way?'

'Professor Blackwood's trip to London. Esme went to see him on Friday and told him Frances was on her way to London.'

'Your point being?'

'He confronted her on Saturday when I dropped her off at the hotel. Why did he wait an entire day?'

'Hmm. I never thought of that.' Hannah frowned, thoughtful. 'Perhaps because he wanted to confront them together and didn't want to run into Frances on the train.'

'In which case, why not go straight to Chiswick and tackle them together?' Aunt Violet shrugged.

'Maybe he did. He found Julian alone at the church getting ready for my wedding, killed him and then turned up at the hotel the next day claiming he had just arrived?'

'Hmm. I'll have to add that theory to our list.' She pointed a teaspoon at Hannah. 'You might be on to something there.' She broke off as the waitress returned and unloaded dishes haphazardly onto the tabletop before withdrawing with a brief, awkward curtsey.

'He claimed to be in Oxford when Julian was killed,' Hannah observed when the girl had retreated. 'To make a case against him we'd have to prove he was in London.'

'He also *claimed* not to have known about Julian's relationship with Frances.' Her aunt draped a napkin over her lap and broke a bread roll into pieces, then paused, her spoon halfway to her mouth as she watched Hannah stir salt into the greyish liquid in her bowl. 'Hannah, you haven't even tasted it.'

'Twice,' Hannah replied without looking up.

'Twice what?'

'You asked me to remind you whenever you sounded like my mother.' The salt cellar landed with a small thump. 'That was the second time today.'

'When was the first?' Aunt Violet's frown showed no memory of such a conversation.

'Before we left Ilchester Place, you asked if my coat was warm enough.'

'Oops. Sorry.' Her aunt pointed her spoon at her bowl. 'This is delicious. Pity the portions are so meagre.'

'Blame the food shortages.' Hannah spread pale-looking butter on a piece of roll and bit into it. The bread was slightly stale, but acceptable. 'Go on, Aunt Violet. You were saying?'

'If Professor Blackwood arrived in London on Friday, where was he until Saturday afternoon? Frances didn't actually go to Chiswick until the day after Julian was killed. So what was she doing on Friday?'

'I doubt she was plotting with her father to kill Julian.'

'That's not such a silly answer.' Aunt Violet nodded approvingly. 'Where were we?'

'Where were you? I'm not on board with this, Aunt Violet. I don't think Frances lied.'

Hannah splayed her hands in front of her before applying her spoon to her soup. 'And something else has been nagging me – why choose digitalis? Poison isn't traditionally a man's weapon.'

'Misdirection?' Aunt Violet suggested. 'It isn't a restricted drug, so any pharmacist would sell it to him.' She returned her spoon to the now empty bowl. 'So, which one of them was it? The father or the daughter?'

'I'm sticking with the professor for the moment.' Hannah spooned up her soup. 'He arrives at St Nicholas Church when Julian is alone on Saturday morning. The professor is calm, nonthreatening, and says Frances has told him everything and he wants to build bridges.'

'Workable so far. Go on.'

'Julian invites him into the vestry where the professor slips something into Julian's drink, and then spots the oversized key to the mausoleum on the wall. We know he's interested in medieval churches, so he persuades Julian to let him see inside.'

'Ugh!' Aunt Violet grimaced but nodded for her to go on.

'Outside the mausoleum, the drug takes effect, Julian collapses, hitting his head on the stone steps, loses consciousness and the professor slips away without being seen. It could be years before the mausoleum was opened again, by which time no one could connect Professor Blackwood to Julian's disappearance.'

'Ingenious, certainly and quite positively evil,' Aunt Violet said. 'So why didn't he complete this plan?'

'He was interrupted? We had several deliveries at the church that morning. Food, flowers, wine deliveries, early guests? He panics at the thought of being recognised after the fact, abandons the key in the lock and makes his escape. Then he lies low for the rest of the day, emerging on Saturday to confront Frances at the Gore Hotel.'

'That sounds convoluted, but plausible.'

'It's only an hour's journey to London by train and another half hour for a hackney to Chiswick. He could have managed it. But won't the police have checked his movements between Esme's visit and his appearance at the Gore Hotel?'

'If Aidan was running the case, then yes, obviously. However, I'm not convinced Inspector Wilson is as thorough.' Hannah turned an idea over in her head. 'If we could pinpoint when Professor Blackwood booked into the Gore—'

'*If* he did,' her aunt interrupted. 'He could have stayed somewhere else, so when he appeared on Saturday, no one thought of asking him where he was the day before.'

Hannah chewed at her bottom lip as her mind ran through the possibilities. 'When we spoke to him, the professor didn't seem at all curious about Julian leaving Oxford late last year.'

'Maybe he assumed Frances had broken off their association? As her father he would expect obedience so probably didn't give it another thought. He was probably glad to see the back of him.'

'Good point.' Hannah nodded. 'But I still don't know why he disapproved of Julian. He was friends with his aunt and uncle and if he wasn't exactly fond of Benjamin, he apparently tolerated him. What did Julian do to turn him against him?'

'Married his daughter, apparently!' Aunt Violet laughed.

'Forget the professor for a moment. What about Esme? You could be right, and she was jealous of Frances. Did keeping their secret become too hard for her to endure, so she revealed it to the professor out of spite?' She raised her sandwich, from which she had taken a bite. 'This *is* really good. The egg is cooked perfectly, and the mayonnaise makes it less eggy.'

'How can an egg be too eggy?' Aunt Violet gave her an ironic look.

'I don't know, but it can.' Hannah wiped crumbs from her lips with her napkin. 'Haven't you ever started eating one then stopped halfway through because it's too, well, eggy?'

'I cannot say I have, no.'

'Ah well.' Hannah popped the last piece of sandwich into her mouth and wiped her fingers on her napkin. 'Now what was I going to say? Ah yes, I remember. Esme. Her mother is an invalid after contracting rheumatic fever. Could her heart have been affected so her doctor prescribed digitalis?'

'Of course!' Aunt Violet brought her hand down hard on the

table. 'As her carer, Esme would have access to her mother's medication. Good point, Hannah.'

The rattle of china brought the waitress running. 'Is there anything else you want, ladies?' She shot a nervous look at each of them, her order pad clutched tightly to her chest with one hand and a menu in the other.

'Er…' Hannah hesitated, her inherent manners too ingrained to order more food unless her aunt set a precedent. 'What do you think, Aunt Violet?'

'Hmm.' Her aunt retrieved the menu from the girl's outstretched hand and scanned it with a smile. 'I'll have the suet sponge with raspberry jam.'

'Bread and butter pudding for me, please,' Hannah said, resolving not to eat anything but consommé and crackers for supper.

'Are we being too clever and jumping to a too obvious conclusion about the digitalis?' Hannah ventured when they were alone again. 'Esme didn't strike me as being stupid. She must know the police would make the same connections we did.'

'True, and can we prove Esme was even in London, let alone somehow managed to administer the drug to Julian before noon last Saturday?'

'Exactly.' Hannah sighed. 'I have this feeling we are talking ourselves into a bigger puzzle, which sounds good, but with no proof backing it up.'

'Then let's forget about poison and murder for now and enjoy our dessert.'

Twenty minutes later, and comfortably replete after her dessert of layered slices of buttered bread covered with cream, seasoned with cinnamon and plump sultanas, and followed by cups of hot and fragrant tea, Hannah followed her aunt into the street, having pressed a generous tip into the underage waitress's hand.

'That was an excellent luncheon,' Aunt Violet addressed Hannah over the long bonnet of the motor car. 'Most satisfactory.'

'And yet wholly vegetarian,' Hannah nodded in agreement. 'Who would have thought?'

Her aunt narrowed her eyes as she hauled open the driver's door. 'One day, you'll go too far, young lady.' She scrutinised the sky, which had clouded over during the last hour.

'I'd better secure the tonneau for the return journey. Give me a hand, would you, Hannah? The wretched thing can be hard to handle.'

* * *

On the way home from Oxford, a thunderstorm turned the already inadequate roads into a quagmire and at one juncture, they had been forced to enlist the help of an obliging local farmer to pull their motor car from a water-filled rut outside Beaconsfield.

By the time they reached the outskirts of the city, Hannah ached all over and could hardly keep her eyes open, so their farewells and promises to meet up again the next morning were brief and perfunctory.

After breakfast, Hannah was on her way to the well-stocked library compiled by Darius's grandfather for a quiet hour after breakfast, when she was drawn to where Travis was helping Aunt Violet out of her coat in the entrance hall.

'I didn't hear the door.' Hannah changed direction and approached them. 'I assume you've had breakfast?' Hannah's glance at the hall clock told her it was after ten. 'But I'm sure you wouldn't turn down some coffee.'

'If it's the same as you served me the other day, I won't say no.' Her aunt swept the upper landing with a lingering, almost hopeful look before peering through the dining room door that stood ajar. 'I trust I'm not disturbing your newly married bliss?'

'I wish you were,' Hannah replied enigmatically. 'Darius didn't get home until dawn, so he's still in bed.'

'In bed, is he?' Aunt Violet raised an eyebrow. 'Then what are you doing down here?'

'Hush!' Hannah flapped a discreet hand as the butler carried her aunt's coat reverently to the hall cupboard. 'Travis, would you arrange for some coffee for Miss Edwards and me? We'll be in the sitting room.'

'For Miss Edwards, it will be my pleasure.' Halting, he dipped his head in a formal bow and backed away.

'I wish you wouldn't say things like that.' Hannah opened the sitting room door and stepped back to allow her aunt to pass inside. 'Travis is easily shocked.'

'Butlers are never shocked.' Aunt Violet glided past her. 'And don't pout. Allow me to enjoy my small entourage of admirers. It makes the dullest day worth getting up for.'

'It's not as if it's a small entourage either,' Hannah muttered, following her inside.

'Have you come to any further conclusions after our jaunt into Oxfordshire?' Aunt Violet kicked off her shoes, then sank her toes into the thick Turkey rug and lounged in the corner of a brocade sofa.

'Well.' Hannah perched on the edge of the sofa opposite. 'Professor Blackwood is our most promising candidate thus far.'

'Oh, I don't think it's him.' Aunt Violet raised her stockinged feet onto a footstool, giving all the appearance of being settled in for a long stay. 'If killing an unsuitable son-in-law was a reason for murder, the newspapers would be full of them.'

'It's still possible though.' Hannah had turned every detail over in her head endlessly while she lay in bed waiting for Darius to come home. 'Suppose the professor already knew about Frances and Julian because he'd snooped through her belongings when she was out and found their marriage certificate, or Julian's letters?'

'Wasn't he more likely to confront her than wait for an opportunity for murder? Annulment, for instance. They hadn't actually lived together so there could be grounds. My money is back on Miss Toliver.' Aunt Violet lifted one foot and scratched the heel with a fingernail. 'Jealous women can be single-minded and ruthless in such situations, which makes a powerful motive for murder.'

'I suppose you're right.' Hannah backtracked. Said aloud, it sounded ridiculous. 'I thought Professor Blackwood's account held a subtext which has been bothering me. Esme doesn't strike me as guilty either. If she loved Julian, then why kill him? Wouldn't she be more likely to get rid of Frances and be on hand to soothe his broken heart?'

'Now that makes more sense, but isn't what happened.' Aunt Violet tutted and scrutinised the door. 'Now, where's Travis with that coffee?'

Her aunt's imperious demand appeared to have summoned him, for the butler arrived bearing a tray which he placed on the low table in front of her with much ceremony while virtually ignoring Hannah.

'And you've even brought some of Cook's famous Florentine biscuits.' Aunt Violet clutched a hand to her throat and gazed up at him. 'How thoughtful.'

'Always a pleasure to serve you, Miss Edwards.' Travis's lips twitched, but he made no move to leave until Hannah gestured briskly for him to go. He started, then recovered himself and addressed Hannah. 'Is there anything else, madam?'

'No, thank you,' Hannah said through gritted teeth. She waited until he had retreated before adding, 'After that performance, Aunt Violet, you can pour.'

With a one-shouldered shrug, her aunt swung her feet over the side of the sofa and reached for the coffee-pot. 'Incidentally, I rang Cavan last night when I got home.'

'How is he? I haven't spoken to him since the day after the wedding.' Hannah relaxed as the rich coffee aroma reached her.

'He seemed to enjoy hosting the family, even if it was because of Iris's brief incapacity. He said he'd like to do it more often.'

'What *is* Cavan doing these days?' Hannah asked. 'I heard he had given up his London surgery to work from his house. I hope becoming a widower hasn't made him a recluse?'

'He spends a lot of time at the hospital in Queen Square these days, apparently.' Aunt Violet broke off to take a slow sip from her coffee cup. 'He's studying the effects and treatment of soldiers returning from the front with shell shock.' She lowered her cup, frowning. 'I'm sure we've had this conversation.'

'You started to tell me that day in Cavan's garden, but then Mama ordered us inside to talk to the police,' Hannah replied. 'I'm glad it's now recognised as an actual neurological illness and not just cowardice. I must invite him to supper when things are more settled.'

'Settled with the war or with you?' Aunt Violet gave her a sideways look.

'Me, I suppose. I had all sorts of ideas on how to take up the reins of the household when I moved in, but this murder has occupied all my thoughts lately. I haven't spent more than ten minutes with Cook and have simply let her get on with things.'

She slid an empty cup and saucer within reach of the coffee-pot, which her aunt obligingly filled.

'You cannot act like a guest in your own home permanently, Hannah. Take control.'

'I know, but I've been busy.' Hannah shrugged, conscious she was making excuses, her coffee spoon making tiny yet annoying ticks against the china. 'What did Cavan say when you called?'

'According to him, heart failure is a complication of rheumatic fever, therefore Mrs Toliver might well have been prescribed digitalis.' Her aunt added milk to both cups. 'Aidan told me the dose Julian Aldrich received was larger than a doctor would use.'

'Would Esme *know* what a fatal dose was?' Hannah asked. 'Although she could probably just double or treble the amount her mother took.'

'That's where you are mistaken.' Her aunt pointed a finger at her. 'Cavan said the toxic dose of digitalis is about one and a half times larger than a therapeutic dose, so even a small amount can result in severe poisoning.'

'Now that *is* interesting.' Hannah sipped her coffee as she considered this. 'Did someone intend the dose to make Julian ill, but they gave him too much and killed him instead?'

'You'd have to ask the murderer that.' Aunt Violet plucked a Florentine from the plate and bit into it. 'And if it *was* Esme, she wasn't at Somerville last Saturday morning as she claimed, but murdering Julian in Chiswick.'

'Aidan will have access to witness interview notes, won't he? I could ask him.' Hannah placed her barely tasted coffee on the low table between them and approached a low table in the corner, where a candlestick telephone resided on a low table.

'I didn't know you had two telephones,' Aunt Violet observed through a mouthful of biscuit.

'Three, actually.' Hannah raised her chin, preening a little as she lifted the earpiece. 'Apart from the main box in the hall, there's one in our bedroom.'

Aunt Violet muttered something Hannah could not make out, but suspected it was less than complimentary. Before she could ask her to repeat it, the operator's voice spoke into her ear. Hannah asked to be put through to Scotland Yard and after a wait, a male voice asked where to direct her call.

'I wish to speak to Detective Chief Inspector Farrell.' She was about to add who was calling but the line crackled and a deep male voice responded to her request. 'Oh, er, just a moment.' Hannah removed the earpiece and covered the speaker with her hand.

'What's the matter?' Aunt Violet asked from the sofa, a second Florentine in her hand.

'Aidan isn't there,' Hannah replied in a fierce whisper. 'It's Inspector Wilson.'

'Well, don't just stand there. Ask him.' Aunt Violet waggled her fingers in a 'go on' gesture.

'Um, all right.' She removed her hand. 'Inspector Wilson, how nice to hear your voice.' Aunt Violet snorted a laugh, which Hannah hoped he had not heard. 'Might I ask you a question about the investigation into the murder of Julian Aldrich?'

Several seconds of silence ensued, then his voice came again. 'That depends on what it is, Mrs Clifford. I'm aware of your special relationship with Detective Chief Inspector Farrell, but I'd like to remind you this is a police matter.'

'Of course, Inspector, and I assure you it concerns nothing confidential.' She rolled her eyes at her aunt, who grinned. 'We, meaning my aunt and myself, have recently discovered that Miss Esme Toliver works at Somerville College.' She hoped the mention of Aunt Violet might soften him, as their relationship was common knowledge amongst Aidan's colleagues.

'That's correct, Mrs Clifford.' His baritone voice did not change. 'She's a volunteer there.'

'Would you know if their pharmacy stocks digitalis?'

'Somerville is currently a wartime convalescent establishment, not a hospital. However, I imagine they keep certain drugs and medicines on hand.'

'What about digitalis?' Hannah insisted, trying not to sigh. *Was he being deliberately obtuse?*

'If the drug is on the list provided to the police by the establishment,' he replied in a slightly bored tone, 'I can guarantee all witnesses in connection to the recent murder have been taken into account.'

'I'm sure it has, Inspector.' *Which tells me absolutely nothing.* 'And was Miss Toliver in Oxford all day last Saturday? Or at least not in Chiswick.'

'I can say with confidence that investigators have corroborated all witness alibis, madam.'

'I see. Well, thank you, Inspector. I'm sure your investigation has been very thorough,' she said, putting emphasis on the word 'your'.

'Thank you for your interest, madam. It's much appreciated. Good day.'

He hung up abruptly.

'What a pompous man.' Hannah rammed the earpiece back into place. 'I was about to ask about Mrs Toliver's medication but lost my nerve.' She slumped back down on the sofa. 'However, if Esme was anywhere near west London on the day Julian died, he would know about it.'

The door clicked open and Travis paused on the threshold. 'My apologies for disturbing you, madam, but there's a lady at the front door demanding entry.' He drew himself up to his full height, his upper lip curled in disdain.

'Did she give a name?' Hannah groaned. Did they *have* to go through this ritual every time someone called?

'Miss Matilda Gilmartin, who claims to be an acquaintance of yours, madam. I told her to wait, and I would enquire whether you are at home.'

'That journalist?' Aunt Violet stiffened. 'I realise she's an engaging young woman, but you need to be careful, Hannah. Her career will always take precedence over friendship. And you can do without a lecture from Aidan about talking to the press.'

'I'm being discreet. Besides, she was supposed to call after luncheon, but having invited her, I can hardly turn her away. As you see, Travis, I am at home. Kindly show her in.'

'As you wish, madam.' Unsmiling, Travis bowed and withdrew.

'He didn't mean *are* you at home, dear,' Aunt Violet said while refilling her coffee cup for the second time. 'Rather are you at home to callers?'

'I know exactly what he meant.' Hannah schooled her voice so as not to snap. 'It's 1918, not 1875.'

16

'Miss Matilda Gil—' Travis began, but got no further as Matilda swept past him.

'I'm so sorry to arrive earlier than planned, but a witness to the Betts trial failed to appear, so the judge adjourned the entire court until tomorrow.' She plumped down on the space beside Hannah, since Aunt Violet showed no signs of moving.

'Miss Edwards! How lovely to see you again.' Matilda hauled her oversized bag into the space beside her, forcing Hannah to inch sideways to make room. 'I was hoping to run into you again sometime. Have you given some thought about the interview on the Representation of the People Act?'

'Hannah mentioned it in passing.' Aunt Violet blinked, taken aback, but instantly recovered. 'I'm flattered you should ask, although I'm not a leading light in the WSPU any more, if I ever was. Why would anyone be interested in my opinion?'

'You underestimate yourself, Miss Edwards.' Matilda hauled the bag onto her lap and delved inside. 'As a local business-woman, featuring in my newspaper would be to your advantage.'

'I beg your pardon?' Aunt Violet looked Matilda slowly up

and down with an excellent impression of Lady Bracknell. 'Why do I require any further advantage?'

'I meant in the industry,' Matilda explained, unfazed. 'Book-selling is a field widely dominated by men, so I thought—'

'Hmmm. I'll think about it. I suggest you call and make an appointment, Miss Gilmartin. Hannah will give you the number.' She flicked Hannah a sideways look, ignoring her niece's frantic eyebrow dance.

'May I take your bag, miss?' Travis had followed her in and flicked a critical look at the offending object that was taking up a major portion of the squab between the two women.

'It is rather large, isn't it?' Matilda replied apologetically. 'A steward mistook it for a portmanteau once and tried to put it in the hold of a ferryboat. But I'll keep it with me, if you don't mind. Oh!' She leapt to her feet and made for the door. 'I think I left my favourite pen in my coat pocket. At least I hope so.' She flapped a hand at Travis as she passed. 'Don't worry, I'll fetch it myself.'

Travis followed her out, more confused than offended.

'That was very pompous of you, Aunt Violet,' Hannah whispered as they awaited Matilda's return. 'I thought you admired her determination to function in a man's world?'

'I do, but I haven't forgotten her veiled threat to expose my relationship with Aidan in her newspaper during the Cornelis case. That was underhand, though probably not surprising. It's how journalists work.'

'Which proves she's good at it. And she didn't print a word about you or Aidan.'

'Only because you exposed the murderer, giving her a better story. Oh, hush, she's coming back.'

'Found it!' Matilda held up black fountain pen trimmed with what appeared to be real gold.

'Very nice.' Aunt Violet raised an admiring eyebrow.

'It's a Waterman Eyedropper. My father gave it to me for my twenty-first birthday, and I'd hate to lose it.'

'Your father has excellent taste.' Aunt Violet smiled. Matilda had apparently gone up in her aunt's estimation. Hannah wondered what she'd make of his being a High Court judge.

Hannah started the interview, or whatever Matilda had decided this meeting was, with a detailed description of their visit to Professor Blackwood and Esme Toliver – with a mention of Ruby Webb – during which Matilda didn't interrupt once and made copious notes in a notebook as oversized as the bag it came out of.

'Then we enjoyed a pleasant luncheon at The Angel Cafe,' Hannah added. 'Although the weather deteriorated on the way home and we were drenched.'

'That was clever of the killer to leave the body in a tomb to avoid discovery, perhaps for years. Both ingenious and cunning,' Matilda observed when they had finished.

'If that was the intention, he failed.' Aunt Violet laughed humourlessly. 'He left the mausoleum door open and the reverend lying on the steps.'

'Which suggests he was interrupted!' Matilda tapped her bottom lip with the end of her pen.

'An excellent point, Miss Gilmartin,' Aunt Violet exclaimed. 'I wonder if the police came to the same conclusion?'

'Please, call me Matilda,' she said. 'Perhaps that hasn't occurred to them?'

'Or they have already worked that out,' Hannah added. 'But what difference does it make unless we have some idea of when the murder was committed? Currently we have a timeframe of over two hours during which the reverend was given the digitalis and subsequently died. We asked if Esme, had access to digitalis, but thus far DI Wilson has been unhelpful.'

'Huh, the police often are.' Matilda made a dismissive noise in her throat. 'The idea of anyone but their pompous selves solving a crime sends them into a panic. And what about Benjamin Aldrich's death. Does anything about it strike either of you as noteworthy?'

'The stories didn't differ significantly,' Hannah replied, although she felt there was more to it but without a particular aspect to refer to, she kept her thoughts to herself.

'In my experience, no one ever tells the whole truth,' Matilda said. 'Whether deliberately or because certain aspects get missed in the telling.' Hannah recalled Darius saying a similar thing.

'Which is why I was wondering if you could look up old newspaper reports for Oxford in the summer of 1916 that relate to death by drowning?' Hannah asked.

Matilda lifted the pen away from her mouth. 'I have a friend at the British Newspaper Archives in Colindale who might help. But unless there is a connection between the two incidents, I doubt it will tell us anything. Was his death suspicious?'

Hannah shook her head. 'Not according to the inquest.'

'It's what Detective Chief Inspector Farrell would call "a line of enquiry",' Aunt Violet interjected. 'I shall be putting the same question to him when I next see him.'

'Do let me know what he says,' Matilda asked. 'It would make a good quote for my newspaper.'

'You can't print anything about this, Matilda!' Hannah said, more sharply than she intended. 'At least, not yet. Unless someone is formally charged. Even then you'll be guilty of sensationalism.' The implications of telling this journalist anything began coming back to her with dread. 'There's a word for it, isn't there? Now what was it?'

'*Sub judice*,' Matilda and Aunt Violet said simultaneously.

'Pity,' Matilda muttered. 'It's drama and scorching headlines which sell newspapers. Did anyone report seeing any strangers at the church that morning?'

'Not that we know of.' Hannah shook her head. 'Apart from my wedding party there was no one other than the ladies who came to arrange the flowers, but they were all locals.' A memory surfaced suddenly. 'Wait a moment. Penny was inside the church and saw Reverend Aldrich at his desk in the vestry when someone closed the door. She couldn't see who it was though.'

'It might have been my sister,' Aunt Violet said. 'Madeleine went to check on the flower arrangements. She claims no one struck her as being out of place and if anyone can spot a pigeon among the starlings, it's my sister.'

'I think Penny was there before that,' Hannah said, frowning. 'Aunt Violet, is that an actual saying? I've never heard it before.'

'I just made it up. But it's appropriate, don't you think?'

Matilda giggled, and Aunt Violet's expression softened, suggesting she might warm to the newcomer. At that moment, Travis returned with a tray. 'I assumed your guests would like more refreshment, madam, so I took the liberty of preparing a new coffee tray.'

'Good thinking, Travis,' Aunt Violet waved a leisurely arm in his direction, like Cleopatra commanding a serf. 'You're a gem.'

'This smells wonderful.' Matilda eased forward until she was perching on the edge of the squab. She lifted the lid of the coffee-pot and inhaled it. 'I haven't had coffee this good for ages. Would anyone mind if I played mother?'

'Go ahead.' Hannah's bemused smile mirrored Aunt Violet's as they watched her fill cups and hand round milk and sugar.

'If we discount Ruby Webb,' Hannah said, her hands wrapped around her third cup of coffee of the day, 'we have two possibilities: Professor Blackwood or Esme Toliver. Neither of whom seems likely candidates for violence.'

'Oh, I don't know.' Matilda looked up briefly from her cup. 'I would have never taken Dr Crippen for a killer, but he murdered his wife and chopped her into pieces.'

'You've seen Crippen?' Hannah stared at her. 'Face to face?'

'Across a courtroom, which isn't quite the same, but yes.' Matilda preened slightly. 'It was my first murder case.'

'Ugh.' Aunt Violet gave an exaggerated shudder. 'And we shouldn't yet discount Ruby. She had a day off on Saturday but refused to say where she spent it or with whom.'

'I'll add her to my list, then.' Matilda set down her cup and scribbled in her notebook.

'Perhaps we are on the wrong track and Julian's murder has nothing to do with Benjamin Aldrich at all.' Hannah sighed.

'Or...' Matilda paused for effect. 'Julian Aldrich knew something that his killer didn't want revealed? Something one of his university friends did when they studied together?'

'The gate porter told DI Wilson that Julian used to mix with a rowdy crowd in his first year.' Hannah added. 'Maybe they got up to some high jinks that got out of hand?'

'But why now?' Aunt Violet asked no one in particular. 'He left the university over a year ago.'

'And became an ordained priest.' Hannah raised a hand in emphasis. 'Perhaps his conscience wouldn't let him keep that secret. He either told someone or the person it involved, and they murdered him to protect it?'

'A plausible theory,' Matilda agreed. 'But we don't know what secret, if there is one, or who it involved, so we are no further ahead.'

They fell silent for several moments, each occupied with their own thoughts.

'Well.' Matilda was the first to speak, her contemplative gaze sliding between them. 'While you two were talking to suspects in

Oxford, I had a root through our morgue and found these.' She produced a thin sheaf of yellowed paper with curled edges from the depths of her bag and spread them on the table.

'The morgue?' Hannah stiffened, shifting the tray to avoid accidents.

'Not that kind of morgue.' Matilda laughed. 'It's where we keep copies of back editions of the newspaper. I didn't have time to make notes, so borrowed a few to show you. Be careful with them as I must put them back before they are missed.'

'You shouldn't have done that, Matilda. You could get into trouble for taking these,' Hannah mumbled, but her statement lacked conviction.

'One needs to take risks to achieve one's goals, Mrs Clifford.' Matilda exchanged a look of mutual agreement with Aunt Violet. 'And no one is likely to miss twenty-year-old social pages, so I'm probably safe.'

She slid a page in front of Hannah containing a blurred photograph of a handsome couple outside wrought-iron gates. 'This one is of Miss Lydia Fortescue and her escort attending a society wedding in 1895.'

'Frances's mother?' Despite the inferior quality of old newsprint, the image was that of a porcelain-skinned woman with wide eyes framed by thick lashes and a cupid's bow mouth, her dark hair arranged on top of her head in a froth of curls à la Queen Alexandra.

Before Hannah could examine it, Matilda covered it with another. 'And this one is the same lady with another young man at a New Year party later that year.'

'She was very beautiful.' Hannah compared the two photographs.

'And popular.' Matilda pushed another page across the table. 'And here she is again at Henley Regatta that following year with a third handsome, and evidently wealthy, young man.'

'Let me see.' Aunt Violet waggled her hand until Matilda obliged.

More pages showed the same lady with various other people, both male and female, taken at the Cheltenham Races, or outside various London restaurants and nightclubs.

'It looks as if the photographers followed her around.' Hannah flicked through them until she came to one which snagged her attention. 'Goodness! This one has you in it, Aunt Violet!'

'Where?' Aunt Violet straightened, her eyes narrowed and suspicious.

'I wondered if you would spot her.' Matilda sat back in her chair. 'I didn't until I read the caption at the bottom.'

'Miss Lydia Fortescue in the company of the Hon Jonathan Cadogan-Blair,' Hannah read aloud over her shoulder. 'Accompanied by Miss Violet Edwards and Harry Fordham.'

Aunt Violet swung her legs onto the floor and almost snatched the page from her hand, scanning the page rapidly. 'Goodness! I remember this. It was a birthday party, but for the life of me I cannot remember whose. I couldn't have been more than seventeen.'

'And who is Harry Fordham?' Hannah dragged out the name, a hand reaching for the page, but her aunt moved it out of her reach.

'*Was* Harry Fordham. He died in '09.'

'I didn't realise,' Hannah said gently. 'Sorry.' She relaxed back in her seat while exchanging a rueful look with Matilda.

'I couldn't find any references to Miss Fortescue after that.' Matilda's voice was overloud. 'That is, apart from her marriage announcement the following year and a death notice in 1910. How old is Frances Aldrich?' she asked thoughtfully.

'Twenty-one or two, I think,' Hannah replied.

'Are you thinking what I am?' Matilda looked from Hannah to Aunt Violet and back again in anticipatory silence.

Hannah did a swift mental calculation. 'Are you saying one of these young men could be Frances's natural father?'

'Why not?' Matilda shrugged. 'It's not unheard of for a society hostess to get into a delicate situation, resulting in her being quietly married off to a nondescript man to keep her respectable.'

'That's the stuff of gutter press and scandal rags!' Aunt Violet snapped, staring daggers at Matilda. 'You cannot assume something like that without proof. Is that why you came? To put forward some libellous theory?'

'Matilda isn't trying to castigate anyone any more than we are, Aunt Violet,' Hannah said, surprised at her aunt's vehemence when she was more than capable of doing the same herself. 'We're just throwing wild theories about.'

'Is it that wild?' Matilda's hazel eyes widened, unruffled. 'Frances told you she wondered why her mother married a university professor when she had the likes of Viscount what's-his-name chasing her?' Matilda flicked through the pages of her notebook. 'I recorded the names of those I could find who were photographed with Miss Fortescue in the year or so before Frances was born.' She held her pencil in the air and read from the page. 'Mr Peter Randall, Grantley Smythe-Potter, John Cadogan-Blair, which you have already seen, and a Viscount Percival Rathbone.'

Hannah glanced up at this last name. 'Aunt Violet, didn't you mention Lydia's past infatuation with a lord's son?'

'Possibly.' Her aunt shrugged, non-committal. 'If we're merely speculating and not accusing anyone, I also recall an Alfred

Leverton-Fanshawe from those days who inherited the peerage when his brother died. But we're talking about over twenty years ago.'

'Well, then.' Matilda chewed the end of her pencil. 'My next task is to find out where these men are now. It might be a long shot, but it's worth looking at. Interestingly, I couldn't find any pictures of Professor Blackwood. With or without Lydia.'

'Maybe he was a homebody in his youth too and didn't like parties?' Hannah suggested, but neither reacted.

'You want to track them down?' Aunt Violet scoffed. 'And do what? Ask each of them if they fathered a child on Miss Lydia Fortescue in 1896?' She huffed. 'We'll get shown the door immediately.' She shook her head.

'We're going to have to be more subtle than that.' Matilda shoved the pile of newspaper clippings back into her bag and closed the flap. 'I'll contact my friend at the archives and see what he can come up with. He owes me a favour.' Rising, she dragged the shoulder strap over her head. 'This has been fascinating, and I'll get back to you if I find anything, but please don't summon the butler – it slows everything down and I'm quite happy to show myself out. Oh, and I'll call you soon about that interview, Miss Edwards.'

'I'll look forward to it,' Aunt Violet replied, and looked as if she meant it.

Hannah walked Matilda to the front door. 'Will you promise not to print anything until the case is solved?' she demanded.

'I'm a journalist, Hannah. I have business cards to prove it.'

'The murder is one thing, but would anyone care what a dead woman did with a society playboy over twenty years ago? But it would hurt Frances Aldrich, and after what she's been through lately, I wouldn't want that.'

'I'll think about it.' Matilda hauled the strap of her bag over her head. 'And I'm not a monster. I don't set out to ruin people's lives.'

On a note of mutual understanding, Hannah closed the door on her guest and returned to the sitting room, hoping she wouldn't regret having involved Matilda. Entering the room, she found Aunt Violet on her feet, her shoes back on and ready to depart.

'I had better go too, darling. I ought to put in some appearance at the bookshop today to check the place is still standing.' She pecked Hannah on the cheek. 'I thought I heard some movement upstairs a moment ago, which tells me Darius is awake, so I'll make myself scarce.'

'It's unnecessary, as I'm sure he would love to see you.' Hannah's smile faded as she spotted her aunt slide a folded-up sheet of paper into her pocket.

'Aunt Violet, what's that?' Though she did not require an answer. 'Did you take that newspaper clipping when Matilda wasn't looking?'

'I only borrowed it. Which is exactly what Miss Gilmartin did.' Aunt Violet's sheepish stare turned to defiance. 'I preferred not to mention this in front of her, but I need to make a call to Chelsea.'

'What's in Chelsea?' Hannah asked, her curiosity piqued.

'I'd rather not go into it until I've spoken to a friend who has a better memory than mine.'

'You're being very enigmatic, Aunt Violet. But if you think it's important, I won't ask questions – provided I can come too.'

'Well, if you insist.' Her aunt marched to the front door while speaking over her shoulder. 'I'll collect you at ten tomorrow morning. And make sure you're ready because I don't intend to wait.'

Hannah sighed. 'It's not as if I have any other plans for the day.'

17

Darius's familiar tread on the stairs brought Hannah into the hall seconds after her aunt's roadster careened out of the drive.

'Was that Aunt Violet's voice I heard just now?' With one hand clamped around the newel post, he swung over the bottom two steps onto the polished floor, just as he used to during his schooldays. His hair curled below his ears, darkened and still damp from his bath, the scent of his Floris cologne making Hannah smile as delicious memories returned as he wrapped her in an almost suffocating hug.

'It was. We've just had coffee with Miss Matilda Gilmartin.'

'The journalist gal?' He pulled back slightly but still grasped her upper arms. 'You aren't stepping on DI Wilson's toes about this Reverend Aldrich murder, I hope?'

'His toes are quite unharmed. But we do think there might be more to this murder than what happened in Chiswick. Both Frances and the reverend had pasts, so the answer might lie elsewhere.'

'I thought DI Wilson had investigated that side of things in Oxford. What do you hope to find out he hasn't?'

'He did, but maybe he didn't ask the right questions. So far, DI Wilson hasn't found anyone with a firm reason to want Julian Aldrich dead.'

'I only met the reverend twice to discuss our wedding, but he seemed to be a reasonable chap,' Darius said. 'Second-guessing the police is never advisable, my love.' Releasing her, he planted a loving kiss on her head as if to dilute his warning, then approached the hall mirror where he tweaked the Windsor knot in his tie.

'Is something worrying you?' he asked, addressing her reflection over his shoulder. 'Or are you angry at me for not coming home for dinner last night?'

'Dinner? You weren't home for the sunrise.' She tried not to sound too critical, but her disappointment of the evening before returned in full force.

'I'm so sorry.' He winced, turned from the mirror and shot his cuffs. 'I tried, but everything got away from me.'

'What do you mean by everything? Or aren't you allowed to talk about it?'

'Not really, but since I've given you the worst honeymoon anyone could have, I'll offer you a few crumbs, metaphorically speaking.' He gave the hallway a swift glance, grasped her hand and drew her back into the sitting room, where he eased her onto the sofa she had just left. 'You know the revolutionaries have held the Romanov family captive for over a year?' In response to her slow nod, he added, 'Our government has been trying to get them smuggled out of Russia, but no one knows where they are being held.'

'I thought the King was going to help them? Has he decided against it? They are his family. Separated by thousands of miles, perhaps, but still family.'

'It seems so. The political situation is... delicate. Some

members of the government feel the Tsar is nothing but a blood-stained tyrant, so they are reluctant to step in. Thus, the King has perhaps no choice, although I also think Queen Mary had something to do with the decision not to get involved.'

'Do you have any idea where they are being held?' Hannah asked.

'We think perhaps Siberia, but having spent most of the night poring over maps and going through snippets of information from our agents abroad, we're not sure.'

'Siberia?' Hannah dragged out the word into three syllables. 'Wasn't keeping them under house arrest enough? I cannot imagine how those lovely girls are coping with imprisonment. And that poor, sick boy. He's only thirteen.'

'I wish it was up to me, darling, but other factions are at work here.' He wrapped an arm around her shoulders. 'There's still hope. Now, what else is making those lovely eyes dull? Wasn't your trip to Oxford enjoyable? I heard the weather was pretty dire.'

'Oxford was quite interesting. It's not that, only I don't want you to think I'm complaining, but—' He tucked in his chin with a downward look that conveyed disbelief. 'I know, I'm being selfish, but I always thought married life would be... different. I was practically raised here in this house, so I don't understand how living here makes me feel, well, lonely.' His heartfelt sigh prompted her to add, 'I'm not blaming you. Truly. It's just that I loved being alone in my home in Chiswick Mall. It was my sanctuary and if I needed someone to talk to, which wasn't often, I had Ivy, whom I've hardly seen since we moved in. She has the other staff to keep her company now and if any of them see me coming in the halls, they bob a swift curtsey and dart away. Besides, I would only interfere in their work if I chatted about the garden or the weather every time I came across a housemaid.'

'It's how my parents ran the household.' He tightened his arm around her and propped his chin on her head. 'My grandfather was worse. He had the servants turn to the wall when a member of the family walked by.'

'He didn't?' Hannah jerked up her chin and stared up at him. 'I thought only royalty did that?'

'My grandparents thought they *were* royalty.' He gave a low, rolling laugh, then lifted his arm to tuck her head back beneath his chin before lowering it again. 'It never occurred to me you would find everything here so alien.' He stroked the back of her neck with his thumb. 'I thought I was giving you something we both wanted, but I've allowed this wretched job to come between us. I feel I've let you down.'

'You've done nothing of the kind.' Guilt lanced through her, as the last thing she wanted was to upset him. She twisted on the squab and cradled his face in her hands, the skin soft and fragrant from a recent shave. 'I'm the one being spoiled and self-indulgent.'

'We could move back to Chiswick, if you prefer.' The disappointment in his voice made her regret the entire conversation. 'I don't care where we live and it's a perfectly adequate house.' His use of the word 'adequate' told her he didn't believe that for a moment.

'No, Darius. We cannot do that. Your father would be so disappointed. The reason he retired and handed this house over to you was because he envisioned you growing old here with a family like he did.'

'I know, but if you aren't happy—'

'I *am* happy, so ignore my silly mood. I know you would spend more time here if you could.'

'If it were up to me... but it isn't.' His warm breath in her ear sent warmth along her spine. 'Can you bear it for a while longer?'

'If only we knew how long, it would make the wait easier.' She lowered her hands into her lap. 'Ignore me, I'm being childish. It's up to me to occupy myself, so I'm going back to the bookshop to work. Maybe not full-time, but it will stop me from moping.'

'What about your volunteer work at the Endell Street Hospital Library?'

'I suspect I'm about to be decommissioned, if that's the word. Dr Murray has started accepting influenza patients, so to avoid the risk of infection, for the foreseeable future, all civilian staff are no longer required.'

'A wise precaution. I wouldn't want you catching it.' Darius placed his flat hands on his knees and pushed to his feet. 'How about we arrange a small supper party here next week? Say, Thursday? We could invite Aidan and Aunt Violet. Maybe even Cavan and your Miss Gilmartin?'

'That's a lovely idea, but I think I'll save the delights of Miss Gilmartin for another occasion. I'm going to Chelsea with Aunt Violet this morning, so I'll ask her if she and Aidan are free.'

'What's in Chelsea to interest your aunt?'

'I've no idea. She's being mysterious about it too.' She stepped closer and adjusted his tie, which was already perfect, but she needed an excuse to touch him. 'Will you be home for dinner?' The alternative being Hannah would dine alone again, but this time she kept her dismay to herself.

'I will. And that's a promise.' He leaned down and pressed his mouth to hers, prompting her to wrap her arms tighter around his neck and pull him lower until he laughingly protested. Neither of them noticed the door click open until a discreet cough separated them.

'My apologies, sir, madam.' Travis halted on the threshold, shifted his feet, and stared at the floor. 'I came to fetch the tray.'

* * *

Aunt Violet halted the roadster on a curved front drive where a uniformed doorman had directed them in through a set of gates, while assuring her the motor car would be safe.

'You know we aren't in Chelsea, Aunt Violet?' Hannah viewed the building from the passenger seat – a brick-built structure with white stone facings and a sign with the words Beaufort House in stone above the double front door. 'We passed the British Library back there, which means we're in Bloomsbury.'

'I know it isn't,' Aunt Violet said irritably, slamming the driver's door. 'Celia Pell called last night and told me she had made a mistake.'

Hannah followed her up three stone steps to where a row of numbered buttons beside the glazed double doors identified the building as a series of apartments, and reminded herself to ask who Celia Pell was and how she fitted into this drama, but it could wait until another time. 'Who lives here?' she asked as they waited to be buzzed into the building.

'Someone I used to know,' her aunt replied enigmatically, leading the way into an entrance hall that looked like a hotel, complete with porter's desk with a bell and a 'Ring for service' notice. Aunt Violet swept past into a hallway between a row of evenly spaced doors with polished brass knockers. Halting at the end, she pressed the bell below the number four and, after a brief wait, a man in mismatched trousers and waistcoat wearing an enquiring expression that declared him to be a manservant, opened the door.

'Miss Edwards and Mrs Clifford to see Mr Cadogan-Blair,' Aunt Violet said. 'He's expecting us.'

With an obsequious bow and a smile of acknowledgement, he led them along another hallway and into an elegant sitting room decorated in shades of coffee and cream with accents of ochre, with a wide window that overlooked a manicured lawn.

The room contained several bookcases, a bureau at one end and a standard lamp behind an overstuffed high-backed chair with a human-sized indentation in the squab; a very masculine space but also a sparse one with neither framed photographs, nor ornaments or knick-knacks on the polished surfaces.

'Please take a seat. I shall inform Mr Cadogan-Blair you are here,' the manservant said and retreated.

'Cadogan-Blair?' Hannah began. 'Isn't that one of the names Matilda had on her list of Lydia Fortescue's—'

'Hush!' Aunt Violet said as the door opened and a tall, slightly stooping man joined them with slow, measured steps. Immaculately dressed, he wore a multi-coloured silk cravat at his throat, a pristine white shirt and black suit. His skin was pale and stretched over his skull as if he had lost weight recently, his thin, dark hair combed neatly over a pinkish scalp as if to disguise the loss. His eyes were light blue and retained a sparkle which told her he was younger than he seemed but was not in good health.

'Violet Edwards, as I live and breathe,' he said in a deep, cultured voice that turned into a laugh, ending abruptly in a cough that took several seconds to subside. 'Not that I do either very well these days.' His lips twisted in a self-conscious smile. 'You are still as exquisite as ever.' His eyes shone, showing he was not trying to flatter her but seemed surprised at what he was looking at.

'Hello, Jonny.' Aunt Violet left her chair, her arms outstretched to give him a guarded embrace and gave light as air kisses to either cheek. 'And I don't believe you for a moment.'

'I might be a worn-out version of myself these days, Violet, but I have a photographic memory for beautiful women and could never forget you.'

'That's the Jonny Cadogan-Blair I remember.' Aunt Violet flushed. 'How have you been?'

The question seemed to amuse him, as he offered a dismissive flap of his hand before turning towards Hannah. 'You must be Madeleine's girl? Violet said she was bringing you. It's lovely to meet you.' Hannah started to rise, but he waved her back into her seat.

'It's nice to meet you too.' Hannah took his proffered hand, which sat in hers like a collection of bones wrapped in skin, so she had to make a staunch effort not to flinch. 'You know my mother?'

'I did once. She hated me.' Chuckling, he eased backwards into an overstuffed chair by the fire, a seat Hannah assumed he must spend a good deal of his time in. 'She called me a bad influence on her little sister. Little did she know, Violet was the ringleader.' The blue eyes sparkled again, and a smile appeared that showed he had once been a handsome man. 'Got us all into some tricky situations, did your aunt.' He turned to look at Aunt Violet. 'Remember that party at Rupert's house where we all got so tipsy on champagne, we ended up in the fountain at Kensington Gardens in our evening duds?'

'Hannah doesn't need to hear about that, Jonny.' Blushing, Aunt Violet fussed with her gloves.

'Oh, yes I do.' Hannah refused to be relegated to an afterthought in their reminiscences. 'You never mentioned that particular occasion, Aunt Violet.'

'And I don't intend to now.' She stiffened and inhaled, signifying the subject was forever closed. 'We've come to ask you something rather personal, Jonny.'

'Sounds intriguing.' He crossed one ankle over the other and relaxed back in his chair.

'We aren't here to reminisce. Well, we are, but specifically about someone we both knew. Lydia Fortescue.'

'Ah, Lydia.' His gaze shifted towards the window that gave a rectangular of clear blue sky. 'Another beautiful girl. She died, you know. A horrible accident in Regent's Park. Her carriage hit a kerbstone and toppled over. Tragic.'

'So I heard.' Aunt Violet removed the folded newspaper clipping from her bag and handed it to him. 'Do you remember this?'

Peering at it, he removed a pair of spectacles from a top pocket and put them on, squinting at the page. 'Good heavens. I certainly do. Not specific occasions, but these faces bring a lot back.' He reeled the names off in the same way Matilda had, pointing at each one as he did so. 'There's old Peter. Killed at Mons, you know. There's Harry and Percy. Good old Percy, could never hold his whisky. And here's you, Violet, looking stunning as ever. Lydia, of course, and me. Gosh, don't we look young?' A shadow crossed his features for a second before he smiled again. 'What was it you wished to know?'

Aunt Violet patiently explained the circumstances surrounding the murder of Reverend Aldrich, the connection to Lydia's daughter, and her own wish to help a close friend in the police. Hannah gave her an ironic look at the last part, but her aunt stoically refused to meet her gaze. 'I'm not saying they asked us or even need our help, but that photograph brought back memories I cannot quite recall. It occurred to me you might help with things.'

'What sort of things?' he asked, peering over the top of his spectacles.

'Secrets I wasn't privy to as a girl of eighteen,' Aunt Violet replied enigmatically. 'Lydia, for instance.' She held his gaze for several seconds as numerous emotions crossed his face. Among them sadness and recognition.

'Ah, I think I know what you're getting at. The rumours about why she married Arthur Blackwood in such a hurry, eh?'

Aunt Violet nodded. 'It was awkward for Lydia at the time, because everyone knew she had such a strong attachment to you. We all thought you'd marry her at one stage.'

'So did Lydia.' He removed the spectacles and held them on his lap. 'I was a total fool in those days. Thought I owned the world, and I could have anything I wanted. I should have married her, but I was too vain and stupid to see it.'

'No one in our circle had heard of, or met Arthur,' Aunt Violet went on, most likely for Hannah's benefit. 'When she announced their forthcoming wedding, everyone came to the most obvious conclusion, that...' She let the rest hang between them.

'Is that why you came to see me after all these years, Violet? To accuse me of fathering Blackwood's daughter?' He aimed a sly wink at Hannah before continuing. 'I assure you that is not true and if Lydia were alive, she would refute it.'

'I apologise, Jonny, however—'

He halted her with a raised hand. 'I'm not insulted, Violet. It's not as if you're the only one who has asked me that question.' He rubbed both hands down his trousers, a wry smile on his lips. 'I was young and reckless, but gentleman enough not to despoil a young woman and then abandon her. It was said she married Arthur on the rebound, and maybe she did. However, I believe their child was a honeymoon baby and all above board. I heard they made a go of it in the end.'

'In the end?' Hannah ventured.

His brow furrowed thoughtfully. 'I heard there were a few bumps in the road at first. But then isn't that how most marriages start? Anyway, they both adored their daughter who turned out to be a delightful child. When Lydia was killed, Arthur took the girl out of London within the month.'

'Did you know he became a lecturer at Merton College?'

'Did he really?' Jonny's eyebrows rose. 'That doesn't surprise me. He was a first-class swot at Cambridge.' His eyebrows scrunched together, and he studied the ceiling for a second. 'Odd then that he chose Oxford and not our alma mater. Makes all those scraps we had after the boat race a waste of time.'

'And you, Jonny. What about you?' Aunt Violet asked, implying her reason for coming was answered and she could revert to more personal matters.

'Me?' He sighed. 'When I heard Lydia had died, it was a low time for me, having to face the fact I had passed up the chance of having my own family.' He released a slow, shuddering breath before his smile returned. 'Didn't change much, though. I remained devoted to my hedonistic lifestyle, care of my indulgent papa.' He snorted a laugh, then grew more serious again. 'Until he stopped indulging me. He threatened to cut me off if I didn't shape up and make something of myself. His idea of that was to buy me a commission in the army. I entered as a captain at the age of thirty-seven and spent the next two years up to my knees in French mud.' He held both arms out from his sides and looked down at himself. 'The joke's on the old man, eh?' His coarse laugh turned into another protracted cough.

'What happened to you in France, Jonny?' Aunt Violet asked when he had got it under control.

'What, this?' He tapped his chest with the flat of his hand. 'Gas attack at Loos. I got my men out, though, which makes up for everything. I'm a different person now, in more ways than one. Won't make old bones, but then who does these days?' He propped his glasses back onto his nose and stared at the clipping in his hand. 'Now, who else was there? Ah yes, there's dear Limmy. I had a soft spot for her.'

'Lydia's friend?' Aunt Violet said. 'I forgot that's what we called her.'

'What sort of name is Limmy?' Hannah asked.

'It was a nickname,' Aunt Violet replied. 'Rather a cruel one, I'm afraid. Short for limpet, because she never left Lydia's side.'

'Pretty girl, but shy and overeager to please,' he continued. 'I can't recall her actual name. Dodson, Hobson, something like that. I wonder what happened to her? Probably married with a half dozen offspring by now.' His bemused chuckle developed into a hacking cough that seemed to go on for longer than the last one.

He pummelled his chest with a fist as if to force air into his lungs, the colour draining from his face until his lips took on a blue tinge.

'Jonny!' Aunt Violet cried out, leaping to her feet to rush to his side, just as the manservant reappeared. He was there so quickly, Hannah was convinced he must have been waiting on the other side of the door.

'I'm sorry, madam, miss, but this has obviously been too much for him and he tires easily these days.' The manservant slid a firm hand beneath Jonny's arm and eased him to his feet while glaring accusingly at each of them. 'I must prepare his medicine, and he needs to rest.'

'Sorry, ladies.' Jonny gasped between breaths as the manservant supported him from the room. 'Dashed nuisance but – cannot – be helped.'

'We'll see ourselves out.' Aunt Violet pressed his arm. 'Goodbye, Jonny. And thank you.'

He nodded mid-cough and gave a vague wave as the door closed behind him.

'Poor man,' Hannah murmured, following her aunt slowly back to the motor car. 'He's quite frail, isn't he?'

'I doubt he'll live much longer.' Aunt Violet's lower lip trembled. 'You should have seen him, Hannah. He was magnificent when he was young. The handsomest man I had ever seen, and such times we had. No drawing room was the same without us. We followed him like courtiers to their king without a thought for the consequences.'

'Huh! And what consequences do the offspring of the wealthy ever have to face?' Hannah said, aware she sounded cynical.

'You're right.' Her aunt sighed. 'We were horribly indulged, and the things we got away with would have ruined the reputations of most young people.' Halting beside the motor car, she replaced the newspaper clipping in her bag then withdrew a handkerchief she used to blow her nose. 'I hate the horrible war that has done this to him.'

Hannah patted her shoulder, helpless to offer anything but meaningless platitudes so she chose silence and waited for Aunt Violet to compose herself before guiding her into the driver's seat. She toyed with offering to drive them both back, but her aunt needed the distraction. Aunt Violet rarely showed emotion and scorned overt displays in others as a lack of decorum.

'I feel we achieved nothing, though.' Hannah skirted the bonnet and settled into the passenger seat. 'I was hoping we might unearth some dark secret, which would explain why someone would want to prevent Frances from marrying Julian Aldrich. Now we have no clue where to look next.'

'Do you think Frances was a honeymoon baby?' Hannah asked. 'That could be the story they gave when the pregnancy was announced. It might not be true.'

'I thought the same myself,' her aunt replied. 'But if Lydia married Blackwood to stay respectable, and it wasn't Jonny, then who was Frances's father?' She sighed. 'I shall have to go back to Celia's and do some more digging.'

'Does it matter whose daughter Frances is? How does that relate to Julian Aldrich's murder?' Hannah said, mildly irritated that they might be going down a rabbit hole.

'Maybe it doesn't, but thus far nothing has come to light, which would explain why anyone would want to kill him.'

'I just feel we're wasting our time,' Hannah said despondently.

'What makes you think that?' Dry-eyed, Aunt Violet stared straight ahead and started the engine. 'Aidan always says negative information can sometimes be every bit as important as the positive.'

'Whatever that means,' Hannah murmured.

18

Feeling guilty at not having kept in closer touch with Frances than she had promised, Hannah drove to the Gore Hotel the following morning. The porter behind the desk in the entrance hall confirmed Mrs Aldrich had just had breakfast and directed Hannah to the first floor. As she traversed a long corridor lined with identical doors, Hannah experienced an impulse to run, as her last experience with hotel rooms at Alfred's Gentleman's Club a few months earlier came back to her, but when Frances answered her knock with a welcoming smile, her nerves vanished.

'How nice of you to call.' Frances had evidently spent some time shopping as she was dressed entirely in black, with a black marcasite necklace and a matching clip in her upswept hair.

She grasped both of Hannah's hands and drew her inside a luxurious bedroom decorated in deep blue and gold, with a canopied bed at one end opposite a marble fireplace, empty now as the day was warm. A casement window stood partly open, and the sounds of traffic could be heard from the street.

'This is delightful,' Hannah said as Frances gestured her into a matching sofa placed strategically at the end of the bed.

'It's charming, isn't it?' Frances smiled weakly. 'I've spent more than one evening here. I've only recently had breakfast, but I could order refreshments should you wish?'

'Not for me, thank you.' Hannah placed her bag in the space between them. 'I ought to apologise for not calling before, but—' She was about to speak of not wishing to interrupt the grim task of arranging a funeral, but Frances interrupted her.

'Please don't concern yourself. I don't feel neglected, and I've kept busy with the funeral arrangements. It's to be a small affair, of course, since Julian had no family.'

'What about Mr Aldrich's aunt and uncle? Have they been informed of what has happened?'

'I assume either the police or the archdeacon would have done that. I'm sure they'll attend if at all possible, even though Scotland is a long way, and it's difficult to travel such distances, what with the railways giving precedence to servicemen.'

'I assume Reverend Aldrich is to be buried at St Nicholas?' The churchyard had been closed over fifty years before due to lack of space, but Hannah knew it was customary for a clergymen to be buried within their own church grounds.

Frances nodded. 'The archdeacon didn't seem to mind that Julian had been in the post such a short time, and designated a space for him inside the church wall. It will be nice to be able to visit his grave whenever I'm in town.'

'Is it likely Julian's aunt and uncle might want him interred near them?' Hannah asked.

'In Scotland?' Frances snorted. 'I doubt it. And as his widow I wouldn't allow it.' Her eyes glittered with determination. 'Oh dear, that sounds rather spiteful of me, doesn't it? Only things have been somewhat strained between them since Benjamin died.'

'Because they left Oxford soon after the funeral?' She tried to recall if Professor Blackwood had said the same thing but it eluded her.

'They did. Mrs Aldrich was in a state of collapse at the funeral. Julian and I called on her a few days later when her husband was at work. She said she couldn't bear to stay in the house where Benjamin grew up because there was so much of him everywhere she looked.'

'That's understandable when she lost her only child.'

'Exactly. She lost her child. But she raised *two* boys. Julian was only six when he went to live with her, but Benjamin seemed to be the one she cared about.'

'Grief is an all-encompassing emotion, Frances. This was days afterwards, you say? She must still have been coming to terms with her loss and searching for reasons for it. That's perfectly natural.'

'I know that now. And she didn't blame Julian at all, only the way she looked at him it was as if she couldn't bring herself to look at him either. It was hard on Julian, and they left Oxford before things could go back to normal.' She inhaled a ragged breath. 'And now they never will.'

'Frances.' Hannah prepared her next words carefully. 'I feel I should tell you that my aunt and I went to Oxford the other day and spoke to your father.'

'I know. Father told me.' Frances reached across the space between them and covered Hannah's hand with hers. 'It puzzled me at first, but you found Julian's body, so it stands to reason you'd feel involved.'

'We do, and to be honest, this isn't the first time we've done this sort of thing.'

'So I've heard.' Frances arched an amused eyebrow. 'Dr Soames told me you and your aunt discovered who murdered his wife. She was your best friend, I believe?'

'She was.' Hannah swallowed as sad memories returned. 'It's not intentional. I mean, we don't go looking for murder victims, but we appear to have stumbled across more than our fair share.'

'I find amateur sleuthing fascinating, and if it helps you discover who killed Julian, I'd be very grateful. The police don't seem to be getting anywhere. Or not that they have informed me, anyway.' She eased closer and lowered her voice. 'There's something which has been bothering me, and I cannot get it out of my head.'

'Go on.' Hannah's pulse raced as she sensed a moment of revelation. 'Whatever you wish to tell me, I will respect your privacy.'

'It seems a dreadful thing to even contemplate, but is it possible my father killed Julian?'

'Your father?' Whatever Hannah expected her to say it was not this.

'Don't look at me like that. I know it's a dreadful thing to suspect about a parent, but Father has shown a different side to him lately.' She licked her lips before continuing, which showed how hard it was for her to vocalise her thoughts. 'The day you brought me here in your motor car and he was waiting for me; he was very angry.'

'I remember, but he seemed to calm down before I left.' Hannah recalled his manner had shifted to overt politeness when he realised she was present.

'I agree, he did – but once we were up here, he released this... this torrent of abuse. He called me an ungrateful child who couldn't be trusted and how could I have contemplated a marriage without consulting him. He insulted Julian too, saying he should have asked for my hand. I told him there would be no point as he would have withheld his blessing, at which he shouted louder, saying Julian should be man enough to accept it. He railed at me for ages until a maid went to fetch the manager who pounded on the door, demanding to know what was happening.'

'That sounds very frightening. He didn't hurt you, did he?'

'Oh no. Father's never laid a hand on me. He uses words to get his feelings across, not violence. But the effect could not have been greater. And I didn't demand he go home; he stormed out in a temper when the manager threatened to summon the police.' She massaged her hand repeatedly with the other.

'Why do you think he might have killed Julian when he doesn't believe in violence— Oh!'

'Exactly.' Frances took in her shocked expression. 'Julian was poisoned. The act of someone who doesn't act on impulse. Someone who thinks things through.'

Leaving a little while later, the spring sunshine warmed Hannah's face as she crossed to where the Swift was parked and climbed into the driver's seat. Before starting the engine, she stared up at the row of blank windows and contemplated what to do with what Frances had told her.

She didn't know how long she sat there until the driver of drayman's lorry shouted for her to move. With a wave of acquiescence, she drove off, but had still not come to a decision.

19

Hannah did not hear from her aunt at all that evening, and when she telephoned the next morning, there was still no answer. Frustrated, she saw Darius off to his office after breakfast and drove to the bookshop, surprised to find Aunt Violet had not yet arrived.

'How lovely to see you, Miss Merr— Mrs Clifford,' Penny greeted her at the shop door. 'I've missed seeing you at your desk.'

'I've been absent for less than a week, Penny,' Hannah laughingly reminded her, then greeted the new manager, which he grudgingly returned.

Apparently unhappy about an invader in what he considered his territory, Mr Hendry mumbled an excuse about having work to complete and scurried into a corner, where he hid behind an oversized ledger.

'Don't mind him, missus,' Penny explained in a whisper. 'He thinks women don't belong in the literary world. Having to work with three of us is more than he can stomach.'

'Well, he'd better get used to it then.' Hannah shrugged out of her coat while shooting the manager a hard look which he failed to see as he kept his head bent over his work.

'Is my aunt not here?' Hannah indicated the vacant desk by the door and the equally empty hook where her aunt always stowed her things.

'She didn't say she weren't coming in.' Penny scanned the room as if she had only just noticed Aunt Violet was not there. 'I expect she'll be in later.'

'That's a nuisance. I had something I wanted to share with her.'

'About the body at the wedding?' Penny blurted, her eyes widening behind her spectacles. 'Does Inspector Farrell know yet who killed the vicar?'

'No, Penny. Did you and Archie enjoy the day?' Hannah asked, quickly changing the subject.

'Oh yes, it was lovely. And Papa was so delighted to be invited to the reception. He says people he marries don't usually do that. And talking of Archie...' She withdrew a brown envelope from her pocket. 'He wrote this at the station while waiting for his train to leave. He says he's made lots of friends and seems to be enjoying it so far, but he still hasn't mastered tying his puttees, so they don't unravel.' She returned the folded sheet of oilskin carefully into her pocket. 'I expect he'll get used to it. He promises to write again when he arrives.'

Hannah lifted Bartleby onto her lap and stroked his fur, responding in all the appropriate places, but doubted Archie was having as much fun as his letter claimed. 'Is it my imagination,' Hannah said when she had finished, 'or has this animal lost weight?'

'He's a bit off his food.' Penny's face fell. 'I've done everything I can to tempt him, but he won't have it. He misses Archie almost as much as I do.' She swiped a hand across her cheek as a stray tear escaped.

'Poor Bartleby.' Hannah held the cat closer until his body

vibrated in a gratifying purr. 'I'm glad he hasn't forgotten me. I'll see if Travis can find something at home to tempt him.'

On her Aunt Violet's suggestion, Penny had moved into the flat above the bookshop while Archie was away, adding a distinctive feminine touch to the place with a collection of china ornaments and some homemade cushions.

'I'd appreciate that, missus, 'cos if Archie comes back and finds him thin and sad, he won't be pleased with me.'

'I'm sure he'd never blame you.' Hannah bit down on her bottom lip as the word 'if' sounded loudly inside her head.

'It looks as if Miss Edwards has taken the morning off, but I told her I would be in today, so I'll wait for her a while longer.' Hannah eyed Penny, who looked comfortably settled in for a long chat. 'In the meantime, is there anything you'd like some help with? I wouldn't like to feel I was interrupting your work.'

'There are six cases of books at the back which need unpacking.' Penny's eyes rounded, oblivious to Hannah's sarcasm. 'I would have started on them, but them cases are too heavy for me alone, and his lordship is unlikely to lift a finger.' She narrowed her eyes at the manager, who had not moved from his corner. 'If you're willing, we could do them together.'

'Well, we'd better get started then.' Hannah set Bartleby down on the polished floor and he scooted away in pursuit of a stray fly.

They worked steadily together for most of the morning, unpacking books and entering the details into the inventory, shadowed by a sorry-looking Bartleby.

At one o'clock, and with still no sign of her aunt, Mr Hendry appeared from behind his desk in his coat and hat and explained he had an appointment at Lincoln's Inn.

'Did you know about that?' Hannah asked Penny as the jangle of the doorbell followed him out.

'Why would he tell me?' Penny shrugged. 'We get a lot of orders from the lawyers there, and he likes to think he's on a par with them, so to speak.'

Muttering to herself that communication around here was going markedly downhill, Hannah turned as the doorbell clanged again, and Aunt Violet strode inside.

'I'm glad to see you.' Hannah crossed the floor towards her. 'I was afraid I had misunderstood, and you weren't coming in at all today.'

'Not so loud, darling, I have a slight headache.' Her aunt dropped her bag on the floor and massaged her temple with the fingers of one hand. 'However, despite my minor incapacity, I remembered we were supposed to meet up today.'

'Late night, was it?' She kept her voice low, but Penny's conspiratorial look told her she was wasting her time.

'Something like that.' Aunt Violet eased carefully into the chair behind her desk. 'No Mr Hendry?'

'Lincoln's Inn,' Hannah and Penny said simultaneously, causing Aunt Violet to screw up her eyes as if in pain.

'Perhaps you shouldn't have come in at all,' Hannah said, feeling no sympathy. 'Where were you last night? I telephoned twice.'

'She was probably out looking for murderers.' Penny grinned over a pile of books clutched to her chest.

'You have a customer, Penny,' Hannah said, pointedly indicating a man in a long overcoat who signalled for attention from beside the till.

'Ah, so I have.' Penny discarded the books onto a nearby table and retreated.

'Should I ask what caused your headache, or do I already know?' Hannah said.

'You can stop looking so smug. I had dinner at Celia Pell's last night, which turned into something of a replay of our days as debutantes. Totally self-indulgent, as most of the stories were embellished to make the tellers sound less reprehensible.'

'Remind me again, who is Celia Pell?'

'I don't think you've met her, darling. We were beautiful young things once and while my principles were forged by Emmeline Pankhurst, Celia married money and became a society wife with no interest in contradicting her husband's politics. I still regard her as a friend who remembers every scandal and wedding since 1903 and the names of who was left off the invitations. Does that give you an idea?'

'Indeed, it does, and now I don't regret having never met her. Your evening sounds – eventful. Champagne or gin?' Hannah asked.

'You know me better than that. I never get drunk on gin; it makes me maudlin.'

'Champagne, then.' Hannah smirked.

'It was very good champagne too.' Aunt Violet sounded offended. 'It never used to affect me this way. And don't you dare say it has something to do with my age.'

'I wouldn't dream of it. And your sobriety aside, I have something to tell you about Frances Aldrich. Well, not about her, per se, but something she said.'

'Really?' Aunt Violet directed a swift look at Penny, who had finished with her client and was pretending not to listen from behind a bookshelf, the top of her head clearly visible in a gap in the shelf above.

'Tell me on the way.' Aunt Violet grabbed Hannah's jacket from the back of her chair and handed it to her. 'I spotted Darius's Swift when I came in so we can go in that. I didn't feel up to driving today.'

'Now why doesn't that surprise me?' Hannah caught the garment before it ended up on the floor. 'And on the way where? You've only just got here.' Slinging the jacket over one arm, she grabbed her hat and bag and followed her aunt to the door.

'Will you be back before closing?' Penny called after them. 'Or shall I lock up?'

'Thank you, Penny. I know we can always count on you.' Hannah didn't hear what it was Penny muttered under her breath as the door closed, but perhaps it was for the best.

'I never realised how penetrating a motor engine sounds when one is not quite up to par.' Aunt Violet pressed the top of her nose with her thumb and forefinger. 'Could you perhaps not rev it so hard?'

Hannah resisted an urge to roll her eyes and eased up on the accelerator by a fraction of an inch. 'Now will you explain?'

'When I mentioned the Aldriches lived in Scotland, Celia dismissed that completely. She maintained everyone assumed that because her husband was Scottish.'

'Did she know where they went?' Hannah hoped it wasn't far. She didn't relish another trip out into the country on unmade roads.

'Naturally. Celia keeps tabs on everybody.' Aunt Violet delved into her bag and withdrew a used envelope with something scrawled on it. 'Celia says they went to live in Putney after Benjamin died.'

'Putney? That's not far at all. What is it, seven miles from here?'

'Well done, darling. That's almost spot on.'

'I can see your consumption of alcohol hasn't affected your penchant for sarcasm.' Hannah swung the motor car wide to overtake a tradesman's cart, smiling when Aunt Violet groaned and brought a hand to her forehead.

* * *

Howards Lane, a pedestrian side street off Lacy Road in Putney, was built in the middle of the last century. It was an area once filled with market gardens where the houses were primarily inhabited by shop workers, bank clerks and small business owners experiencing moderate poverty due to the war but were better off than many.

The substantial red brick Victorian villas sat shoulder to shoulder, each with square bay windows, the paintwork freshly painted, and featured heavy oak doors with a stained-glass panel at eye level.

'Perhaps no one is in?' Aunt Violet asked when Hannah's knock was left unanswered after a full minute.

Hannah stepped back onto the path, her neck craned to examine the upper windows. 'Someone is there – I can see a face behind the voile curtains.'

'Don't stare, Hannah. She might see you. Try again.'

Hannah hesitated. 'It feels rude and aggressive to knock twice. After all, we don't know her.'

'*You* don't. And don't be silly, I— Wait, I hear footsteps.'

The door was opened tentatively by a woman of about Aunt Violet's age, but for whom time had not been so kind. Deep wrinkles encased hazel eyes that must once have been pretty and still held a sparkle. Her complexion was clear but looked dull, and she possessed the round figure and thickened waist which her aunt had somehow escaped.

'May I help you?' she asked. Her voice, both clear and high, was in stark contrast to her appearance, but her expression was open without suspicion.

'Surely I haven't changed that much,' Aunt Violet replied with slightly false laughter. 'I know it's been years, but—'

'Violet?' The lady's jaw sagged, which did little to improve her looks. 'Violet Edwards, is that you? Well, you took your time looking me up.'

'Still the same, Louise, straightforward as ever.' Aunt Violet laughingly presented Hannah. 'You remember my sister, Madeleine? Well, this is her younger daughter, Hannah.' Without waiting for a response, she rushed on. 'Don't keep an old friend on the doorstep when we've come all this way.' Though this was hardly accurate as the distance was less than four miles and had taken a mere half hour.

Aunt Violet marched past her into the entrance hall, almost dragging Hannah behind her. 'I don't mind if your maid hasn't cleaned up today, I'm not fussy.'

'It's not that, but I—' Louise hesitated, then seemed to make up her mind and relaxed. Mrs Aldrich stepped back, throwing a nervous look behind her which seemed odd as she was clearly alone. 'As you're here, you might as well come in.'

Hannah and Aunt Violet were showed into a neat parlour at the rear of the house, decorated with floral wallpaper in hyacinth blue and pale grey; a marked and surprising contrast to the homes Hannah had visited where brown furniture and cabbage-green fabrics predominated.

Having invited them into the cramped but homely parlour, their hostess gestured for them to sit in the mismatched but comfortable chairs around a Morris-tiled fireplace, empty of coal.

As Mrs Aldrich took her seat in an upright, if faded velvet upholstered chair, her air of clueless confusion disappeared, her eyes sharpening as they settled on each of them. 'Now, I doubt this is a casual visit, Violet.' Her spine straightened and she clasped her hands in her lap. 'You were always a lady with a purpose.'

'Then we won't waste your time.' Aunt Violet inclined her

head in respectful acknowledgement. 'We came about your nephew, Julian.'

'You know he's dead?' she replied dully, a flash of pain entering her eyes.

'We do,' Hannah said. 'I assume the police told you what happened?'

'Actually, no.' Louise stared past Hannah to the pretty rear garden beyond the window. 'His murder was reported in the *Hammersmith and Fulham Chronicle*. I contacted the bishop to ask if it were true, which was rather silly of me as it was all there in black and white. He replied with his condolences and sent me details of the funeral. Is that why you came, because you saw it in the papers? Though I'm surprised his name would mean anything to you after all this time.'

'No.' Aunt Violet launched into an explanation of the circumstances of finding Julian's body in the mausoleum of St Nicholas's church where Hannah was married last Saturday.

'Julian married you? How lovely.' Her gaze went to Hannah, and she smiled, but it faded quickly. 'Wait, Saturday that was when—' Her face paled.

'It was, but he wasn't discovered until afterwards. Which is why Aunt Violet and I were involved.'

'Louise,' Aunt Violet began carefully. 'Did you know Julian was married?'

'Married? No.' She frowned. 'Was it that girl, Esme? I knew they were close at one time, so it shouldn't be a surprise. But it's odd that he didn't tell me.' Implying Julian and his aunt were still in touch after the Aldriches left Oxford when everyone they spoke to said this wasn't the case.

'It wasn't Esme Toliver.' Hannah exchanged a look with Aunt Violet. 'Julian eloped with Frances Blackwood.'

'Frances?' Louise gasped. 'Arthur Blackwood's girl? Well, I never.'

'Louise, if you didn't know about Frances,' Aunt Violet began, 'who did you imagine was arranging the funeral?'

'I... I suppose I assumed the Church had taken care of it.' She looked nonplussed as if this had not occurred to her. 'When the bishop said he would forward the details to me, I assumed—' She rose and slid open a drawer in a bureau and withdrew a handkerchief, where several more had been neatly folded. 'I don't understand. Hearing he was murdered was devastating enough, and now you say he was married.' She swung round to face them. 'Frances didn't do it, did she? She didn't kill Julian. Is that what you came to tell me?'

'No.' Hannah shook her head and exchanged a loaded look with her aunt, who responded with an affirmative nod.

'I don't understand.' Louise flapped the unused handkerchief. 'Not when I read it in the newspaper and not now. Who would want to kill Julian? He didn't have an enemy in the world.'

'The police are doing all they can to find the culprit, but it's proved a difficult question,' Aunt Violet said. 'Have you spoken to the police? I'm sure it's only a formality, but they always interview everyone who knew the deceased.'

Louise nodded. 'The same day I received details of the funeral. A local constable came and asked me a few questions, but I couldn't tell him much. I've only seen Julian a handful of times since we left Oxford. The last time being Hugh's funeral.'

'Professor Blackwood told us about the accident where your son, Benjamin, drowned.' Aunt Violet softened her voice to show sympathetic understanding.

'You've spoken to Arthur?' Louise paled, then her expression cleared. 'Goodness, I haven't seen him since the inquest.'

'That must have been such a hard time for you,' Hannah said.

'The worst in my life.' She straightened, her chin lifting as if she had to brace herself against the arrival of bad memories. 'I cannot believe it's been two years, when every second of that afternoon is as clear in my mind as if it happened yesterday.'

'I had no idea you had lost Hugh.' A frown of annoyance crossed Violet's face, probably towards Celia for not having included it in the gossip. Or had last night's champagne wiped that from her friend's mind?

'Anyway.' Aunt Violet schooled her face into gentility. 'It's so nice to see you after all these years, Louise, despite the circumstances.'

This comment elicited no more than a vague smile from Louise, who asked, 'What-what did Professor Blackwood tell you?'

'About what happened on that day, and that he didn't know his daughter and Julian had married. It came as a surprise to him too.'

'I imagine it would.' Varying emotions crossed her face which Hannah found difficult to identify. Was she resentful, troubled or simply resigned? 'Frances,' she murmured to herself. 'I had no idea he knew her that well.'

'What would you have said if you had known about Frances?' Aunt Violet asked, apparently the same thought having occurred to her.

'What a strange question.' Louise bridled slightly, her knuckles whitening as she tightened her grip on the chair arms. 'Why wouldn't I be glad he had chosen a wife? All clergymen need a supportive spouse to help with their parochial work. I didn't expect it to be her, though. She seemed young and rather immature. Poor child,' she said vaguely, her gaze drifting again to the window. 'It must have been a terrible shock for her.'

'I cannot imagine what losing a child and then a husband

must have been like for you, Louise,' Aunt Violet said. 'Now Julian too, who was clearly more like a son than a nephew.'

She nodded, her eyes distant, as if sorting through her memories. 'Julian was six when his parents died of tuberculosis within weeks of each other. Hugh and I came to Oxford to help them until they recovered, but they never did. Naturally, we took Julian in. Benjamin was only a baby, so they grew up as brothers.'

'Do you get back to Oxford often?' Hannah asked. Though according to Professor Blackwood, neither Louise nor Hugh had been near their son's grave since the accident.

'Er, not really. Seeing Benji's name on a gravestone upsets me. I prefer to imagine my boy has simply gone away for a while. I know it's silly, but it helps me cope.'

'It must have been hard for Julian too – losing Benjamin?'

'He jumped into the water after him, you know? He did his best, but by the time he dragged him out it was too late. If he had been with them or got there a couple of minutes earlier, he might —' She released a ragged breath, her lips clamped together. 'Julian was so upset. It was soon after that he decided to go into the Church. Hugh told him not to feel guilty as it wasn't his fault, but he was determined.'

'Were Julian and Benjamin close?' Hannah asked.

'There was the age gap, which meant they shared few interests. Julian never had much time for Benji once he started studying at the university.'

'They didn't get on?' Hannah persisted.

'I don't mean it like that. Only... Well, I think he was jealous. That's what Hugh said. He always told me not to favour Benjamin, but how could I not? He was my son and Julian was our nephew.' She gave a small start. 'It's not that I didn't love Julian. I did, but he was... different. He preferred to spend time alone and kept his thoughts to himself. Not like my Benji, who was always ready with a smile, a prank or a tall tale to tell. Perhaps Julian took more after his father, my brother-in-law, who was a stern, silent man.' She placed her crumpled handkerchief on the table in front of her like a silent announcement. 'But that's enough sad talk. I want to hear what you've been doing all these years, Violet. I doubt you're still carrying banners and breaking windows in Downing Street. Though I'm surprised you never married. You had a veritable entourage of eager young men after you in those days.'

'She still does,' Hannah couldn't resist adding, earning a critical look from her aunt.

Aunt Violet then launched into a catalogue of 'do you remembers,' which Louise responded to with wry smiles that suggested the younger Limmy Hobson was very much on the fringes of the various japes her aunt and her friends got up to.

With Louise's attention exclusively directed at Aunt Violet, Hannah wandered to the bay window that overlooked the rear garden. She looked out on to a patch of lawn surrounded by swathes of shrubs and flowerbeds, where all colours of blooms jostled side by side with no space in between. A tiny paved area at the far end was surrounded by a curved pergola, from which hanging fronds swayed gently over a table and chairs in the brightest spot. It made Hannah smile.

'I'm sorry, my dear, am I being tedious?' Louise's voice caught Hannah mid-thought as she tried to identify as many flowers as she could.

'No, of course not.' She turned to face the two women. 'I was just admiring your garden. It's truly lovely.'

'Thank you. I've been working on it these last two years. It gave me something to focus on after—'

'Of course, I understand perfectly.' Hannah cocked her chin at the door as a signal to Aunt Violet that it was time to go. 'We apologise for intruding on your grief. I assume we'll see you at Julian's funeral?'

'Of course, and I'm dreading it.' She brought a handkerchief up to her nose and blew noisily. 'But I owe it to him to be there. He might not have thought of me as such, but I always saw him as my child.'

20

Hannah arrived home late after her trip to Putney to find Darius had kept his promise to be home for dinner. However, she had been so distracted, she had not arranged the meal in advance with the cook.

'Cook loves to have free rein over the kitchen,' Darius replied, with no sign he cared about her failures as a housewife at all. 'And these pork chops are superb, so I have no complaints. It's Travis you'll need to pacify, as he's a stickler for the lady of the house being in charge.' He popped the last bite of a bread roll into his mouth and chewed. 'What have you and Aunt Violet been up to recently?'

'Oh, you know what us underemployed ladies are like: all gossip, shopping and tea parties.'

'And you expect me to believe that?' He chuckled. 'I'm no expert on ladies' matters, but I guess whatever occupied your time relates to the reverend's murder?'

'We haven't solved it, if that's what you're asking, which is quite frustrating. Anyway, I've hardly seen you for the last two nights, so I have plenty to tell you.' Without waiting to see if he wished to hear it, she rushed on, 'First, Aunt Violet took me to see an old acquaintance of hers.' She launched into an account of her visit to Jonny Cadogan-Blair and how subdued her aunt was during the journey home. 'She barely said a word, and that's not like her.'

'Mustard gas is a hellish thing. I hate that we have resorted to using it.' Darius nodded, placed his cutlery in a straight line on his empty plate, and tossed his napkin onto the table. 'I doubt that it took all day. So what else have you been up to?'

'Since you ask, Aunt Violet discovered where Julian Aldrich's aunt lives.'

'Didn't you already know that? Scotland, wasn't it? I cannot imagine you've been there and back in one day.'

'Misinformation, apparently. She lives in Putney. She's widowed now and quite a sad lady, but then she's lost her son, husband and now her nephew in the space of three years. No one deserves tragedy like that.'

'Poor woman. I assume you didn't have to deliver the news of this latest death?'

'No. She saw it reported in the *Fulham and Hammersmith Chronicle,* so she already knew.'

'I meant to mention it, but I spoke to Aidan today,' Darius said when the conversation stalled. 'He's almost office-bound, so was pleased to hear from me. I invited him to stop by for a post-prandial drink this evening. Depending on how his mother is, naturally.'

'Heavens, I almost forgot about his mother. How is she?'

Hannah had contemplated visiting Mrs Farrell, but since Endell Street cancelled visiting hours, she'd assumed all hospitals had done the same.

'He visited her at the hospital this afternoon.' He rose from the table and strolled to the sideboard where he poured a cup of coffee from the tray, a second cup held up in invitation. Hannah nodded acceptance and he poured another before returning to the table, placed it in front of her and resumed his seat.

'He said little, but I could tell he's worried. The doctors are hopeful, but she isn't rallying as quickly as they expected.'

'Well, she's in her late sixties. The influenza must have taken it out of her.'

'He says she's very weak but still alert and keeps questioning him about the hotel. Barks orders like a sergeant major, apparently, but in a much softer voice.'

'Did Aidan say anything about the case?' Hannah stirred milk into her cup. 'There are so few suspects, and DI Wilson has nowhere else to look. He's not as intuitive as Aidan and might focus on the most obvious.'

'What do they say? The spouse is always the first suspect?' Darius said. 'If so, she's not the first attractive woman to have turned to murder to solve her problems.'

'I know.' Hannah peered at him over her cup. 'You were engaged to a murderess once, remember?'

Travis, who had slipped into the room on silent feet to clear the table, froze in place, a plate in each hand. 'Will that be all, sir?' His eyes flickered nervously between them.

'Yes, thank you, Travis. We'll serve ourselves with drinks.' Darius kept his bemused gaze fixed on Hannah as he spoke.

'Oh dear,' Hannah said when he withdrew. 'Another black mark against me.'

'He's heard worse.' Darius scraped back his chair and rose. 'Care to join me for a brandy?'

'I would, but I'd rather wait for Aidan to get here, as more than one will make me decidedly squiffy.' She wondered if Aunt Violet had recovered from her hangover and would be coming with him.

'Would it be ungentlemanly of me to say I would like to see that?'

'Another time, perhaps. We must attend a funeral tomorrow.' She glanced up at him as a thought struck her. 'You are coming, aren't you? We didn't know the reverend well, but I feel I owe it to Frances.'

'Don't worry. No one questions a request for time off for funerals these days, so I'll be there. You never know, there might be a dramatic confession over the gravesite.'

'I wish you hadn't said that.'

Just then, the doorbell sounded, followed by Travis's rhythmic click of heels on the hall tiles. They both fell silent in readiness to welcome their guest.

* * *

'Is Aunt Violet not with you?' Hannah asked when Travis showed Aidan in, alone.

'Hmm.' Aidan dragged out the sound. 'She's fragile this evening so turned me down, saying she's going to have an early night. Where on earth did the pair of you go last night, or did you make another trip to Oxford?'

'My aunt's social life has nothing to do with me. Not on this occasion, anyway.' Hannah's cheeks warmed as Darius led the way into the sitting room.

Goodness, had he had them followed?

'I could do with this.' Aidan sighed appreciatively when Darius returned from the sideboard with two glasses of brandy, settling on a sofa opposite the one Hannah and Darius occupied.

'I probably shouldn't ask,' Hannah began. 'How is the case progressing?'

'There are several current files on my desk right now, but I assume you mean the Aldrich murder?' He took a restrained sip from his glass before continuing. 'DI Wilson thinks he's made a case against Professor Blackwood.' He picked a copy of Edith Wharton's *Summer* from a table at his elbow that Hannah had brought home from the bookshop to read.

'Aidan, I don't think that's your sort of book.' Hannah accepted the glass Darius handed her without looking at it. 'Unless you are interested in the New York elite and the limitations placed on women in a patriarchal society.'

'No? Ah well, you could be right.' He snapped the volume shut and replaced it. 'I'll leave that one for Vi.'

'You were saying?' she prompted.

'What? Oh yes. Records at the Gore Hotel show he booked in on Friday morning and asked the porter to take his luggage to his room before hailing a hackney as a matter of urgency and left.'

Hannah frowned. 'When I drove Frances to the hotel on Saturday afternoon, he gave the impression he had only just arrived.'

'Exactly.' Aidan tilted his glass at her. 'Which isn't exactly lying, but the result is the same. Wilson accepted his word he arrived the day after, but he should have checked. My rule to repeat witness interviews paid off in this case. He won't make that mistake again.'

'It sounds circumstantial,' Darius observed, 'but might stand up in court.'

'That's what I'm banking on.' Aidan leaned forward and rested his forearms on his knees, cradling the empty glass between his hands. 'Besides, we cannot find anyone else who benefits from Julian Aldrich's death.'

'The professor didn't seem capable of murder to me,' Hannah said, but was in no position to correct the police if they believed him guilty.

'Murderers rarely do.' Aidan grimaced. 'And protective fathers can be surprisingly ruthless.'

'You don't seem very pleased, Aidan.' Hannah placed her untouched drink on the table in front of her. 'You're usually more enthusiastic about having a villain in your sights.'

'That obvious, is it?' Aidan sighed. 'I intend going over the evidence again in case we've missed something. Perhaps I was mistaken to leave this case to an inexperienced man like Wilson, but I seem to have lost my drive to pursue villains lately. Attending crime scenes and questioning witnesses always enthused me, but these days I sit behind a desk half the day and attend meetings the other.'

'That's not like you, Aidan.' Darius crossed one ankle over the other, his glass held high so he could release his trapped jacket flap from beneath him. 'Surely there's satisfaction in seeing your team succeed?'

'Not as much as I imagined it would.' He took a large mouthful of his drink, sighing with pleasure as it went down. 'I had my eye on that friend of Mrs Frances Aldrich, but DI Wilson excluded her.'

'If you're referring to Esme Toliver, I doubt she's a serious candidate,' agreed Hannah, even though she had toyed with the idea herself at one point. 'She was working at Somerville for part of the day. I doubt she had time to get to London and back without it being noticed—' She inwardly groaned as she realised what she had said.

He looked up sharply, an eyebrow raised in her direction. 'Information you could only have received if you had spoken to her. In case you're wondering, I know all about your visit to Oxford.'

Hannah gave an embarrassed shrug, but instead of his customary lecture about meddling, he waved her away.

'Are you planning to arrest the professor?' Hannah remained uneasy at the way this was going. That Frances's father had been less than candid about when he arrived in London was interesting, but did that make him the murderer?

'That triumph will be Inspector Wilson's, as this is technically his case. Best keep it quiet until then. Don't want the man to bolt, do we?' His uncompromising stare told her he expected her to respect his decision.

She nodded, still troubled, then remembered her manners. 'Aidan, I'm so sorry. I haven't asked how your mother is.'

'Not good, I'm afraid.' Aidan rubbed the back of his neck and studied the floor. 'She hasn't rallied at all. It's all rather disconcerting, as I cannot remember her ever being ill.'

Hannah did not know what to say that wasn't trite or dismissive, and opted for a sympathetic smile.

21

Darius halted the Daimler outside St Nicholas Church and turned to talk to Hannah while he left the engine ticking over. 'I'll park in the mews and see you inside.'

'I cannot help thinking that by attending a funeral here a week after our wedding will spoil our memories of the day,' Hannah said, not moving from the passenger seat.

'If finding a body here hasn't done that already, then today certainly won't.' He leaned across and squeezed her hand reassuringly. 'That church has witnessed every human happiness and tragedy over the years. Our wedding was a good memory and will join the countless others absorbed into the church's stone walls. No one can ruin that.'

'How did I find a husband as clear-headed as you?' Hannah released a sigh, and with it all her former worries dissipated.

'Funny, when I thought *I* was the winner in this marriage.' He planted a lingering kiss on her cheek. 'I imagine the entire congregation will make the effort to attend the occasion. It's seldom a minister gets murdered. There might be standing room only, so you go and secure some seats and once I have parked the motor car, I'll join you.'

Easing from the seat onto the path, she closed the door and waved him off from beneath the lych-gate before making her way along the path towards the church. She felt self-conscious in her black silk mourning dress, handmade for her grandmother's funeral five years before, and the same one she had worn for Lily-Anne's funeral.

Inside the coolness of the church, her footsteps barely made a sound on the stone floor, a habit ingrained in her by a pious nanny. Immediately she was assailed by the smells of childhood Sundays – a mixture of beeswax polish, damp stone and decaying flowers.

It seemed almost the entire parish had turned out to see their minister buried, but whether from respect or morbid curiosity over the circumstances of his death was uncertain.

Making her way to the front, Hannah found herself behind a group of young women, whose ages ranged from late teens to about thirty, huddled together in grief with crumpled handkerchiefs held to their faces. Were they the reverend's admirers who the housekeeper had mentioned?

She spotted Frances and Esme in a front pew and was about to approach them when Professor Blackwood arrived with Louise Aldrich on his arm. Hannah almost didn't recognise her in a layered gown in unrelieved black, topped with a wide-brimmed matching hat and a veil that obscured the top half of her face.

Professor Blackwood was wearing a charcoal-grey suit and black tie with a matching armband around his upper right arm. He handed Louise into the pew behind his daughter before joining her. Louise bent her head and leaned a hand on the back of the pew where the girls sat and whispered something to Frances, then touched Esme's shoulder.

Frances's face when she turned to acknowledge her father looked drawn and very young-looking beneath her hat and veil.

As Hannah debated whether to approach them to offer her condolences, or wait until after the service, she wondered if Professor Blackwood had accompanied Louise from Putney, or had they renewed their former acquaintance in the churchyard? With no time to think further about it, the sudden appearance of Mrs Berry distracted her.

'It's kind of you to attend Reverend's burial, Mrs Clifford. Especially when his passing almost ruined your lovely wedding.'

Hannah hated the word 'passing'. Why not simply 'death', which felt more natural? Although in the reverend's case, his dying had been anything but.

'Thank you, Mrs Berry,' she replied with more confidence following Darius's words in the motor car. 'I assure you, nothing was spoiled, and my husband will join me presently.' Her attention remained on the group in the front pew, so she didn't catch what the housekeeper said next until the woman's impatient tone penetrated her thoughts.

'What was that you said, Mrs Berry?' Hannah blinked, frowning.

The housekeeper raised her voice slightly as if peeved she had to repeat herself. 'I said, how nice to see your mother has also made an effort to attend.'

'You must be mistaken,' Hannah replied, puzzled. 'My mother isn't here.'

'Yes, she is. She's that lady sitting with that professor chap,' Mrs Berry said confidently. 'I recognised her straight away. She helped with the church flowers at your wedding.'

Hannah was about to correct her, but the housekeeper had already turned away.

Urgency propelled Hannah back to the porch where she

found Darius talking to Cavan on the church steps. He looked up when he saw her and smiled.

'Cavan was kind enough to move his carriage so I could put the Daimler in the mews,' he said with a grin, a hand extended to shake the doctor's hand.

'You're welcome, Darius,' Cavan replied, turning to take Hannah's hand. 'Good morning, Hannah. It's a day for sad memories, eh? Now, if you'll excuse me, I must pay my respects to the family.' He saluted each of them before strolling away.

Hannah watched him go sadly. The last time they had been at a funeral together was that of his wife, Lily-Anne.

'Looks crowded in there.' Darius looked past her into the packed church and rubbed his hands together. 'Did you get a seat?'

'I haven't tried, to be honest. I've just had the most peculiar conversation with the housekeeper.'

'Look out!' Taking her elbow, Darius steered her aside as two matrons swept into the porch and passed them into the nave on a rustle of black taffeta.

'Who are they?' Darius whispered.

'I don't recognise them, although I'm hardly likely to know everyone in the village,' Hannah replied. 'Professional funeral attendees attracted by the murder, possibly. I believe most parishes have them.'

Darius chuckled and slipped an arm around her waist. 'Now, what were you saying about a housekeeper?'

'Mrs Berry,' Hannah repeated with emphasis. 'She just said—' She broke off at the sound of rapid hoofbeats of a hackney on the road, accompanied by a commanding male voice as the contraption came to an abrupt halt at the lych-gate. The carriage door was flung open and Matilda Gilmartin jumped down onto the road, handing the fare to the driver before bounding towards them.

'Matilda, what are you doing here?' Hannah stared at her. 'If you're hoping to get a story, this is hardly the time.'

'Miss Gilmartin, what an unexpected pleasure.' Darius greeted her with an outstretched hand, showing more grace than Hannah had given her. 'I don't believe we've met.'

'Oh, er, no. We haven't. And it's very nice to meet you, Mr Clifford.' Matilda shook Darius's hand with a self-conscious smile Hannah had never seen before. She might even have been blushing.

Hannah fretted, wishing the journalist would explain as they needed to get into the church or the ceremony would begin without them.

'I'm sorry I didn't call, but I had no time,' Matilda gushed, a hand pressed against her midriff as she tried to slow her breathing. 'Listen. I noticed one of those clippings I brought was missing and thought I must have left it somewhere, so I went back to the archives again—'

'I'm really sorry about that,' Hannah interrupted her, guilt-ridden. 'Aunt Violet, er, borrowed it. But I'll get it back to you, I promise.'

'That's not important!' Matilda hefted her bag to her waist and delved inside. 'I found something you ought to see.' She pulled out a clipping and held it out.

'What is it?' Hannah rapidly scanned a photograph similar to the others she had unearthed: a group of smiling young people gathered outside the Savoy Hotel in Piccadilly.

'Who are these other people? I don't recognise any of them,' Darius asked, peering over her shoulder.

'That's Lydia, Frances's mother.' Hannah tapped the photograph with a finger. 'This man looks like a younger version of

Professor Blackwood. But I don't know the other couple. I cannot see the woman's face properly. She must have turned her head away just as the shutter clicked.'

'It was taken about two years after Blackwood and Lydia were married,' Matilda said, still slightly breathless. 'Do you notice how Blackwood is not looking at the camera, but at the woman behind him with the other man?' She tapped the page hard with a finger. 'Read the caption.'

Scanning the small print, Hannah read aloud. 'Mr Arthur Blackwood with Mrs Lydia Blackwood, at a celebration for the...' She glossed over the next part and went to the names at the end '...in the company of Mr and Mrs— Oh!'

'What is it?' Darius split an enquiring look between them.

'I'll tell you later.' Hannah thrust the page into her bag. 'Where's Aidan?'

'Was my name mentioned?' Aidan's spoke from behind her.

Hannah swung around to where he stood with Aunt Violet and DI Wilson. There was no sign of any uniformed officers who would be necessary for an arrest, but she had no time to worry about that just then.

Aunt Violet bussed both her niece's cheeks while Aidan gave Matilda a suspicious look.

'Miss Gilmartin.' He acknowledged her with a curt nod.

'You don't have to glare at her,' Hannah said under her breath. 'Matilda isn't here to cause trouble. In fact, she has some interesting information for you.'

'Although that's not totally out of the question, either,' Matilda said, returning his critical look with defiance, her chin raised.

Hannah rolled her eyes. 'Are your officers inside the church?'

'They're close by.' Aidan shoved both hands into his pockets and rocked on the balls of his feet. 'I don't want to spook the professor. Can't have him making a run for it.'

'It's not him you need to worry about.' Hannah handed him the clipping.

'What's this?' He gave Matilda another hard look before accepting it.

'Miss Gilmartin brought it from her newspaper office. You need to see it.'

'Well, well.' Aidan's eyes glinted. 'It appears we've been on the wrong track. Vi, take a look at this, would you?'

Frowning, Aunt Violet scanned the page over his shoulder. 'I should have known.' She exhaled through pursed lips. 'Well spotted, Hannah.'

'It wasn't me. Matilda found it.' Hannah nodded to where the journalist preened beside Aidan, who was doing his best to ignore her.

'Where is this lady now?' Aidan asked.

'In the front pew with Professor Blackwood, Frances and Miss Toliver,' Hannah said.

Aidan nodded. 'Then let's keep that to ourselves for the time being.' He handed the newspaper clipping over his shoulder to Inspector Wilson.

'What am I looking at, sir?' DI Wilson peered at it.

'Did you take all the names of everyone who was at the church in the three hours before the Clifford wedding?'

'Er, yes, sir. It was a short list.' Inspector Wilson tugged his notebook from his pocket and flicked through the pages. 'Here it is, sir. Apart from the housekeeper, the gardener, Miss Wells and Miss Moffatt, there were only the ladies who arranged the flowers who all vouched for each other. The only other person present that morning was the bride's mother, Mrs Merrill. I assumed—'

'Never assume, Wilson.' Aidan interrupted him. 'Aren't I always saying, corroboration is the key?'

'You are, sir, but I fail to understand why an additional flower arranger is relevant, sir.' His face turned a deeper pink. 'I'm still of the opinion Professor Blackwood is our best bet.'

'Let's not do anything for the moment.' Aidan folded the page and slid it into an inside pocket. 'We'll move once the leading mourners have gathered at the vicarage for sherry.'

'Yes, sir.' DI Wilson retreated, followed by Aidan, leaving Hannah with Darius, Matilda and Aunt Violet inside the porch.

Hannah watched him go, thoughtful. Did he expect the woman to bolt? If she was going to do that, then why come to the funeral at all and risk being exposed? 'What do we do now?' she asked no one in particular.

'What we came for,' Aunt Violet said. 'Attend a funeral.'

'I'm still in a fug, but I assume you both know who the murderer is?' Darius asked.

'We do,' Aunt Violet said. 'And well done, Hannah, for getting there first. You and Miss Gilmartin have been busy.' She turned an enquiring look on Matilda. 'Will you be joining us? I'm sure you'd like to see this to the end.'

'I'm hardly dressed for a funeral!' Matilda issued a deprecating laugh and glanced down at her navy-blue skirt topped with a crisp white blouse and matching straw hat.

'Sit between us at the back,' Aunt Violet said. 'I doubt anyone will notice. They'll be too busy staring at DI Wilson trying to hide behind a pillar.'

They hurried to find seats as the organ burst into life with the opening chords of *My God, my Father*.

The Archdeacon of Middlesex conducted the committal service and delivered a moving sermon, emphasising the regrettable loss of a young man, orphaned early, who had been robbed of his full potential, which left several elderly ladies in tears. Hannah couldn't see Frances's face from the back pew where they sat, but her permanently bowed head clearly showed her deep distress.

At the last notes of the final hymn faded into silence and hymn books thudded onto the pews, and as the congregation shuffled to its feet and joined the procession into the churchyard, the round notes of the church clock struck the hour.

22

After the interment was over, most of the villagers drifted away from the graveside back to their own homes, leaving only a handful of family and acquaintances in the vicarage sitting room, where a footman, co-opted from Cavan's staff, handed out miniscule glasses of sherry at the door.

Aidan entered last and glared at the three policemen, each of whom had claimed a glass, and confiscated them with a stern, 'You lot are supposed to be working.'

Frances and Esme stood together by the French windows with Louise Aldrich, their combined focus trained on the garden while clutching glasses of sherry they had yet to taste. Professor Blackwood stood beside the wooden fireplace, one foot raised on the fender, staring into the empty grate.

'He looks very calm.' Hannah tried not to stare. 'Do you think he knows that less than an hour ago he was the chief suspect?'

'Who knows?' Aunt Violet replied in an undertone. 'I'd still like to know what he was doing on Saturday morning, if not murdering Julian Aldrich?' She raised an enquiring eyebrow at

Aidan, who placed his half-drunk sherry on the mantel, tugged down his waistcoat and strode towards the three women.

'Mrs Aldrich,' Aidan began. 'I should like to offer my condolences on the loss of your nephew. However, may I ask you a few questions about the death of Julian Aldrich and when you saw him last?'

'Is this really the time and place, Chief Inspector?' Professor Blackwood intercepted him. 'Can you not show respect for a grieving lady?'

'I understand, Professor,' Aidan replied calmly. 'However, this is a police matter.'

'Even so, you cannot seriously—' Professor Blackwood's face suffused with red, but Louise raised a hand, silencing him.

'Arthur, let me handle this.' She rose to her full height. 'Chief Inspector Farrell, is it?' she asked, regarding him steadily. 'What do you wish to ask me?'

'Louise, you don't have to say anything!' Professor Blackwood threw her a pleading look to which she responded with a dismissive shake of her head.

'When my colleague interviewed you recently,' he indicated DI Wilson, who nodded. 'You said you were not in touch with your nephew, Julian Aldrich.'

'Ah yes, I remember. There wasn't much I could tell him, I'm afraid. I haven't seen Julian in over two years. He did not attend my husband's funeral last year, although he sent flowers.'

'That's not what she told us,' Hannah whispered to her aunt. 'She said—'

'Hush!' Aunt Violet placed a hand on her arm.

'That's not quite true, though, is it, Mrs Aldrich?' Aidan said pointedly.

The tension in the room stretched as they waited for her

response, the only sounds that of a door closing somewhere and the clearing of a throat.

Louise looked as if she was about to offer a denial, but in the face of Aidan's calm expression, she changed her mind. 'As you already know the answer to that question, I wonder why you bothered asking it.'

Professor Blackwood stepped between them. 'Louise, I wouldn't advise—'

'It's too late, Arthur.' She cut across him and kept her attention on Aidan. 'I'll make it easy for you, Chief Inspector. I saw my nephew, Julian on the fourth of May.'

'Did she just admit it?' Hannah gasped.

'Looks like it.' Aunt Violet nodded.

'What are you saying, Mrs Aldrich?' Frances eased closer and laid a hand on her forearm. 'How could you have seen Julian that day?'

'It's all right, dear.' Louise patted Frances's hand. 'I know what I'm doing.'

'Mrs Aldrich, is this a confession?' Aidan cautioned. 'Because if so, I feel I ought to warn you, it's unwise to incriminate yourself.'

'I suppose it is.' She made a dismissive sound in her throat. 'But I feel sure everyone here is eager to hear what I have to say.'

'Well, *I* certainly am,' DI Wilson muttered under his breath, tugging his notebook from a pocket.

'And me,' Matilda added, her pencil poised over her ubiquitous notebook, which was considerably larger than the policeman's.

'I knew Julian better than anyone,' Mrs Aldrich began. 'No one will convince me he tried hard enough to locate Benji in the river that day. He was a strong swimmer so could easily have pulled him out. Instead, he let my Benji die.'

'That's not true!' Frances interjected, staring first at her father, and then Louise.

'Is that why you murdered your nephew, Mrs Aldrich?' Aidan said gently. 'Because you believe he killed your son?'

'I do!' Louise's lower lip trembled slightly. 'I put Benji's behaviour, his jealousy, down to boyish high spirits, which, with hindsight, was possibly poor judgement on my part. I accept that Benji made Julian's life more difficult than necessary, but I loved Benji. How could I not? He was my son.' She lifted her black-clad shoulders in resignation, as if a plea for understanding.

'I cannot believe you felt that way!' Frances stared at her with a horrified gaze. 'Not being able to save him devastated Julian.'

'Have you forgotten?' Louise turned on Frances, her face twisted with fury. 'Benji shouldn't have goaded him that day, but when Julian hit him, he struck his head on that tree trunk. Julian knew he was injured but he still let him drown,' Louise spat.

'He was stunned, true, but only for a moment.' Frances frowned as if trying to remember. 'Julian didn't really hurt him. And it had rained heavily during the previous days; the river was swollen higher than usual. Even so, Julian warned him not to jump but he wouldn't listen!'

'It's natural you would defend him.' Louise snatched her arm from Frances's and turned her head away, as if not seeing her face meant she didn't have to hear anything she didn't want to.

'Frances—' Professor Blackwood wrapped an arm around his daughter's shoulders.

'No!' Frances shrugged him off. 'She's wrong, Papa. The inquest said Benji's injury was from hitting his head on an object in the water when he jumped. It wasn't Julian's fault. Surely, you cannot believe he would let Benji die?'

Hannah took a step closer, ready to comfort her, but Darius's small shake of his head kept her where she was.

'I... I wasn't certain,' Professor Blackwood replied. 'I always thought it odd Benjamin could drown in a river where he had swum since childhood.'

'My husband wouldn't listen either.' Louise snorted dismissively. 'He told me Benji was gone and I must forget it, and after the funeral he insisted we move to my childhood home in Putney.'

'Putney?' Esme spoke for the first time. 'We thought you had gone to Scotland.' Frances frowned, looking to the professor for confirmation.

'Er, no.' Professor Blackwood shook his head. 'I– I said that to comply with Hugh and Louise's wishes to have no contact with anyone they knew in Oxford.'

'Why you, Papa?' Frances demanded. 'Why did they tell you?'

'I think it's time you explained, Arthur.' Louise pressed his arm in a gesture of intimacy developed over time.

Frances apparently saw it too as she glared at each of them in open shock. 'Explain what?' she demanded. 'What's she talking about?'

'We all knew each other when we were young, Frances, dear. Your parents and I were part of a group of close friends who went everywhere together,' Louise said, when the professor seemed unable to form his words.

'You knew my mother?' Frances faltered, hearing this for the first time.

'We did. Lydia was madly in love with Jonny Cadogan-Blair, but when he refused to marry her, she became engaged to dear, patient Arthur.' Louise's bitter laugh as she stared up at him was in contrast to the possessive grip she had on his upper arm. 'He was her Captain Brandon to Lydia's Marianne Dashwood.'

'Louise, please,' the professor snapped, frustrated, refusing to look at her.

Her face softened, as if recalling happier memories. 'We had some happiness of our own, though, didn't we, Arthur? Then, after Benji was born, Hugh's brother became ill, so we went to Oxford to help and stayed there. Hugh never really minded he wasn't his.'

'Papa?' Frances gasped, her eyes widening as she realised what Louise was saying. 'You and Mrs Aldrich?'

'We agreed, Louise. It was over. Forgotten.' Professor Blackwood's face hardened, although Louise's stricken expression told Hannah she had never forgotten it. 'Marriages are often fraught at first, but after you arrived, Frances, everything between your mother and me changed.' He reached for her hand. 'I'll explain everything later, but—'

'No!' She snatched her hand away. 'I don't want to hear it.' Without another word, she shoved past him and made for the door. One of the uniformed officers stepped forward to prevent her, but Aidan gestured to him to stay.

'Let her go.'

'Frances!' the professor called after her as the door banged shut, and with a final, lingering look of contempt at the professor, Esme followed.

No one spoke for a full minute, and silence seemed to expand and fill the room.

Darius grabbed the sherry decanter from the sideboard, poured a large measure into a glass, and carried it across the room, offering it to the professor. He accepted it gratefully, and when Darius led him to a chair, the man did not protest. Once seated, he downed half the glass and sat with his head down, and both hands grasped around the glass.

'I... I didn't always know. About Benjamin.' Professor Blackwood seemed to shrink as all eyes turned towards him. 'It wasn't until after Lydia died, that Louise told me the truth. That's when I applied for the post at Merton, so I could be close to him.'

Aidan thanked him with a slow nod before turning back to Mrs Aldrich.

'Would you care to sit, Mrs Aldrich?' Aidan showed her to an empty chair. 'I feel you have a lot to tell me, so you may as well make yourself comfortable.'

Louise seemed to find this amusing and agreed, sinking onto the squab. 'I suppose you want to know what happened that morning?'

'When you're ready.' Aidan nodded.

For a long moment it looked as if Louise would not answer, but then she inhaled a slow breath and began. 'Julian wrote to me a few weeks ago informing me he and Frances Blackwood were married. That he wanted to put past resentments behind him. He asked for my forgiveness.'

'Forgiveness for what?' Hannah asked impulsively, earning a sharp glance from Aidan.

'Isn't it obvious?' Louise shifted her gaze to Hannah. 'For letting Benji drown when he could have prevented it. What else could he have meant?' Her eyes glinted with anger. 'His ultimate insult was to marry the half-sister of the boy he killed, when my Benji would never have such fortune.'

'But—' Hannah blurted, then bit down on her words when Aidan held up a hand, silencing her.

'Go on, Mrs Aldrich.' Aidan's voice was soft, cajoling.

'That morning at the church, I watched from behind a laurel hedge when Julian came out of the vicarage with the house-keeper. They exchanged a few words, and she left with a large shopping bag. I knew she'd be gone a while; those shop queues are mind-numbing.' Louise rolled her eyes as if in sympathy. 'Julian went across to the church, and I followed. I couldn't find him at first, then I heard him humming and found him in the vestry.'

'Was he surprised to see you?' Aidan asked.

'He was but pleased as well. I hadn't answered his letter, you see. I even brought him a late wedding gift – a pair of crystal sherry glasses etched with his initials. He was delighted with them, and even more so when I produced a bottle of sherry.'

'I assume the bottle contained a tincture of digitalis,' Aidan asked.

A flicker of triumph entered Louise's eyes, but she offered no response.

'Of course!' Hannah blurted in a stage whisper. 'That's why the police couldn't find any digitalis in the teacups. She doctored the sherry.' Then something occurred to her. 'Wait, no one told us Reverend Aldrich drank sherry that morning.'

'And why would they? Now hush!' Aunt Violet flapped an impatient hand at her. 'I want to hear this.'

'I planned to be long gone before he opened the bottle,' Louise went on. 'But Julian insisted we toast his future.'

'Do you know what time this was, Mrs Aldrich?' Aidan asked.

'I'm not sure. After eleven, I think. He said he was due to meet with the groom at noon, which was why he was wearing his vestments.'

'I see.' Aidan nodded at a puzzle solved. 'Julian drank the sherry you gave him. Then what happened?'

'It was extremely good sherry.' Louise levelled her gaze at Aidan, savouring the moment. 'I could have done with a drink myself but didn't dare.' She shrugged lightly. 'Revenge can be wearing, you know. Anyway, Julian said he had forgiven himself for what happened to Benji, and he had found his peace.' She poked a sharp finger at her own chest. 'What about *my* peace?'

'You interpreted his words as a confession rather than regret?' Aidan said.

'What else was I supposed to take from that? I always knew what he did. When Julian started to feel dizzy, and said his vision was blurry, I panicked a little. I didn't expect such a quick reaction and hoped to be long gone before then. I couldn't risk us being found together. Then I saw the tomb through the vestry door. If I could get him inside, it was possible no one would have found him for days, if ever.'

Aidan's jaw tightened. 'How did you plan to do that? The tomb is kept locked.'

'I'm a resourceful woman, Chief Inspector.' She smirked. 'I gambled on the oversized key hanging on the wall having something to do with it. Turns out I was right, so I got the gate unlocked. Julian was barely conscious by then, and I only had to drag him a few paces. I've always been strong, but he was heavier than I expected, and I-I dropped him onto the stone steps inside the fate. He must have hit his head as that's when he stopped moving altogether.' She scowled as if reliving the frustration she felt. 'I had just got the wooden door open when I heard voices.'

Hannah shot a nervous look at Cavan, who occupied an upright chair beside the fireplace. His jaw went rigid, and he gripped his knees with both hands, the knuckles white as he stared at the floor. She wanted to offer sympathy but feared moving would break the spell Louise had spun around them all.

Matilda scribbled furiously in her notebook and murmured something that included the words 'cold-blooded' followed by, 'My boss is going to love this.'

'Go on, Mrs Aldrich,' Aidan prompted, after aiming a hard glance at the journalist, which she ignored.

'I returned to the vestry,' Louise said. 'Put the sherry bottle and glasses into my bag just as a lady came and assumed I was a relative of the bride, so I stayed a while and helped with the flowers. Then when no one was looking, grabbed my bag and left.'

'You left?' Hannah snapped, horrified. 'As Julian lay dying on the mausoleum steps?'

'I told you, I didn't know the drug would affect him so quickly.' Louise bridled, as if this turn of events was not her responsibility.

'Thank you, Mrs Aldrich, I appreciate your candour.' Aidan glanced at DI Wilson, his attention on the notebook in his hand. Once reassured his colleague had recorded everything, he gestured to the other two officers.

'Mrs Aldrich,' Aidan spoke calmly. 'I must inform you that you will be taken to the local police station, and from there, they will remove you to Scotland Yard in the morning to formally charge you.'

'Is that really necessary, Chief Inspector?' Professor Blackwood protested.

'Your best strategy would be to remain silent at this juncture, Professor.' Aidan gestured to the two officers, who needed no instructions about what to do next.

'Arthur,' Louise said gently, 'I appreciate you intervening on my behalf, but I don't need it. I knew exactly what I was doing and have no regrets.' Rising, she smoothed down her full skirt, tweaking each of her gloves into place. 'I'm ready now, Chief Inspector.'

Hannah watched as the older woman was escorted from the room. Flanked by the officers, she seemed diminished somehow, as if all the grief and anger had drained out of her.

Professor Blackwood slammed his now empty glass on the table and leapt up to follow, protesting furiously he would get her the best lawyer he could find, but was blocked by DI Wilson who stood between him and the door.

'Professor Blackwood!' He turned at Aidan's commanding tone. 'I haven't finished with you.' He waited for him to resume his seat, then asked, 'When did you realise Mrs Aldrich had murdered her nephew?'

'I didn't. Not at first.' Professor Blackwood seemed unable to meet Aidan's eye, his gaze going from a painting on the wall then to his feet. 'The day I confronted Frances at the Gore Hotel; she told me about the digitalis. I knew then Louise was involved. Instead of returning to Oxford I went to Louise's home in Putney.' He closed his eyes and swallowed. 'She told me everything. I tried to persuade her not to come today, but she refused. She even seemed proud of what she had done.'

'Sounds like none of his women listen to him,' Aunt Violet said under her breath.

Hannah hushed her but could not prevent a small smile she hid behind her hand.

'Why protect her, Professor, when you risked being suspected yourself?' Aidan asked.

'That possibility occurred to me, yes. You forget, Inspector, I lost my son too, and it was easy to blame it on Julian for not trying hard enough. But I came to realise I was mistaken. However, when Esme Toliver told me he had eloped with Frances, it occurred to me that maybe Louise was right about Julian. Maybe he did kill Benjamin and when everyone expected him to announce his engagement to Esme, he courted Frances. Why else but for her money? Lydia's money.'

No one spoke for a full minute, the air thick with tension broken only by a clearing of a throat and the closing of a door somewhere in the house.

'Don't leave just yet, Professor,' Aidan said finally. 'I'll need a statement from you.'

'I wish to speak to my daughter first.'

'Then I'll ask one of the officers to escort you.'

* * *

Once all the police work was completed, the remains of the funeral party adjourned to Cavan's house across the road where his housekeeper served them all welcome cups of tea.

'It will be a long time before I enjoy a sherry without some unpleasant connotations,' Hannah said from where she and Darius occupied a sofa in Cavan's sitting room.

'A very satisfactory ending, if I may say so, Chief Inspector.' Darius saluted him with his teacup.

'I don't deserve your praise, Clifford,' Aidan muttered. 'I went along with Professor Blackwood being the culprit. Worse, I almost allowed DI Wilson to arrest him and that woman would have gone free.'

'Don't be too hard on yourself,' Hannah pleaded. 'It was only Aunt Violet remembering some gossip from years ago that pointed us in that direction.'

'Even so, I should have asked Wilson to look deeper into this drowning affair.'

'Why would he?' Aunt Violet said from the sofa opposite. 'It was an accident that happened three years ago. I only hope Frances can forgive her father one day.'

'So Hugh Aldrich was a pharmacist?' Darius said when Hannah had told him what she had read on the newspaper clipping that had brought it all together for her. 'Well done for spotting it, darling.' He nudged Hannah gently with an elbow.

'I dread to think what might have happened if Julian had shared that bottle of sherry with someone else. It might have even been Frances!' Hannah rapidly stirred her tea, the spoon clicking the sides until Aunt Violet took it away from her.

'I believe she knew that and changed her mind,' Darius said thoughtfully. 'Which is why she risked staying with him to ensure only he drank it.'

'An interesting perspective, but you are being too generous.' Matilda raised her pencil in the air. 'Didn't you hear her say she only stayed because Julian insisted on a toast? I'm more inclined to believe she wanted to see the results of her careful planning.'

'With a mind like that you ought to join the police force, Miss Gilmartin,' Aidan's slow smile appeared, banishing his former professional detachment.

'Now there's a thought.' Hannah saluted Matilda with her own cup.

Darius slid an arm around Hannah's waist from behind and squeezed, showing he understood what she was feeling. She left it there, taking comfort from his touch.

'I always said poison was a woman's weapon,' Aunt Violet said. 'Women are far less inclined to violence, even in the most drastic circumstances.'

'I'm not sure that's true, Aunt Violet.' Hannah said thoughtfully. 'What about the nurse who shot that soldier at Endell Street Hospital a couple of years ago?'

'Guns don't count.' Aunt Violet sniffed.

'By the way, Aunt Violet, where *were* you last night?' Hannah asked. 'I telephoned you three times, and you didn't return any of my calls. At one stage we even considered a search party.'

Instead of an answer, her aunt levelled an intense look at Aidan. He had his back to them at the open French doors, hands in his pockets and his gaze on the garden where birds flitted between the laurel hedges. After a few seconds, he appeared to have heard her and turned his head to aim a brief but firm nod in her aunt's direction before turning back to his contemplations.

'We spent most of the evening at the hospital.' Aunt Violet placed her cup on a low table and clasped her hands on her knees. 'I'm sad to say that Mrs Farrell died last night.'

A round of low, sympathetic murmurings and gasps of disbelief circled the room.

'Oh, Aidan. I'm so dreadfully sorry.' Hannah's breath hitched, and she chastised herself for being flippant earlier. 'I thought she had rallied and was on the mend.'

'That's what we all thought. Including her doctors.' Aidan sounded neither angry nor bitter, only resigned while accepting heartfelt sympathy from Darius and then Matilda.

'This virus is a strange phenomenon which is spreading fast. A three-day fever not unlike pneumonia and just as unpleasant,' Cavan said, as if addressing a lecture hall. 'Most people would expect to recover, but it's possible your mother had an underlying condition which prevented her from fighting the virus.'

'Thank you for explaining it, Dr Soames, but speculation won't help Mrs Farrell now,' Hannah said, trying not to sound sharp, all the while feeling wretched. Cavan was an excellent doctor, but he could be detached and insensitive at times.

'No, of course not. I'm sorry.' Cavan seemed to realise his faux pas and retreated to the fireplace where he retrieved his sherry.

'What's happening with your mother's hotel?' Darius asked, earning a sharp, 'not now' look from Hannah. It appeared men had few social rules where sudden death and grief were concerned. Or did their upbringing focus on endurance rather than sensibility?

'Limping along with my intermittent help,' Aidan replied calmly. 'But it needs someone at the helm. With Mother gone, I'm torn whether to employ a full-time manager or step in permanently.'

'What do your instincts tell you?' Aunt Violet said, her eyes soft with sympathy, which showed they had already had this conversation.

'That I would let Mother down to consign the business to someone who didn't care about it like she did. She worked for years to bring it up from a boarding house to a first-class establishment that hosts foreign diplomats, members of parliament and even obscure European royalty.'

'You're seriously thinking of leaving the police, then?' Hannah asked, recalling a previous conversation with her aunt.

'If I'm to make an even half respectable job of it, then yes,' Aidan replied with a wry smile. 'She employed twenty-five staff, so there are their livelihoods to consider, and someone needs to keep a tight rein on income and expenditure.' He pushed away from the French doors and came to sit in a chair beside Aunt Violet. 'I think this latest case has shown me it's time to make a change. To focus on the good things life can bring and not the worst of human nature. Louise Aldrich coldly murdered a young man she had raised from infancy in an act of misplaced revenge. And look around us? We are in the middle of the most cataclysmic war we have ever embarked on. It makes me despair for us all.'

'The war won't last forever.' Aunt Violet placed a reassuring hand on his arm. 'We'll get our lives back and we'll need some normality to look forward to. What better than a place of life and laughter to dance the night away?'

'You could be right, and running a hotel might be the making of me, but I cannot do it alone.' He turned a sheepish smile on Aunt Violet. 'What do you say, Vi?'

'I'm not sure what to say.' Aunt Violet's bemused gaze swept the company before settling back on his face. 'Isn't it a little late to try to make me into a respectable woman?'

* * *

MORE FROM ANITA DAVISON

Another book from Anita Davison, *Murder in the Reading Room*, is available to order now here:

https://mybook.to/ReadingRoomBackAd

ACKNOWLEDGEMENTS

I'd like to thank the brilliant team at Boldwood for all the work they have done in bringing this series to life, especially Isobel Akenhead, for her enthusiasm for my characters and her intuitive ironing out of plot holes. To copyeditor, Gary Jukes, and proofreader, Rachel Sargeant, who deserve credit for sorting out my wonky sentence structure. Also, my appreciation goes to the creative team for the stunningly beautiful covers that convey Hannah and her era so accurately. Not forgetting the Marketing and Publicity departments, Marcela Torres, Megan Townsend, Wendy Neale, Ben Wilson, Grace Cooper, Isabelle Flynn.

Special appreciation goes to my agent Kate Nash who took a chance on me at the beginning and continues with her help and encouragement, and to her fabulous team at KNLA. I could not do any of this without you all.

ABOUT THE AUTHOR

Anita Davison is the author of gripping historical cozy mysteries, including the Miss Merrill and Aunt Violet Mysteries.

Download your exclusive bonus content from Anita Davison here:

Visit Anita's website: www.anitadavison.co.uk

Follow Anita on social media here:

facebook.com/anita.davison

x.com/anitasdavison

instagram.com/anitadavison3740

goodreads.com/anitadavison

ALSO BY ANITA DAVISON

Miss Merrill and Aunt Violet Mysteries

Murder in the Bookshop

Murder at Midwinter Manor

Murder in Covent Garden

Murder at the Wedding

Murder in the Reading Room

The Flora Maguire Mysteries

Death On Board

Death at the Abbey

Death of a Suffragette

Death by the Thames

Death on a Train

POISON
& pens

POISON & PENS IS THE HOME OF
COZY MYSTERIES SO POUR YOURSELF
A CUP OF TEA & GET SLEUTHING!

DISCOVER PAGE-TURNING NOVELS FROM
YOUR FAVOURITE AUTHORS &
MEET NEW FRIENDS

JOIN OUR
FACEBOOK GROUP

BIT.LYPOISONANDPENSFB

SIGN UP TO OUR
NEWSLETTER

BIT.LY/POISONANDPENSNEWS

Boldwood

Boldwood Books is an award-winning fiction publishing company seeking out the best stories from around the world.

Find out more at www.boldwoodbooks.com

Join our reader community for brilliant books, competitions and offers!

Follow us
@BoldwoodBooks
@TheBoldBookClub

Sign up to our weekly deals newsletter

https://bit.ly/BoldwoodBNewsletter

Printed in Dunstable, United Kingdom